"Quirky . . . intriguing . . . [with] recipes to make your stomach growl."
—*Reader to Reader*

"A foodie's delight that includes an enticing look at Southern Oregon's beauties and appended recipes."
—*Kirkus Reviews* on *Killing Me Soufflé*

"The close-knit group of family and friends, the warm details of baking and running a bakeshop framing the story, and delicious-sounding recipes add up to a satisfying cozy."
—*Booklist* on *A Smoking Bun*

"*A Batter of Life and Death* is a delightful cozy mystery that will keep you turning pages. . . . Grab a few napkins, because you'll be drooling all over the pages as you read."
—Fresh Fiction

"Clever plots, likable characters, and good food . . . Still hungry? Not to worry, because desserts abound in . . . this delectable series."
—*Mystery Scene* on *A Batter of Life and Death*

"[With] *Meet Your Baker*, Alexander weaves a tasty tale of deceit, family ties, delicious pastries, and murder."
—Edith Maxwell, author of *A Tine to Live, A Tine to Die*

"Sure to satisfy both dedicated foodies and ardent mystery lovers alike."
—Jessie Crockett, author of *Drizzled with Death*

Also
by Ellie Alexander

Meet Your Baker

A Batter of Life and Death

On Thin Icing

Caught Bread Handed

Fudge and Jury

A Crime of Passion Fruit

Another One Bites the Crust

Till Death Do Us Tart

Live and Let Pie

A Cup of Holiday Fear

Nothing Bundt Trouble

Chilled to the Cone

Mocha, She Wrote

Bake, Borrow, and Steal

Donut Disturb

Muffin But the Truth

Catch Me If You Candy

A Smoking Bun

Sticks and Scones

Killing Me Soufflé

Laying Down the Latte

A Bakeshop Mystery

Ellie Alexander

St. Martin's Paperbacks

This is a work of fiction. All of the characters, organizations, and events portrayed in this novel are either products of the author's imagination or are used fictitiously.

Published in the United States by St. Martin's Paperbacks, an imprint of St. Martin's Publishing Group.

EU Representative: Macmillan Publishers Ireland Ltd., 1st Floor, The Liffey Trust Centre, 117-126 Sheriff Street Upper, Dublin 1, DO1 YC43, Ireland.

LAYING DOWN THE LATTE

For information, address St. Martin's Publishing Group, 120 Broadway, New York, NY 10271.

www.stmartins.com

ISBN: 978-1-250-32622-5

Our books may be purchased in bulk for specialty retail/wholesale, literacy, corporate/premium, educational, and subscription box use. Please contact MacmillanSpecialMarkets@macmillan.com.

Printed in the United States of America

St. Martin's Paperbacks edition / September 2025

10 9 8 7 6 5 4 3 2 1

Thank you to the team at Hacienda Belen for giving me a private coffee tour. I learned so much, and I'm still dreaming about your coffee.

Acknowledgments

To my own "Team Torte" Spencer Calquhoun, Tracy Charlee Darlington, Mary Ann McCoy, Ericka Turnbull, Tish Bouvier, Kat Webb, Flo Cho, Kayla Baucom, Jennifer Lewis, Lily-Ann Gill, and Courtny Drydale! Thank you for all your ideas, support, and suggestions and for always cheering on my writing!

A special thanks to the Tech Guy, also known as Gordy, for spending countless hours touring coffee farms and tasting in Costa Rica to make sure I got that piece of the story right. So much coffee!

to Emigrant Lake

Oregon Shakespeare Festival

The Merry Windsor

Lithia Park

Ashland Police

tovte

A Rose By Any
Other Name

Puck's Pub

The Green Goblin

Ashland

to Crater Lake

Chapter One

They say that you have to travel the world to find home. I had certainly found that to be true. After spending a decade sailing from one romantic port of call to another on a boutique cruise ship, I found my way back to my hometown of Ashland, Oregon, where I had been about as close to blissfully happy as one could be ever since. It was fairly impossible not to be swept up in Ashland's charms—the bustling plaza with its locally owned shops and restaurants, the Siskiyou Mountains nestling us in with a cozy evergreen hug, the creative energy that pulsed through town, the artists who also called this place home, and the warm and welcoming spirit of community that connected each of us.

This morning, my beloved Ashland was washed in a golden glow as I walked to Torte, my family bakeshop. Sunlight kissed the top of Grizzly Peak, lighting up the flaxen hillside like fire, though the thought of fire made me shudder.

Recent summers had seen a swath of wildfires that tore through southern Oregon's dense forests and cocooned Ashland in a thick, unrelenting blanket of smoke. This summer felt like the days of old, with brilliant, blue, cloudless skies that seemed to stretch out for miles, hot afternoons perfect for a refreshing iced coffee, and cool evenings punctuated by a symphony of stars. Fortunately, this summer had been smoke-free. I stopped and looked around for something to knock on. The bark of one of the towering pines would do. I rapped on the wood, not wanting to jinx the clear blue skies.

I turned off Mountain Avenue onto Main Street and breathed in the crisp, clean air. Bungalows and Victorians lined the two-way road, each with lush grassy lawns, flower beds overflowing with cranberry red and canary yellow geraniums, and front porches adorned with bird feeders and colorful windsocks. I loved the eclectic nature of the neighborhood. At this hour, it was just me and the wild deer that nibbled on climbing roses and bedded in groups beneath clumps of grapevines. Downtown wouldn't be alive with activity for another few hours. As a baker, I was used to greeting the dawn alone, and to be honest, it was my favorite part of the day.

I breathed slowly as the houses transitioned into old Elizabethan façades, and the Carnegie Library came into view. My morning walks were a time to clear my head and center myself for the day. I'd always loved the quiet meditation of a sleepy town, but now that I was pregnant with twins, my morning solace felt especially important—the calm before the storm of the coffee and pastry rush.

Instinctively, my hand went to my little bump. I couldn't quite believe Carlos and I were having twins. Twins. It had taken some getting used to, but now that my belly was starting to swell and my feet ached by the end of a long day running up and down the stairs with heavy trays laden with sticky orange morning buns and custard tarts, it was impossible to ignore the reality that in a few months our little family was going to double in size.

I continued along Main Street, where royal banners in eggplant purple and gold announced upcoming performances at the Oregon Shakespeare Festival (affectionately known as OSF to locals). My best friend, Lance, was the artistic director at the world-renowned theater company that attracted actors and patrons from around the globe. There was nothing like taking in a show at the outdoor Elizabethan theater on a warm summer night, guided by the constellations above. Lance drew in audiences for his outrageous and whimsical production of Shakespeare's comedies, his heart-moving renditions of the tragedies that left not a single dry eye in the house, and his slant toward showcasing new and upcoming playwrights, making his stage a place where every actor, regardless of age, color, disability, or sexual identity, had a home. His productions had received critical acclaim and a litany of awards. His penchant for playing into the stereotype of a diva director only endeared him more to tourists. He could often be found casually strolling through the plaza in a well-cut suit, stopping to pose for photos with his adoring fans. He deserved the praise, and those of us lucky enough to know the real Lance understood that behind his demure, coy smile was a man deeply attached to Ashland and those he loved.

Recently, he had added to his ever-growing accolades by launching a new endeavor—the Fair Verona Players, a theater troupe hosting small, intimate productions at vineyards and Lithia Park. We'd opened the season at Uva, the winery on the outskirts of town that Carlos and I owned and managed. I was curious to see if one of Lance's passions would overshadow the other. Thus far, he seemed to be balancing both with ease. However, he and his longtime partner had recently gotten engaged, and wedding plans were about the only thing we discussed these days.

I was thrilled for Lance and Arlo. Lance had popped the question at a beachside bonfire a few weeks ago, proposing to Arlo with a Ring Pop and the sweetest profession of his love. The spontaneous act shocked all of us. For someone who tended to curate every aspect of his life, watching him lean into love—even the messy, sandy, unpolished parts— had been a delight.

Ever since, not a conversation had gone by without a mention of the wedding. Lance was in his element and would find a way to bring up the subject with any poor, unsuspecting stranger and certainly our group of friends. His ever-growing list of wedding possibilities seemed to expand by the hour, and each idea was more elaborate than the last. He'd floated everything from a private island ceremony where guests would be helicoptered in and marooned for the weekend to having Cirque du Soliel performers descend from the ceiling on silk ribbons for their first dance. Every time I thought he had finally settled on something, a new absurdly extravagant idea would emerge.

Case in point: before I turned off the lights last night, he texted me asking how I felt about doves. "Picture this: we arrive at the ceremony in a crystal carriage pulled by white horses and surrounded by a synchronized release of one hundred doves. Trained doves that would perform choreography before landing on floral perches."

I responded, "One hundred doves?"

He immediately shot back, "Forget it. You're right. Too cliché. Too pedestrian. Forget I ever mentioned it. Banish the thought. It's overdone and so 1990s. I hear you."

My thoughts started to swirl as I passed the bookstore and the Crown Jewel, with collections of silky summer scarves and glittery earrings on display. Summers are typically our busy season at Torte, Uva, and our seasonal ice cream shop, Scoops. There was never a dull minute between all the time spent baking, constructing wedding cakes, catering private events, mapping out staff schedules, ordering inventory, and—believe it or not—planning ahead to fall and the holiday season. But this week, there was even more than usual to do. Two of my senior staff, Sterling and Steph, recently departed to take on head chef roles at an ailing restaurant on the southern Oregon coast. We'd hired their replacements, who were getting up to speed, but it was still an adjustment. Additionally, a fortuitous invitation from Valentina, one of our former colleagues from the *Amour of the Seas*, the cruise ship where Carlos and I had met, had me preparing to venture to the coffee capital of the world for a tasting tour and an immersive weekend at her family coffee farm in Costa Rica.

Valentina had managed the espresso bars on the cruise ship. She was an aficionado when it came to not only pouring a perfect shot or crafting exquisite latte art but also about every aspect of coffee growing, production, and roasting. We had been good friends during our time at sea and kept in contact. Like me, she decided to give up her vagabond lifestyle to help grow and expand her family's offering on their coffee farm tucked high in the Costa Rican mountains.

Unbeknownst to Andy, our resident barista, Carlos and I had a little secret up our sleeves. With the changes brewing at Torte and in our personal lives, we'd decided to bring him along on our Costa Rican adventure. Andy dropped out of college at Southern Oregon University to explore his passion—coffee roasting. He'd spent the last year tinkering with roasts and perfecting his talents on roasting equipment housed on his grandmother's property. His coffees were a true art form and had attracted a cult-like following. And now Carlos and I were ready to invest in Andy. We'd priced out commercial roasting machines and intended to promote him to coffee manager and head roaster. It was a win-win for all of us. Torte would be able to bring our roasting in-house instead of procuring beans from other coffee roasters, and Andy would lead the charge on the ever-rotating coffee menu, combining new signature blends for the bakeshop, and would manage our growing team of baristas. He was ready for more responsibility, and hopefully, a weekend of intensive coffee education in Costa Rica would give him an extra boost of confidence and some new tools to level up his roasting game.

I couldn't wait to tell him. He was always the first to arrive, so I knew we should have a few minutes to chat before the rest of the team showed up.

Torte came into view as I passed by the Lithia bubblers in the center of the plaza and the information kiosk covered with posters and flyers for summer jams at the park, acting classes, book club meetups, and white-water rafting tours on the nearby Rogue River. Torte's candy apple red and teal blue awnings greeted me, along with the current front window display. It was an ode-to-summer theme. Bethany, our lead baker, and Rosa, our front-of-house manager, had teamed up to create the luscious and delectable window set. Marzipan grapes, strawberries, and peaches filled tiered cake stands intermixed with lacquered tarts, pots of honey, tea cakes, bite-sized sandwiches, and chocolates. Filmy gauze in pale and forest green was draped from the rafters and fluttered down like willowy trees. Strings of honeybee lights gave the window a buzzing glow. Vases with fresh-cut wildflowers and floral teapots finished off the scene.

I was blown away by Bethany's and Rosa's creativity and artistic eye. Everything in the window was so tempting that I wanted to reach inside and swipe a glossy marzipan berry. I resisted the urge and headed down the brick stairwell instead.

When I reached the bottom, I unlocked the door and flipped on the lights. Our commercial kitchen and baking stations were located in the basement. Shortly after I moved back home, Mom and I had taken on a massive remodeling project—moving our entire operation downstairs. It had been a bigger undertaking than either of us had initially imagined, but the final result was worth it.

The basement was naturally cool, a welcome gift on days like this when temps would rise in the afternoon, flirting with triple digits. I ran my fingers along the exposed brick walls and fluffed up a pillow on the couch as I passed the comfy seating area in front of the atomic fireplace. There was no need to light the fireplace today.

Along with the couch, there was a collection of chairs,

a coffee table, and bookshelves filled with books and games for customers to enjoy while they lingered with iced cinnamon spice mochas and slices of bourbon pound cake.

The open-concept kitchen was my favorite spot in the bakeshop. It was light and bright, with ample counter space for rolling out sheets of puff pastry dough. The space was meticulously organized, with a cooking station near the gas stove and a pastry-decorating counter with extra overhead lighting for those fine piping details. We designed special drawers to house our extensive collection of sprinkles, edible glitter, and pastry knives. The pièce de résistance, as Lance would say, was our wood-fired pizza oven that consumed the far back wall. Neither Mom nor I had had any idea a rustic oven was hiding behind old Sheetrock. The construction crew had discovered it during renovations—like a gift from the pastry gods. We baked our breads, pizzas, and hand-rolled pretzels in the oven, giving everything a beautiful smoky finish.

I started the opening checklist by lighting a bundle of applewood in the pizza oven and heating the main ovens. Then I brewed a pot of decaf and grabbed the custom order sheets. We kept our pastry cases stocked with a selection of signature baked goods and offered daily specials based on whatever was in season. We also baked bread for a variety of wholesale accounts, predominantly restaurants and hotels in town, who used it in their sandwiches and to accompany warm bowls of soup.

While the coffee brewed, I printed out Andy's plane ticket and quickly assessed the inventory in the walk-through fridge. For today's specials, I wanted to bake something quintessentially summer and settled on a peach cobbler with a bit of a twist. The peaches were ripe and juicy, picked from the nearby orchards, and hand-delivered to our door.

I washed my hands with lemon and lavender soap, poured myself a cup of decaf with a splash of heavy cream, and got to work peeling, pitting, and dicing the peaches. Soon my hands dripped with the sweet juice. I mixed the peaches with cinnamon, brown sugar, a touch of salt, and lemon juice. I scooped cornstarch into a small Tupperware, added water, and shook it with the lid on until the cornstarch had dissolved. The mixture would ensure that my cobbler didn't end up runny. There was nothing worse than a runny cobbler or soggy pastry crust.

Once I'd added the mixture to the peaches, I set them to the side and cut cold butter into cubes. Then I forked the butter with flour, brown sugar, and oats until it formed a crumbly, sand-like texture. Next I pressed it into greased baking dishes and slid them into the oven to bake for ten minutes.

I sipped my coffee and leafed through the custom orders. There were requests for birthday cakes, baby showers, a retirement cake, and three wedding cakes. The wedding cakes took top priority, because they required extra time to cool in the fridge so the crumb coat (or first layer of frosting) could set before they were assembled and finished to each happy couple's specifications.

My phone buzzed with a text. Lance, of course.

It was like he was in my head.

"We must discuss cake. Square? Round? Tiers? Individual? I will only admit this to you, but I can't keep up with the trends."

I chuckled as I gave him the advice I gave every one

of our wedding clients, which was to pick a style and flavors that were meaningful to him and Arlo. Trends in cakes came and went like the rise and fall of dough in the oven—puffing up with excitement and sinking back into obscurity. The only thing that mattered was whether or not Lance and Arlo were pleased with the cake design.

"Fine. Way to be practical. Sending you inspiration pics now."

He proceeded to bombard me with dozens of radically unique designs. We'd bake whatever they wanted, and I knew it was a losing battle to attempt to rein Lance in. He loved the drama.

My timer dinged, but I didn't need it. As I teach every new baker, a chef's nose is their best guide for doneness. Without fail, I could always smell when a batch of cookies or a cake was ready. The base of the peach cobbler was no exception. Its buttery aroma with hints of cinnamon wafted through the kitchen as I walked to the oven to remove the pans. I spread a thickened peach layer over each and finished with a final layer of the oat crumble—this time sprinkled loosely over the top.

The door jingled. Andy burst inside carrying a reusable grocery bag filled with containers of beans. His exuberant energy was magnetic. Andy was like Torte's personal golden retriever. He could brighten any room with his wholesome, genuine smile and contagious enthusiasm. He was tall and muscular with shaggy hair. Today, he wore a pair of board shorts and a T-shirt. "Morning, boss. It's already heating up out there." He hoisted the bag onto the island and lifted the first tub. A piece of masking tape secured the lid and had the words "TEST BATCH 24" written across the top. "Since I had the weekend off, I did some more testing, and it sort of got out of hand."

"You roasted twenty-four different batches?" I stared at the shopping bag, impressed by Andy's commitment to creating new blends and recognizing that he might be prone to perfectionist tendencies like me.

"Yeah, I think my grandma is going to kick me out soon. She said she can't smell anything other than coffee beans and that even her sheets are infused with the aroma of my roasts." He lifted his hand to his nose as if to check whether his pores were oozing with the heavenly scent of freshly roasted beans.

"There could be worse things." I tried to wink but only managed to contort my face into a weird half grin.

"That's exactly what I said." He balled his hand into a fist and pumped it against mine. "Who doesn't want to smell like coffee twenty-four seven?"

"Well, that might be taking it a bit too far," I admitted, although my coffee addiction was legendary. I'd given up the caffeine content with my pregnancy, but thanks to Andy, I didn't have to sacrifice the flavor. He'd put countless hours into creating mouthwatering decaf options for me. I was forever in his debt. There weren't many things I cared about giving up during my pregnancy, but coffee was nonnegotiable. It was so much more than just the caffeine for me. It was ritual, comfort, and an integral part of my daily routine.

"We're talking about beans." He ran his hand over the bag. "Nectar of the gods. Java juice. Should I keep going?"

"No." I chuckled. "Although I do have some news that, in a roundabout way, involves your grandma."

Andy raised his thick eyebrows and stared at me skeptically. "My grandma?"

Andy's grandmother had graciously allowed him to take over her yard and garden with his coffee roasting equipment. He had started by tinkering with her old cast-iron skillet on the stove and then expanded to a countertop roaster for beginners. He eventually saved up enough to purchase a used commercial roaster and installed it in his grandmother's shed. As his love for the craft grew, he quickly found himself limited by space. His blends were so popular at Torte that Carlos and I had grand visions of what he might be able to accomplish with a true commercial roastery setup. I had a feeling his grandmother wouldn't mind if his operation moved off her property.

"Yep. Give me one minute." I held up my index finger and hurried to grab the plane ticket from the counter. "As you know, Carlos and I are going to Costa Rica next weekend for a coffee farm excursion, and we decided we needed a stowaway." I pressed the folded sheet of paper into his hand. "Go ahead, open it."

His brow scrunched tight in confusion as he studied the ticket. "This is a plane ticket, Jules. A ticket to Costa Rica with my name on it." Realization dawned on him. His freckles popped like sunbursts as his smile stretched across his boyish cheeks. "Me?" He tapped his chest. "I'm going? What? Really? No way. Are you serious?"

"Dead serious." I nodded solemnly. "Carlos and I have some big plans and ideas in store for you that we can discuss on the flight. Valentina is thrilled that you're coming—I mean, assuming you want to come. I checked with your grandmother, and she thought you were free, but we purchased a refundable ticket, in case the timing doesn't work or you have other plans."

He cut me off, bouncing up and down on his toes. "I want to come. I want to come. I've got nothing major on the calendar, and even if I did, I'd cancel everything for a chance to come to Costa Rica with you. Are you kidding me? Who would turn down an offer like this? I'm in—one hundred percent in."

"I figured." I laughed. "Anyway, Valentina will walk you through the entire process, from how they monitor the flowering cherries to harvesting, washing, drying, roasting, and everything in between. It's a good time of year to visit, because they're preparing for the harvest later this fall, so things are slow on the farm. Valentina has asked for our help with the new espresso bar and pastry counter they're going to open in a converted barn, and in exchange, she's going to share her coffee expertise with you."

"This is amazing. I can't believe it." Andy's mouth hung open in awe as he read and reread the ticket like it was a figment of his imagination. "I've always wanted to go to Costa Rica. It's the coffee heartland." He pressed his hand over his chest with reverence. "Thank you so much for this opportunity. Seriously, Jules. This is my dream."

"We're over the moon to have you accompany us, and I'm eager to learn and refresh my memory right along with you. It's been years since I've visited a coffee farm. I think the last time was when Carlos and I stopped in Costa Rica for one night on the ship."

It was fun to watch him spring around the kitchen like a bouncy ball. "I have so much to do. Pack. Study." He froze. "Oh no, what about coverage here? The new staff are just finally in the zone. Is that going to throw everything off?"

"We've got that covered. In fact, that's the only reason I waited to tell you. I wanted to make sure we were set, and I'm happy to report that we are. Mom and the Professor are going to help, as will Wendy, Mom's good friend who used to assist my parents back in the day when they needed an extra hand. Wendy will cover the pastry counter and dining room, which frees up Sequoia, Bethany, Rosa, Marty, and the new staff to focus on baking and managing the espresso bar." I wasn't at all surprised, but I was delighted that the recent additions to our team were blending in seamlessly and had quickly become an integral part of our small but mighty baking operation. "The Professor even volunteered to help with wholesale deliveries. I've tweaked the schedule at Scoops, so if needed, some of those team members can rotate here, and we're going to close Uva for the weekend. We're only going to be gone for four days, so it's no big deal."

"Wow, you've gone to a lot of trouble—you might even say a *latte* of trouble—for me." He winked and ran his hand over the Tupperware containers.

I groaned and tossed a dish towel at him. "You've been spending too much time around Bethany." Running a bakeshop naturally lent itself to baking puns, and Bethany was our queen of clever catchphrases. She was notorious for wearing T-shirts and hoodies with sayings like BAKE MY DAY and I'M A WHISK TAKER.

"They get in your head, man." He made a face and tucked the ticket in the bag with his assorted roasts.

"Thanks for all of this, Jules. I'm going to make you proud. I'll be sure to thank your mom, Wendy, and the Professor, too. It's so cool of them to step in and help."

"That's what we do at Torte." I checked the peach crumble, which was bubbling and juicy. It still needed another minute or two. "Plus, we get the benefit of your creations, so really it's about that—hook us up with coffee."

"Consider it done." He grabbed his things and started toward the stairs. "I'm already dreaming up a Costa Rican special for today. I'll make yours unleaded." He took the stairs two at a time, repeating, "We're going to Costa Rica. We're going to Costa Rica."

I finished my first cup of decaf while I waited for my bake. Andy's reaction was exactly what I was hoping for. I couldn't wait to fill him in on our other plans, but I wanted Carlos to be part of that discussion.

Soon the kitchen was humming with activity as the rest of the team trickled in. I cut slices of my peach cobbler for everyone to taste, and as promised, Andy returned with a tray of sample coffee. "Try these, you all. It's my Pura Vida latte," he said, passing around mugs after sharing the news of our upcoming research trip. "It's a classic latte with a medium roast espresso, coconut milk, and sugarcane, topped with cinnamon and nutmeg. Hopefully, it evokes the tropics. I'll improve it after we return and I have a chance to apply what I learned."

His baseline was already high. I didn't see much room for improvement, but I was eager for our getaway and to watch Andy immerse himself in his passion. After all, Torte and baking were my passion, and getting to give my staff the opportunity to explore theirs was the best gift I could ask for.

Chapter Two

A week later, after a frenzy of packing and planning, I woke to the sound of Carlos's alarm and a pitch-black bedroom. Our flight was early, even for me, which was saying a lot, given that I work baker's hours.

"Mi querida, it's time," Carlos mumbled, his voice groggy, still clinging to the last dregs of sleep. He reached for me as I started to get out of bed and wrapped me in his warm, strong arms, nuzzling my neck with kisses. "Stay for just a minute."

I returned his embrace. "I'd love to, but we have a flight to catch. The Uber will be here soon." I couldn't believe the trip was finally here. I left him with one last kiss and jumped in the shower, reviewing my mental checklist to make sure I hadn't overlooked any important details. Carlos had already checked us in for our flights. Andy was meeting us at the airport. Our bags were packed. Torte was in the capable hands of Marty, Bethany, Rosa, and Sequoia. Mom and the Professor would rotate throughout the weekend along with Wendy and our new staff.

Check, check, and check.

I lingered in the shower a moment longer, letting the

water wash over me as eager anticipation began to build. It had been years since my last trip to Costa Rica, and I couldn't wait for the warm, tropical breezes and culinary delights. I dried my hair, tied it in a high ponytail, and pulled on a cozy set of travel clothes—soft cotton joggers, a T-shirt, and a zip-up sweatshirt. By the time we landed, I wouldn't need the sweatshirt, but I always tend to get cold on planes. Blame it on all that dry air.

By the time I finished getting ready, Carlos was waiting downstairs with a tumbler of decaf, breakfast to-go, and our luggage. Ramiro, his son, was off on one last adventure with his Ashland High School friends before he returned to Spain for his senior year. His soccer team and friend group arranged a four-day backpacking trip in the Mount Shasta wilderness. They intended to hike eight miles to a campsite and set up near one of the many high alpine lakes. It was an Ashland tradition. I'd taken the same backpacking trip with Thomas, my high school boyfriend (and Ashland's current detective) and a group of our friends the summer before our senior year. I'll never forget spending leisurely days swimming in the frigid lake waters and long evenings sharing dreams about our futures around a campfire. I loved that Ramiro was getting an opportunity to do the same.

We'd invited him to join us in Costa Rica, but—shocker—he opted to hang with his friends instead. That was fine with both of us. I was thrilled he'd made such great connections in his year with us and had a feeling that many of his friendships would continue even once he was overseas. It was so much easier to stay in touch now with FaceTime and social media. After Costa Rica, Carlos and I would have one last week with Ramiro in

Ashland before we sent him home to his mom, stepdad, and little sister in Spain.

I hated thinking about it.

He'd become an integral part of our lives, and I was already grieving not having him here.

"Breakfast, Julieta. You cannot skip it." Carlos offered me an egg and turkey sausage sandwich. "The car is here."

I had no intention of skipping breakfast. Being pregnant made me hungry around the clock. Gone were the days of drinking copious amounts of coffee while working at the bakeshop and realizing it was nearly noon before I got around to eating anything.

A text from Lance came in as I got in the car. I couldn't believe he was up this early. Normally, Lance had vampire tendencies. He preferred post-show midnight cocktails to my baker's hours.

"Fair warning, darling. Be prepared for a potential Richard Lord sighting. Rumor has it he's flying out today to film *Make a Millionaire Match.*"

Richard Lord owned the dilapidated hotel across the plaza from Torte. He'd made it his singular mission since I moved home to do anything and everything in his power to get under my skin. Fortunately, his latest escapade had nothing to do with me and was taking him to an unknown location to film a new reality dating show. I had many questions about said reality show, like how they vetted the contestants. There was no chance Richard had millions in the bank. I pitied the poor woman who got matched with Mr. Lord, but then again, maybe this was his chance to find love. Far be it from me to stand in the way of love.

Richard had certainly thrown himself into preparing

to film the reality show. He'd been tanning, had updated his golf-inspired wardrobe, and even had Botox (although he vehemently denied doing anything to his puffy, ruddy face).

"Thanks for the heads-up. Why are you awake?"

"Centerpieces, darling. Centerpieces. Succulents? Topiaries? Bouquets? Arlo is off in dreamland next to me. How can the man sleep when we have such burning questions to answer?"

Poor Arlo.

He was a saint.

On the short drive to the airport, I polished off the hearty breakfast sandwich and the decaf latte Carlos made me. Andy was waiting for us outside the terminal. It wasn't hard to spot him. The Medford airport was small, and at this hour, there was only one flight departing. Carlos and I were seasoned travelers from our years working on the cruise ship, but it had been a while since I'd reviewed my checklist—making sure to update my phone with an international plan, securing our passports and cash, and confirming my health information.

"Morning, boss!" He waved, picking up his pack and slinging it over his shoulder.

"Have you been waiting long?" I asked, checking my watch. We were right on time.

"I couldn't sleep. I was too excited, so I got here a bit early." He gave me a sheepish grin as Carlos unloaded our bags. Andy's backpack reminded me of an overly puffed marshmallow.

"How early?" I raised one eyebrow.

"Uh, let's just say I've familiarized myself with the

constellations." He motioned to the star-drenched skies. "Do you know how many satellites pass over us? It's a lot. Like, a lot."

I chuckled. I shouldn't have been surprised he was eager and energetic. Coffee was his passion project, and we were soon to be on our way to the motherland. "How much coffee have you had? And what's in your pack? You look a little top-heavy, my friend."

"Not enough. But that's okay. I'm holding out until we get to Costa Rica. Plane coffee is a hard pass. No chance you'll get me to drink that sludge, and I want to keep my palate pristine until we land. I brought twelve notebooks because I'm going to take as many notes and sketches as I can. Plus, my grandma told me to pack extra socks and all the necessities."

"Smart." I nodded with approval and proceeded inside to the nonexistent security line. I scanned the small airport for any sign of Richard Lord lurking nearby. Luckily, I didn't catch sight of him before they announced it was time to queue for our flight.

Boarding and takeoff were smooth, and once we were in the air, I quickly dozed off again. Carlos nudged me awake when the pilot announced we were starting our descent into San José. I lifted the shade and was greeted with swaths of lush, tropical foliage. Endless palms spread out before me, their leaves reaching toward the horizon. It was a canopy of green dotted with brilliant pops of bright pinks and yellows.

"Wow, I don't think I've ever seen this much green." Andy sucked in a breath. "It's magical."

"Sí, she is a beautiful country," Carlos agreed. "And this is only the view from above. Wait until we're up in the mountains, in the coffee fields—you won't believe your eyes."

Andy gushed for the remainder of the flight. "Seriously, you two, I can't thank you enough for bringing me on this trip. It's amazing." We made it through customs and spilled out into a bustling corridor of shops. "Oh my gosh—that's Dulce Coffee. I have to grab a taste."

Andy was already halfway toward the coffee shop and happily sipping rich, local brews before I could respond.

That was fine because I promised Mom I would text her when we landed. I shot her a quick text: "In Costa Rica. We've already lost Andy to an airport coffee tasting."

She responded right away: "I'm so glad you arrived safe and sound. The morning is off to a great start. Marty made a maple honey and bacon flatbread, and customers are literally begging for more of it. Bethany is working on brownies for book club. She cut them into the shape of the book and is hand-piping buttercream to re-create the cover. I'll text you pictures when she's done. Tell Andy to pace himself."

I was glad to hear that Torte was running smoothly—not that I anticipated otherwise. Bethany and Rosa had teamed up to launch our first book club. They were hosting it after hours at the bakeshop. To kick it off, they read *Batter of the Heart*, a romance set in a bakery and featuring an enemies-to-lovers trope. I couldn't wait to see the finished product and pictures.

"Hey, get over here. You have to try this!" Andy waved to us, holding sample coffees in both hands. "Best coffee I've ever tasted."

"And we haven't left the airport yet," I said, gesturing

outside where sunlight beckoned and Valentina Espinoza awaited us.

"It doesn't matter. I already love it." Andy chugged both coffees, handing us sample cups. "Here regular for Carlos and decaf for you." He beamed as we stepped out onto the curb, greeted by a burst of thick, warm air tinged with the aroma of mango and hibiscus.

Carlos and I tasted the strong coffee under Andy's watchful eye.

Valentina jumped out of her Jeep and hurried over to us. She was short and petite with big dark eyes and long dark hair that fell to her shoulders in bouncy curls. She wore a pair of khaki green work overalls and a large, floppy hat. "Pura vida. Pura vida, you made it." She wrapped me in a hug and kissed me on the cheeks, before pulling away to inspect my belly. "Congratulations, I'm so excited for you—twins! You look amazing." She squeezed me again, then she greeted Carlos and Andy with welcoming hugs. "You must be Andy. We're so happy to have you with us for the weekend. Jules and Carlos tell me you are a master at creating balanced roasts. I can't wait for you to teach me your techniques and to walk you through our process."

Her enthusiasm was contagious.

"Teach? Me?" Andy scoffed. "Oh, no. I'm here to learn. I plan to be a sponge and soak up as much knowledge as I can."

She patted his arm and showed us to the Jeep. "You can put your bags back here. Sorry, it's crowded. I had to pick up some supplies on the way. Things have been stressful at the farm. I have to apologize in advance. I've only been home for a few weeks, and things have imploded."

Carlos expertly arranged our luggage next to Valentina's supplies. "Imploded. That doesn't sound good. Can we help?"

Valentina gave him a sad smile. "Having you all here is already helping. It's a long story involving my cousin Miguel, but we have time for that later." She motioned to me and Andy. "Please, get in. The farm is about a forty-minute drive from downtown San José. I thought we might stop at the Mercado Central—or Central Market—and let you explore the stalls and sample some of our regional cuisine and coffee. What do you think? If you're tired and want to rest, that's fine, too. My housekeeper has your rooms ready for you."

I looked at Carlos and Andy. "I'd love to stop at the market if you two are game?"

"Game? Jules, I'm game for *everything* this weekend. *Everything.*" Andy pretended to be offended I had even asked.

"I used to love wandering through the market when we stopped in Costa Rica," Carlos said, turning around to explain the market to Andy. "It's a chef's dream. A full city block of mazes and alleyways bustling with hundreds of vendors."

"That's settled. First stop: the market." Valentina fired up the engine and sped into the sea of traffic exiting the airport. She was the ultimate tour guide as she pointed out landmarks, trees, and neighborhoods en route to San José's famed downtown marketplace. "It's good that we're early," she said, navigating into a parking space in front of the massive market, squeezing the Jeep between two tour buses. She tossed her hat in the back and had Carlos help her tug the soft cover of the Jeep into place to secure our luggage. "The longer the day goes on, the busier and busier it will become with tourists and locals."

"I've never seen anything like this in my life." Andy snapped pictures of the old fading stucco building on his phone. "I promised the team I would document our trip, but I don't think pictures are going to be able to capture the scale. How big is it?"

"It's six thousand square meters. The market was established in 1880 and is one of the largest and oldest markets in Costa Rica," Valentina replied with a touch of pride. "That's why we must stick together. Like Carlos said, you will see it's a maze, and if you get lost in the market, it's nearly impossible to find your way out again."

"Got it. Stick together." Andy gave her a thumbs-up.

The exterior of the market was somewhat utilitarian, with an old-world feel enhanced by faded signage and multiple entrances leading to a labyrinth of narrow passages.

Valentina gave us a brief history of the Central Market as we passed booths filled with bundles of dried herbs and flowers, and fruit stands brimming with vibrant papayas, passion fruit, palm fruit, and noni. "They call this cheese fruit because of its smell and taste. You'll see why." She held up the pale green spotted fruit. "It's an acquired taste, but it is known for its medicinal properties. Try it."

Andy was her guinea pig. His nose wrinkled in disgust as he tasted a piece. "Ew, it does taste like cheese." He closed his eyes and swallowed it. "Maybe blue cheese. I'm usually a fan, but I wasn't expecting that in fruit."

Valentina grinned as she steered us past stalls with fresh fish, clothing, jewelry, coffee, and chocolate. "I like to use it in vinegar to make a salad dressing. It's pungent, but it goes nicely with arugula and cherry tomatoes."

"You're giving me new ideas," Carlos said, pausing to inspect a pastry case displaying sweet and savory empanadas. "I will have to experiment with noni while we're here."

"My kitchen is your kitchen." Valentina addressed both of us. "I was hoping while Andy and I are in the fields and working with the machinery, I might tempt you two to take over in the kitchen if you're willing. I would love your ideas on a menu for the tasting room, although with everything that's happening with Miguel . . ." She drifted off, not finishing her thought.

"Gladly. I'd love to help," I replied. Like Carlos, I felt my mind spinning with potential recipe ideas. Being surrounded by the bustle of the Central Market vendors and the symphony of sounds, colors, textures, and aromas had me salivating and eager to experiment with ingredients we couldn't procure in Ashland.

"I'll take you for ice cream next." Valentina directed us down a narrow corridor. "This way."

We turned onto a tight hallway packed on both sides with more vendors flagging us down to try freshly squeezed guava juice and tamales. Valentina led the march, ignoring their calls until we spilled out into a food court of sorts.

"We call these sodas," Valentina explained. "They're all small, family-owned stalls that serve traditional Costa Rican meals at affordable prices. Do you know why they're called sodas?" she asked, glancing at us like a schoolteacher waiting for her students to catch up.

"Does it have anything to do with soda, as in pop?" Andy asked.

"Yes, good job. They gained popularity in the 1940s and 1950s and were modeled after your American diners or soda fountains, because they were a place in the market where people could grab a quick bite, a snack, and a soda. The name stuck. Now you can find sodas all around the city and throughout Costa Rica."

"Do you have a favorite?" I eyed the closest soda stall, which advertised a daily special of handmade tortillas filled with cheese, meat, and beans. I could definitely eat.

"Sí, but let's get ice cream first. It's an Espinoza family custom that when you visit Mercado Central, you must have a scoop. Come on, this way." She directed us to the stall at the far end of the food court. A canary yellow mural depicting a manual ice cream churn, surrounded by an abundance of bananas, pineapples, and citrus fruit, took up the entire wall near the stand.

The sign read LA SORBETERA DE LOLO MORA.

"This has been here for over one hundred years," Valentina said, joining the small line. "They only make one flavor—it is hard to explain because it's unique, but I think you will love it. It's a vanilla ice cream with cinnamon and cloves. I can't say more. It is delicious, you'll see." She was about to put in our order when a woman dressed in a bright yellow floral sundress with high-heeled sandals and huge gold hoop earrings approached.

"Valentina, what are you doing here? Not guiding tours to make extra money for the farm, are you?" The young woman spoke in rapid Spanish while appraising us. I caught the gist of what she was saying, thanks to having Ramiro live with us for the last year. My language skills had greatly improved, although I still had plenty of room for improvement. She was in her early thirties with expertly curled waves of hair that cascaded down her shoulders, and flawless makeup. "It's unfortunate that the farm is in such dire straits. I'd hate to think you're taking side gigs to cover costs when there's an easy solution."

Valentina sucked in an angry breath and furrowed her brow. "No, Sofia, this isn't a side gig. These are my friends visiting from America."

"Ah, Americans." Sofia pressed her hands together in front of her. "Welcome to Costa Rica, I hope Valentina shows you all our beautiful country has to offer." She checked her expensive platinum watch. "I can't stay, but I'll see you at the farm later. Pura vida."

Valentina muttered something unintelligible under her breath as Sofia swept past us.

"Is everything okay?" I asked. "We have a Sophia in our family, too." I looked at Carlos. It was always hard to describe our beautiful, modern, blended family. His former partner, Sophia, was Ramiro's mom. I never liked using the word "step" to describe my connection with Ramiro. It felt cold, like a barrier not a bond. The same was true for my relationship with the Professor. He would never replace my dad but was a father figure to me, a steady and calming presence in my life. I hoped I could be that for Ramiro, a positive influence in his life, another source of support and someone he could trust. I appreciated Sophia had generously allowed me to be a part of Ramiro's world. We were family. We all took care of one another. Nothing more needed to be said.

"I hope your Sofia is kinder." Valentina crossed her arms over her chest. "I do not trust that woman. Her motives are no good. She's trying to steal the farm right out from under me, and she's not even trying to hide it."

Chapter Three

"Steal the farm?" Carlos and I asked in unison.

Valentina stepped up to the counter to place our order. Then she passed around clear cups with generous scoops of the ice cream. It was the color of saffron, which must have been from the warming spices, and was closer to a sorbet in texture. "I feel bad involving you in my problems when you're here to enjoy the pura vida lifestyle, but yes, Sofia Rojas is my sworn enemy at this point."

I tasted the ice cream, which was like nothing I'd had before. The spicy notes of cinnamon and cloves paired with the creamy base and little specs of shaved ice.

"Your enemy?" Carlos's face was etched with concern as he dipped his spoon into the ice cream. "Why?"

Valentina pointed to a group of chairs nearby. "Let's sit for a minute."

"Why is the woman your enemy?" Carlos repeated, pulling out a chair for me.

"It's a long story. Are you sure you want to hear it? I hate ruining your vacation, but I could use your help. I'm out of ideas. I don't know what to do. I left the ship to come home and expand the farm, and now I think it's likely I'm going to lose it." She stared in the direction Sofia had gone. "I know I shouldn't burden you with my problems, but I have nowhere else to turn."

"No, please, we want to help," I said, knowing that Carlos would feel the same way.

He nodded in agreement. "Sí, sí, please use us however we can be of assistance."

Andy bobbed his head, too.

"Thank you. I'm just heartbroken." Valentina let out a small sigh and leaned against the chair, ignoring her ice cream. "It's my cousin Miguel. We have been partners in the farm for the last ten years, but I'm afraid we have very different visions for the future of Finca las Nubes."

"The Cloud Farm," Carlos interpreted for Andy.

"What a gorgeous name for a farm," I said, taking another taste of the ice cream.

"You'll love it. We are up in the clouds, where the golden bean, as we call the coffee bean, grows best." She paused her story briefly to impart a quick bit of knowledge to Andy about how coffee farms in Costa Rica were located above the clouds in the mountain region of the country. "The farm sits at eighteen hundred meters above sea level, where our volcanic soils are rich in nutrients, and the temperature is cooler so the coffee cherries grow slower, which helps them develop a more complex flavor."

"Like this?" Andy savored his ice cream, closing his eyes, as he took one small bite after another. "This is so good. I'd love to use these flavors in a latte."

"You should. I'll introduce you to Carmen. She's the head of the farmworkers, and she makes a coffee inspired by this ice cream with our medium roast." Valentina smiled, but I could sense sadness or maybe concern behind the smile. "I'll tell you more about acidity and rainfall and why our zone is highly prized for its quality when we get to the farm."

"I brought extra notebooks, so I'm ready for your coffee school, but don't let me get you off topic," Andy said.

Valentina pressed her lips together in a scowl. "I'm stalling because I still can't believe it's true. You see, Miguel and I inherited the farm from our parents. His mom and my father are siblings. Finca las Nubes has been in our family for three generations. Our great-grandfather worked as a coffee picker and saved enough money to buy a small plot of land that eventually grew and became the farm it is today. Miguel and I grew up together. We were more like brother and sister. Our families lived on the property and still do. When our parents decided they were ready to retire, the farm passed down to us. The land is part of me. It's in my blood. I thought it was in Miguel's, too, but I've learned he's trying to sell off his share to a corporate developer—the company Sofia works for, Terra Café International. She's been trying to convince me to sell my shares too, but I would never." She paused to catch her breath. "Now I'm regretting I left the ship, although I suppose it would be even worse if I wasn't here. The farm has been doing fine for generations, but Miguel is intent on growth and expansion. That's part of why I returned home. We were going to do just that—the barn has been renovated to become a full tasting room and coffee bar. We'll sell pastries and whole beans. We can rent the space for special events, and we're expanding distribution and working toward our organic certification. Now Miguel doesn't want to do any of this. He wants to sell to Sofia."

"Oh no, this is terrible news." Carlos sounded dumb-founded. "Can he sell without your permission?"

"It's complicated." Valentina stirred her mostly melted ice cream. "He can sell his shares. We have a fifty-fifty split. I don't think our parents ever imagined either of us would sell. Their dream is for the farm to continue being passed on to the next generation. Miguel and I don't have children, though the plan has always been to keep the farm in the family. But technically, yes, he's free to sell his shares. The problem is that if Miguel sells, it will leave me with a corporate partner."

"Someone like Sofia?" I suggested, polishing off my ice cream and considering whether I should go back for a second scoop.

"Yes, exactly. I would still own half the farm, but Sofia and I do not see eye to eye on how the farm should be managed. She's interested in changing our operations, developing the land, and building a huge coffee showroom. I'm trying to talk him out of selling so we retain control of the farm, but I don't have the kind of money Sofia is willing to put forward. I simply can't compete with her offer. I've spoken with a lawyer and am out of options."

"That's terrible." I reached for her arm. "I went through something similar with the bakeshop when I moved home. I thought my mom and I were going to lose it to a business owner in town who was dead set on getting his hands on Torte, but it all worked out in the end. Maybe there's a solution that hasn't presented itself yet."

"I hope so." She twisted her hair around her finger and stared at the busy market.

Spanish conversations and happy chatter in the romance language reminded me of being back on the *Amour of the*

Seas. As Valentina predicted, foot traffic was already increasing as the lunch hour drew nearer.

She picked up her soupy ice cream. "Sorry to burden you with my problems. Should we have some lunch before it is too crowded?"

We all agreed.

Valentina suggested a soda famous for its casado—a traditional Costa Rican dish served with rice, beans, meat, avocado, egg, corn, and vegetables. She perked up a bit as we enjoyed a leisurely lunch and discussed her ideas for the weekend. I wished there was more I could do in terms of coming up with a solution to save Finca las Nubes. Hopefully, once we were settled on the farm and I had a chance to meet her cousin and the staff, a solution would present itself. Otherwise, our getaway and coffee immersion weekend was going to be a farewell tour to Valentina's beloved coffee farm.

Chapter Four

The drive to Finca las Nubes was like stepping back in time. Valentina wound the Jeep up a bumpy two-lane road through hillsides dripping with color. Pink angel trumpet trees, clumps of wild bamboo, and leafy palms encircled the houses and small grocery stores along the narrow highway. Laundry hung out to dry fluttered in the breeze, and a young mother with a baby strapped to her chest trotted alongside us on a chestnut horse.

"That's so cool." Andy videoed the scene from the front of the Jeep.

We drove higher and higher. A restaurant built into the cliffside advertised strawberries dipped in chocolate and breathtaking views. Downtown San José sprawled out in the distance, a patchwork of colorful rooftops, modern high-rises, and Colonials all clustered together and framed by mountains. Brilliant green slopes of coffee fields rolled downward, blanketed by rows of flowering plants.

A rustic wrought-iron gate with the Finca las Nubes logo carved into it signaled we had arrived at the coffee farm. Valentina hit a button to open the automatic gate.

"Welcome to my home," she said with pride. "You'll be staying in the main house." She pointed down the gravel drive to a creamy yellow two-story stone house with white shutters, columns, and trim. "Miguel's house is up this way, and the fields, worker housing, and production area are on the other side of the property. I'll take you on a full tour after you have time to unpack and get settled."

The house was like something out of a travel magazine. Its open-air design with wooden ceiling fans, dark wood accents, and butter-yellow walls made me feel like I was stepping into a luxury resort. Tiled archways in turquoise and teal and native Costa Rican artwork provided pops of color. The entryway spilled into an open-air courtyard with a massive marble fountain and burnt-orange tile floors. Arched entrances connected the courtyard to a living room, dining room, and kitchen.

The entire back of the house opened out onto a terrace that looked over the coffee fields and onto a luxurious aquamarine swimming pool.

"Valentina, this is gorgeous," I said, unable to focus on any one thing. Jade vines dripped from hanging baskets dangling from the ceiling. Large vases overflowed with peach and tangerine lilies. A deep walnut table in the entryway was set with water pitchers, coffee, and pastries.

"Thank you." Valentina placed her hand on her heart. "Can you see why I don't want to lose this? My family built the house nearly sixty years ago. It's more than a house—it's my home. The farm and these buildings are the only home I've ever known." Her breath caught, and her eyes misted. She blinked away tears and squared her petite shoulders. "It is your home while you're here with us, so please help yourself to a drink and a pastry. This is our estate-grown medium roast blend," she said to Andy, pouring him a cup.

He took it without hesitation, studying the hot liquid and taking the first sip with the utmost reverence. "It's earthy with sweet undertones. Oh, I like the crisp finish. I'm picking up almonds, cashews, and brighter notes of fruit—cherries and tart apple."

"Sí, he is good," Valentina said to me, her smile widening. "You did not exaggerate. He knows his coffee."

"I have a lot to learn, but I know good coffee when I taste it, and this is it." Andy savored another sip. "This is brilliant. I wouldn't taint this with cream or sugar. It's perfect as is."

Valentina patted his arm. "There's so much more for me to show you. Come, let me take you to your rooms. Later I'll introduce you to the team. Everyone is excited to meet you. We have a wonderful dinner planned on the terrace tonight." She showed us to the immaculately styled guest rooms on the second floor and left us to get settled. "Why don't you take a siesta? We can gather in the entryway in an hour if that works for everyone?"

"That sounds lovely," I replied. "Thank you again for being such a gracious host."

Her smile was slightly impish. "Yes, but remember, I have ulterior motives. I'm eager to have you both in the kitchen to help me develop a menu for the new coffee bar." A flash of worry crossed her face. "That is, if the coffee bar will even happen now. Who's to say? In Miguel's plans, the barn is bulldozed, along with everything else generations of our family have built here."

"I'm ready to make sure that doesn't happen," Carlos

said eagerly. "My mind is buzzing with ideas, and I've only had one cup of coffee. Maybe we can speak with Miguel and share our experiences. Growing slow and steady has been good for us."

"Good. I appreciate it. I'm not sure if you can speak any sense into my cousin, but anything is worth a try at this point. See you shortly. Please let me know if you need anything." She made a graceful exit.

Carlos and I explored our room. It was spacious, with the same dark wood accents and arched windows and doors as the main floor. The room was actually two connecting rooms with a canopy bed, dressers, and seating area attached to a living and dining area with a couch, love seat, and kitchenette. French doors led to a balcony with gorgeous views of the fields, as well as the pool, outdoor seating, twinkle lights, and potted palms. It was clear Valentina enjoyed entertaining. She hadn't missed a detail. The kitchenette was outfitted with a bowl of fresh fruit, more pastries, coffee, and sparkling water. The bathroom was stocked with toiletries, pretty bath towels, and coffee-infused soaps and lotions.

I opened the balcony doors. Birdsong streamed inside, along with a tropical wind that sounded like rain rustling through the coffee trees.

"This is paradise," I said to Carlos, who kicked off his shoes and flopped on the bed.

"It takes me back to the ship and meeting you." His eyes held a touch of longing as he patted the empty spot next to him. "Come rest your feet, mi querida."

He didn't have to convince me. The flight and excitement had finally caught up with me. A nap sounded divine.

I snuggled into his arms and rested my head on his shoulder. "This is nice." I sighed contentedly.

"You are glowing, Julieta." He kissed the top of my head.

I sank deeper into his grasp and allowed my eyes to close, but just as sleep started to take hold, I was startled back into reality by the sound of raised voices outside. I jolted upright.

Carlos did the same. "What is that?" He went to the balcony as the shouting grew louder.

I followed him to see two men arguing on the terrace below. One of the men appeared to be in his mid to late twenties. He wore olive green overalls similar to Valentina's with the Finca las Nubes logo embroidered on the chest, a long-sleeved shirt, and a baseball hat. The other man was closer to forty. He wore business casual clothing, black slacks, and a crisp white shirt. His thick black hair fell to his chin in waves. I pegged him as Miguel, Valentina's cousin, immediately. They could have been siblings with their similar features—their big, brown eyes, curly hair, and petite frames.

"Easy, easy. Back off. There's no reason to yell," the man in slacks said to the younger guy, who appeared ready to lunge at him.

"You can't do this! I won't let you do this!" Instead of calming down, the worker's tone grew louder and harsher. "Miguel, you are killing the farm. You are killing all of us. How can you do this? Why would you do this?"

I caught the general gist of their argument. Miguel, as I correctly guessed, tried to smooth the situation, laying on the charm. "Alex, my brother, my friend, you know me. I only do what is best for Finca las Nubes. For you, for everyone. You will be able to live a new life, a better life. You can't live in the shack forever. I do this for you. You can live in luxury. You don't need to stay at the farm. You can buy a big house anywhere."

"I don't want to buy a big house. I love the farm. I love living here. This is my life, and you're destroying it. This sale will destroy the land, too." Alex spat at the ground as he spoke. Angry red splotches erupted on his neck and cheeks. "You can't do this. I won't let you."

"You don't have a choice." Miguel shrugged and stepped away from Alex toward the slatted railing fencing that separated the terrace from the rest of the grounds.

Alex lunged at him.

I gasped. For a second, I thought he was going to push Miguel over the railing. Since the house was angled on a sloping hillside above the coffee fields, the drop from the terrace had to be at least twenty feet off the ground. A fall would be dangerous, if not deadly.

Miguel ducked out of his grasp and smoothed the front of his shirt like he was preparing to give a presentation. "Amigo, don't do this."

Alex fumed. Even from my vantage point, I could see the muscles in his neck and arms bulge and tighten as if it was taking every ounce of self-control not to toss Miguel off the deck. Alex was twice his size. He could easily overpower Miguel, but if Miguel was concerned, his body language gave no indication. He stuffed his hands in his pockets and maneuvered around Alex, strolling toward the French doors of the ground floor. "We're done here."

"You might be done, but this isn't over. I'm not letting you get away with this!" Alex yelled after him.

Carlos turned to me and scowled. "I think Valentina needs us more than she might even realize."

I nodded in agreement, watching Alex storm toward the stairs that led down to the fields. Obviously, Valentina wasn't the only person upset about Miguel potentially selling his shares of the farm. I needed to figure out a solution fast—before things escalated and turned violent.

Chapter Five

The argument between Miguel and Alex had put an end to my nap, so Carlos and I changed into our hiking gear and decided to head downstairs and soak up the afternoon sun on the terrace until Valentina was ready to give us a tour.

The entryway table was still set up with snacks and treats, so I helped myself to melon lemonade, a handful of spiced nuts, and a custard tart. I couldn't take my eyes off the architecture. The grand entrance and courtyard had a timeless element and perfectly blended nature into the hacienda.

Carlos poured himself a cup of coffee. "Valentina has outdone herself. This is so thoughtful of her."

"It's the pura vida way," a voice behind us echoed throughout the room.

I turned to see Miguel casually resting his body against the front door like he didn't want us to know he'd been eavesdropping. "You must be Carlos and Jules," he said, strolling toward us with his hand extended. His charisma came through in his toothy smile and a slight touch of superiority in his eyes.

"We've heard so much about you from Valentina," I said, shaking his hand. "I can see the family resemblance."

He clasped his other hand on top of mine in a show of power and left it there long enough that Carlos finally broke in. "Thank you for having us on the farm."

Miguel broke our connection to shake Carlos's hand but let his gaze linger on me. "Valentina didn't tell me your wife is so beautiful."

Carlos let out a low growl under his breath. He typically wasn't jealous or overprotective. He freely and willingly expressed his love and emotions with me and everyone in his life. It was one of the things that attracted me most. That and his olive skin and dreamy eyes that I never failed to get lost in. However, lately, his paternal instincts had kicked in. I'm used to being independent and protecting myself, but I found his desire to be my constant bodyguard oddly endearing and comforting. It was clear my pregnancy was affecting him, too.

If Miguel picked up on his energy, he ignored it. He popped a strawberry in his mouth. "Valentina says you're going to help her with the menu. I've tried to caution her not to put too much time and effort into this coffee and pastry tasting bar because the farm is about to go through a major transformation. As they say in America—a glow-up, sí?"

I wasn't sure a glow-up was the best way to describe a hostile buyout.

I played it off like this was brand-new information, wanting to hear his perspective. "Oh, really, what kind of transformation?"

Miguel motioned to the terrace. "Come, let's sit and

enjoy the view. I'll show you my vision for our humble family farm. It is time to create something new—something grand here. The land demands it."

I grabbed another tart for good measure and joined him on the deck. The view needed no improvement, but Valentina's touch was evident in the outdoor space as well. Large potted palms flanked the seating area, which consisted of dark wicker couches and chairs with soft blue cushions and yellow accent pillows. Lanterns and hanging baskets overflowing with red ginger and flamingo flowers hung from the pillars and columns. Rows of coffee plants filled the horizon in a rolling sea of deep greens. Their waxy leaves were dotted with clusters of red and green cherries. Tall banana and poro trees were scatted throughout the acreage, offering shady patches for workers to take much-needed breaks from the sun. The shimmering blue swimming pool with a tiled deck, comfortable lounge chairs, and umbrellas beckoned me. I couldn't wait to dive in later. Maybe Carlos and I would have to sneak out for a midnight swim.

In the distance, the volcanic mountain ridges gave the landscape a majestic scale. It reminded me of the way the Siskiyou Mountains surrounded the plaza. Birds that were far off Ashland's migratory path flitted between the trees.

The sky was a soft shade of blue and held the fragrance of coffee blossoms.

"Please sit." Miguel motioned to one of the couches.

I rested my drink on a glass-top coffee table and used one of the throw pillows to support my back.

"You mentioned renovations," Carlos said, sitting so close to me that our knees touched.

I hid a smile. Miguel's oozing charm had definitely put him on edge.

"Yes, what you see in front of you is nothing compared to what it will be in a few years. It is time for our family's legacy to realize its full potential—to do what my grandparents and parents could only dream about." Miguel's voice took on a wistful tone as he told us about his development plans. "We'll expand the fields, taking over two plots from neighboring farms. This area will become a full-scale production center." He gestured to the west side of the property. "No more tinkering with outdated equipment that barely runs. We'll have state-of-the-art facilities and increase our production on a scale my ancestors never could have imagined. Our tasting room will become a full-scale restaurant and high-end dining experience. Every dish will be infused with our golden beans," he continued, pointing to a sweet but small building to the east that looked like a converted barn.

I wanted to ask him about Sofia and his vision for their partnership, but we were interrupted by a woman in her late sixties, who came up the stairs from the fields carrying a basket of bananas. She had glossy white hair cut in a shoulder-length bob and tied back with two small silver barrettes. Unlike Valentina and Alex, she wasn't wearing the farm overalls, but I got the sense she must have spent time in the fields, because she was covered in sun-protective pants and a long-sleeved shirt with a high collar guarding her neck.

"Miguel, I've been looking for you," she said in Spanish before realizing he wasn't alone. "Oh, sorry. I didn't know you had guests."

"These are Valentina's friends, Carlos and Jules," Miguel replied, motioning to us.

Carlos started to get up.

"No, no, sit," the woman said swapping to English as she waved him off with her basket. "I didn't mean to interrupt, but I do need to speak with you about an important matter when you have a minute." She looked pointedly at Miguel. It wasn't hard to catch the intensity in her tone. It wasn't a request. It was a demand.

"What is more important than this?" Miguel countered, and moved back to the couches, encouraging her to do the same. "Carlos and Jules, meet Carmen. Carmen is in charge of the workers. She oversees their housing, food, childcare, schooling, and pay during the harvest. How long have you been at the farm now?" he asked, sitting and patting the spot next to him.

Carmen looked as if she would rather do anything else, but she forced a smile and joined him. "I've been here since before you were born." She set the basket of bananas on the coffee table. "Your grandfather hired me when I was seventeen, and I never left."

I was impressed with the Espinoza family legacy. It was something to aspire to at Torte. Hopefully, future generations of Capshaws would still be running a thriving bakeshop and community hub when Carlos and I were old and gray.

"Carmen is our madre—the mother of our workers." Miguel tried to wrap his arm around her shoulder, but she shrugged him off. He pretended not to notice, but I saw a brief flash of disappointment cross his face. "She is a staunch supporter of the workers and keeps us all in line."

"The reason that Finca las Nubes is the success it is

today is because of our workers. We pay fair wages and provide quality housing with private bathrooms, water, food, free electricity and internet, health care, support, and services for the workers—some of them travel from as far away as Nicaragua and Panama for the harvest season." Her gestures became more animated as she spoke about families. "This is their home. We are known throughout the picking community as the number one place to work because of our care and commitment—providing childcare, ensuring young children have access to schools. Our safe working conditions. The joy that radiates from the fields—the singing—the dinners under the stars. We are the top producer in the region because of our workers. Without them, we are nothing."

Her impassioned speech felt like a plea. A plea that wasn't intended for Carlos and me. I didn't have to guess what might happen to the workers if Miguel's deal went through.

Miguel shifted uncomfortably and addressed Carmen as if he'd read my mind. "Carmen, you worry too much. This isn't the pura vida way. I've told you the workers will be looked after. Terra Café International is a global coffee chain. They understand the vital contributions of the workers."

"No." Her voice turned nasal and pitchy as she shook her hand and wagged her finger in his face like she was scolding a child. "Miguel, you are a dreamer. Valentina is a realist. This is why you make a good team. Terra Café International does not care about our workers. They will cut wages and end the programs and protections we have put into place. Your need to grow and revitalize the farm is going to ruin the lives of dozens of families who have built this farm on their very backs." She blew out a long breath and stood. Her hands quaked like she was trying to contain her emotions but was on the edge of completely breaking down. "I'm sorry to put you in the middle of this, but my heart is broken," she said to me and Carlos before addressing Miguel again. "I'm disappointed in you. You're so quick to give up this land and destroy the lives of everyone who loves it. And for what? Money? Since when did money ever buy happiness, mi hijo?" She walked off without her bananas, shaking her head in disgust.

"Everyone is too serious about the buyout. They resist change and are set in the old ways, but it's time to progress forward." Miguel tried to make light of his exchange with Carmen, but the more time I spent at the farm, the more I realized that no one wanted the sale to go through. I couldn't shake the feeling that everyone's desperation to save the farm might lead to something terrible.

Chapter Six

Valentina found us on the terrace shortly after Carmen left. Andy joined us, looking refreshed and ready for adventure in his khaki hiking pants, matching light earth-toned long-sleeved T-shirt, hiking boots, and a wide-brimmed hat. A retro camera hung around his neck. He had two notebooks and a pen at the ready. He reminded me of an eager college student, overly prepared for the first day of classes.

"Where are your binoculars?" I teased. "We have a regular Indiana Jones in our mix."

"An Indiana Jones, jonesing for more coffee," he bantered back.

I chuckled as a parakeet swooped over us, squawking as it glided into a nearby banana tree.

"If you're ready, we can go now," Valentina suggested. "Everyone has a hat and sunscreen, yes? We'll bring water too. We won't stay in the sun for long, but it does get hot at this time of day."

She was right. In the time we'd been sitting on the terrace, the temp had warmed substantially. Although part of that might have been due to the humidity, which was something we weren't familiar with in dry, arid Ashland.

I dabbed my neck with a napkin and grabbed my sun hat.

"Be sure to stay hydrated," Carlos said, studying me with concern. "Are you too hot already?"

"I'm fine." I knew if I told him the truth, he'd insist I stay back. I was running a bit hot, but that was normal during pregnancy. My doctor and I had discussed the trip, and she approved of the travel and exercise—in moderation. As long as I paced myself and returned to the house if I noticed any signs of heat exhaustion, I would be fine.

"I believe I gave you the rundown on the snakes, spiders, and insects that share our habitat," Valentina said, checking to make sure we were all wearing boots and long sleeves. "I'm glad you've dressed accordingly. Golden orb weavers or jumping spiders are most common, but there are occasional banana spiders—they're rare, but they're highly venomous and aggressive. Keep your eyes on the trees for eyelash vipers and boa constrictors."

"I don't like any of this," Andy said with a grimace. "Snakes, spiders, insects—oh my!"

"We'll be fine as long as we stick to the trails and marked paths. I don't recommend foraging out in the underbrush or looking beneath rocks—that's where you'll find our famous bark scorpion." Valentina wiggled her fingers like a creepy crawler.

Andy stomped twice. "Glad I brought my sturdy boots."

"We'll start at the barn," Valentina said, directing us to the east side of the house along a cobblestone pathway flanked by tropical plants. "We finished the remodel last month, and I'm very eager to hear your thoughts."

The barn didn't look like much from the outside—a rust-brown building with an A-frame roof. But inside was another story. The far wall had been converted into a giant glass window so that the entire backside could open out onto the fields like the terrace. A long, narrow bar with window seating ran the length of the wall. Cozy groups of industrial-style chairs with vibrant pillows and funky iron coffee tables were interspersed throughout the space. The front housed glass cases for pastries, two expensive espresso machines, and another bar with seating where customers could watch baristas make their drinks. Tucked in the corner near the espresso counter was a private coffee tasting room with posters of the lifecycle of a coffee plant, examples of coffee beans at their various stages of ripening in translucent glass canisters, and bags of whole coffee beans and merch available for sale.

"You've done an incredible job, Valentina," I gushed, yet again floored by her aesthetic eye. The barn was a perfect balance of chic meets rustic, preserving the origins of the farm while adding a modern touch.

"I'm happy with how it turned out, but now, with Miguel trying to sell his shares, I fear it will be for nothing. If the sale goes through, all of this will be destroyed."

"Why would they tear down the barn and tasting room?" Carlos asked, running his hand along the smooth wooden countertop. Valentina had managed to blend the indoor and outdoor space seamlessly with her use of natural materials and plants. Vines dangled from the bar and twisted along the shiny glass cases. I could already picture how lively and energetic the space would be filled with happy customers and a delectable display of pastries.

"Would you like to see their plans?" Valentina asked, taking her phone out of the back pocket of her overalls. We gathered closer so she could show us Miguel and Terra Café International's architectural sketches. She swiped through dozens of sketches, drawings, and artist renderings of the new and improved Finca las Nubes.

"It's soulless." Andy was the first to respond. "That's not an improvement. Where's the charm?"

"Yes, soulless—that's the perfect word. I've been trying to land on a description for this monstrosity, and that's it," Valentina cried, tapping her phone screen as if hoping she could swipe away the image permanently. "Miguel seems to think tourists want modern polished coffee experiences, but I keep reminding him that it's our roots that will attract people to visit—to see how we've cultivated the land like our ancestors, generation after generation."

She was right. The new tasting room images starkly contrasted with the rustic charm of the barn. According to the notes accompanying the illustrations, it would be constructed from gray concrete with steel beam supports. Sharp, cold angles defined the new structure inside and out. The cold, minimalist interior was barren and void of any warmth. Polished floors and harsh LED lighting replaced the wooden accents and sweet touches of flora and fauna.

"This area becomes a paved road and parking lot?" Carlos asked, looking from the photos outside to the fields.

"Yes, the natural tiers of the field will be flattened to accommodate processing plants and large-scale storage facilities. Metal silos will stand where rows and rows of coffee bushes planted by my great-grandfather currently grow. They intend to erase our history and our connection to the earth, making this land nothing more than a commodity." She sucked in a breath like she couldn't quite believe it was true.

Again, I was struck by how painful this must be for Valentina. Fast-food coffee culture had shifted the focus from craftsmanship to mass production. Family farms throughout the region had witnessed similar fates, potentially forever altering the landscape of Central America's coffee culture.

There were a variety of environmental activist groups working to protect small family-owned farms. I wondered if there was a way we could connect Valentina with someone who might be able to advocate for preserving her land.

She tucked her phone back into her overalls. "I keep ruining our time together. Please accept my apologies. I never imagined it would come to this." She gestured outside. "Let's take a walk through the fields and up to the processing stations."

"There's no need to apologize," I said, making sure my hat was secure before we traipsed into the sun. "I was just wondering if there's a possibility of working with one of the groups that helps family farms conserve land?"

She held the door open for us and locked it behind her. "It's funny you mention it. I hired an agronomist, Isabel Castillo, who's been assisting to make sure every phase of the production is organic and sustainable. She suggested the same thing. She has some friends who work for groups like that."

"I think you should," Carlos said, falling in step behind me. "They do great work for coffee culture and the environment."

"An agronomist can be essential for studying soil management, crop production, and sustainable farming techniques to improve agricultural efficiency and coffee production. From my research it looks like the most successful farms have hired agronomists. Speaking of that, I've read a lot about the SHB label and how it's prized in the industry for its high quality. Does organic play into that, too?" Andy asked, changing the subject as he took frantic notes, barely bothering to watch his footing.

"You have done your research." Valentina led us along a small pressed-dirt path between leafy banana trees. "SHB, or strictly hard bean, refers to the elevation—between twelve hundred and eighteen hundred meters. What is that in feet? I can't do American math."

"Because we're the only country in the world that measures differently." Andy laughed. "But I happened to excel in my math classes in college, and, full disclosure, I did read a bunch of articles about the coffee region before our trip, so it's fresh in my head. It's four to six thousand feet above sea level."

"You get a gold star," I said, glancing behind me with a grin.

"Cultivating the beans at this elevation results in a premium product." Valentina held back a branch so we could pass under it. "We've been undergoing the transformation process to receive our organic certification for a little over a year. It takes two to three years. That's why we hired Isabel. We've been using natural methods for growing our golden beans since my great-grandfather's time, but there are strict practices and specific requirements to obtain our Rainforest Alliance certification. Isabel can tell you more. She loves talking about this topic and is very enthusiastic. We'll see her shortly."

The pathway was a series of rolling switchbacks flanked by coffee bushes. Bees buzzed from flower to flower, and butterflies in colors that seemed too impossibly brilliant to be real—sapphire blue, tiger orange, and magenta—wafted around us in staggering numbers, landing on our shoulders and hats. Everything smelled sweet, like it had been misted with jasmine.

My cheeks warmed as we trekked through the fields, but I felt rejuvenated from the sensory experience of being part of the farm.

When we arrived at the production area, I was slightly out of breath but captivated by the rugged beauty of the land. There was a shaded nursery where young coffee plants were grown as seedlings until they were ready to be placed in the field. Large forest green shade sails were stretched over long tables filled with seedling trays and drip watering systems.

"This is where the magic begins," Valentina said as we passed by. "I love to watch the beans sprout. They're like my babies. I check on them every day."

We proceeded to the main processing area, which housed a machine that removed the outer pulp of the coffee cherries to reveal the bean, fermentation tanks where the beans would stay for twelve to forty-eight hours to remove the mucilage, or sticky layer, and water channels used to wash the beans after fermentation. Narrow, rickety metal walkways hung precariously over massive concrete tanks below—one misstep and the fall would be long and unforgiving.

"Here, meet some of the team," Valentina said, pausing at the machine. Alex, the employee I'd seen arguing with Miguel earlier, was using a screwdriver to tighten a knob. "This is Alex, our farm manager."

Alex looked to be about Andy's age. He wore his dark hair in long waves that fell to his chin in the same style as Miguel. They could almost pass as twins, except that Alex was a good ten years younger. His Finca las Nubes overalls were stained with grease splatter and dust.

Alex set the screwdriver down and waved hello as Valentina made introductions.

"Is there a problem with the machine?" she asked.

"What?" He startled and shot a glance behind him at the dials, blocking Valentina's view with his body. "No. No. Routine maintenance," he replied, picking up the screwdriver again and getting back to work. "Isabel is looking for you. She's over at the drying patio."

"That's where we're headed next." Valentina paused and looked at Andy. "Do you want to come with us to the patio? Or Alex can show you exactly what each piece of equipment does, if you prefer."

"Really? That would be great. Yeah, cool. If that's good with you, man, I'm here to learn." Andy tapped the tip of his pen against his notebook.

Alex didn't look quite as enthusiastic as Andy, but he gave him a nod and motioned for him to come closer.

We left them and moved on to the drying patio, which was basically a large exposed concrete area where the beans were laid out to dry under the sun. A young woman was raking the beans in a pattern as we approached.

"Valentina, thank goodness you're here." She dropped the rake. "Have you seen Javier? He's furious. He learned about Miguel's desire to make a deal with Terra Café International and he's on a rampage. He said he's going to kill Miguel, and I don't think he's kidding."

Chapter Seven

"Isabel, slow down, slow down," Valencia said, trying to calm her. "Start from the beginning. Why is Javier here?"

Isabel paced to the end of the patio and back. She was in her late twenties with short brown hair cropped in a pixie cut. She wore long, dangling earrings and the Finca las Nubes overalls with a tank top underneath. Her arms were tanned from hours spent in the sun, and her nails were painted in multiple shades of blue with black camo. It was like she'd put her own punk spin on the farm look. "Word has spread. Everyone knows about Miguel's deal, and Javier is furious. He came here looking for Miguel and told me his business would be directly impacted by the sale if it were successful. I explained that none of us want the sale to go through and that it's out of our hands, but he wouldn't listen. He stormed off, saying that he would stop the sale one way or another. I've never seen him like that, Valentina. It was scary."

Valentina remained composed. She drew in a breath and took a moment to collect her thoughts before responding. "When was this, and do you know where he went?"

Isabel chewed on her pinkie. "Um, maybe ten or fifteen minutes ago. I'm not exactly sure. I called down to the house, but you didn't answer. I knew your friends were here." She paused to acknowledge Carlos and me. I gave her a soft smile, wanting to help but not knowing how. "Then I checked with Alex. I didn't know what else to do."

"It's fine. I'm sure it's nothing." Valentina didn't sound convinced.

"May I ask, who is Javier?" Carlos reached down to pick up an errant bean and rubbed its hull off, revealing a green bean beneath the outer layer of parchment.

"Javier Mendez owns a number of successful coffee shops throughout the country, Dulce Coffee. He has locations in San José, on the coast, and in the rainforest," Valentina said. "He's been a family friend and a supporter of the farm for many, many years. We have an exclusive partnership. He procures all his beans directly from us."

"Oh yes. We tasted his coffee at the airport," I said. "Andy was double-fisting cups. He couldn't get enough."

"He's a huge advocate for preserving family farms. He does coffee the right way. The natural way," Isabel added. "His business is built on supporting the local community and Costa Rican farmers. That's his entire brand, which is why he's so angry about Miguel's ridiculous deal. His customers will revolt. Dulce Coffee is Costa Rica."

"Sí, he's not wrong about that." Valentina nodded in agreement. "Locals resist the big international companies and chains who come in and buy up our land. Javier is very vocal about his commitment to protecting our coffee culture."

"It seems like everyone at Finca las Nubes and your colleagues are unhappy about the idea of the sale," I said, repeating the obvious. "Is there a possibility of collectively pooling resources? Could Javier be a potential investor?"

An odd look flashed across Isabel's face that I couldn't quite distinguish. Was it fear? Something else?

"Yes, and what about Julieta's idea of environmental protection groups?" Carlos suggested. "We can also reach out to our contacts from the *Amour of the Seas*, as well as other businesses in southern Oregon, to spread the word. I'm confident we can help you secure more American wholesale accounts."

Valentina tried to smile, but she couldn't disguise the worry in the lines on her forehead. "That's kind of you, but I'm afraid Terra Café International is offering a price that none of us, even if we pool our resources, can match, and we're running out of time. Miguel is motivated. Sofia has been coming around a lot. Every day I wake up waiting for the news that he's officially signed a contract. When that happens, there will be nothing more I can do."

Isabel kicked at the beans she'd been raking. "It's unfair. We have to stop him and Terra Café International. It starts with this farm and then, before you know it, every family farm in the region will be under their control."

I felt like I was stuck in a loop. Everyone on the farm—Valentina, Alex, Carmen, and now Isabel—repeated the same sentiment. Miguel was obviously enemy number one. My thoughts drifted to Richard Lord again. The situation with him and Mom had seemed impossible when I moved home to Ashland. It felt like a foregone conclusion that Torte would slip out of our hands and into his possession, and yet a solution had emerged when I had least expected it. And from a person I never imagined—me.

I refused to give up hope that the same thing could happen for Finca las Nubes.

"Javier didn't say where he was going?" Valentina asked.

"No." Isabel shook her head. "I think he either went to the main house or maybe to Miguel's."

Valentina started to move but stopped and pointed at the large rake. "Why are you raking the practice beans?"

"I want to be as good as the crew," Isabel replied, running her fingers over the spiky tines in the rake. "If I'm advising them on the best ecological practices, I want to show them that I understand every phase of the process. My raking skills aren't great, so I've been working on getting better. It's important for earning their trust."

"Okay, I see. We'll find Javier." Valentina sighed and ran her teeth along her bottom lip. "Would you two like to return to the house? I hate dragging you all around the farm, but I should intervene with Javier and see if I can smooth things over. He's our biggest and most important client."

"Would you like moral support?" I asked, already suspecting that her answer would be yes. I could tell Valentina was flustered, and rightfully so.

She gave me a grateful smile. "If you don't mind, yes, that would be nice. You have so much in common with Javier. It might be a nice distraction from talking about the business."

"Count us in," Carlos said.

"We'll talk later," Valentina said to Isabel. There was

an edge in her tone that told me their conversation wasn't done.

Miguel's house was on the far west side of the property. There were three private houses for staff and Miguel's private residence. Then, a new trail cut up the hillside and led to the workers' quarters.

"This is the hacienda," Valentina said, passing by a white stucco house with a red tile roof. Large wooden beams framed the doorways, and a veranda wrapped around the front, shaded by mango, orange, and lemon trees. "I grew up in this house, and I have so many wonderful memories here of picking oranges for my breakfast and running through the fields. Carmen lives here now."

"It's lovely," I said.

"Alex lives here in what we call la Casita de los Abuelos," Valentina said, pointing out a stone cottage with a porch and a small, fenced garden.

I recalled Miguel referencing Alex's cottage as a shack during their argument. It was far from a shack. The cottage was neat and tidy with bright teal and yellow trim around the windows and bougainvillea draped around the eaves.

"The Grandparents' Cottage," Carlo translated.

"Yes, our great-grandfather lived here when I was young. My grandparents lived in the main house, and Miguel's family lived right up the slope." She motioned to the hillside in front of us. "His house did not look like this when we were kids. Miguel tore down the original cottage and built la Casa Nueva. I should have realized then that he had no intention of preserving the farm."

My eyes followed hers to a modern structure built into the gently sloping hillside. Like the designs for the future coffee bar and tasting room, Miguel's house was a modern geometric concrete box with clean lines and large glass windows. A long deck extended from the full-length doors and windows.

"He must have a good view of the drying patio and processing area," Carlos said.

"Sí, everyone teases he likes to lord over the farm from the hillside."

"We know someone like that." I caught Carlos's eye. Richard Lord took his name to heart. It was good that I didn't need to worry about him harassing our staff while we were away from Torte, because he was off on a secret location filming his reality dating show. Although what I wouldn't have given to be a fly on the wall during taping to see Richard in action.

In order to reach Miguel's house, we dipped back down under the trees. "This is the edge of our property," Valentina said, stepping carefully over a gurgling stream. "The creek belongs to us and then the land above Miguel's house belongs to the neighbors, but if Miguel gets his way, he'll take over their land, too."

A cabin with a thatched roof sat near the stream. Overgrown grasses and wildflowers surrounded it. "Does anyone live there?"

"Isabel is using it temporarily, but it's on my list of projects that need attention. I'm sure you understand, it feels like the list is never-ending, and I worry about putting more money into any renovations at this point." She picked up the pace as the trail took a sharp turn.

We didn't have to wonder if Javier was at Miguel's because we could hear their voices echoing over the fields.

"Put a stop to it now," a man's voice thundered in Spanish.

We were too far down to see anything. The trees obstructed our view, but the sound of their voices carried overhead.

"It's too late, my friend." I recognized Miguel's smooth tone. He should have been a politician instead of a coffee farmer. "Do not worry. You will be taken care of. I've worked it into the deal. Dulce Coffee will continue to have an exclusive partnership with us. Your signature roasts cannot be duplicated. It's in the contract. I'll show you."

"I don't care about paperwork." Javier's voice grew louder as we approached the modern house. "I've spoken with my lawyers. Call it off, or I'll sue."

"It's already done, mi amigo."

I stopped in midstride as the sound of a scuffle broke out, and a deck chair came sailing off the porch. It landed inches away from Valentina's head, shattering as it hit the ground.

"Miguel, stop!" she hollered.

The grounds went silent momentarily.

The next thing I knew, Javier was sprinting toward us like he was trying to make a quick escape.

Chapter Eight

"Javier, stop!" Valentina called as the large man wearing slacks, loafers, and an expensive, tailored shirt breezed past us. His features were striking, and the thin, dark mustache that curled above his upper lip reminded me of an old-fashioned movie villain. It was the kind he could twirl while plotting out his next devious move.

"Your cousin is a disgrace to the Espinoza name and Costa Rica," Javier yelled as he ran past us. He didn't bother to stop. He brushed by, kicking up a wake of dust. "This isn't over, Valentina."

Valentina crumpled over, burying her face in her hands as tears poured from her eyes. "I'm so sorry. I never thought it would come to this."

I wrapped my arm around her. "It's okay. We understand it's complicated."

"I will check on Miguel," Carlos said, heading toward the house. "I'll meet you back at the house."

It was probably better this way. He was a neutral party. The stress had finally reached a tipping point for Valentina. She wasn't in any shape for a rational conversation with her cousin. "Why don't we go back to the house and let things settle?"

"Yes, okay." She wiped tears away with the back of her hand and sniffed. "What about Carlos?"

"He can find his way back." I was more concerned about her well-being at this point. Carlos would be fine.

"I can't believe this is happening while you're visiting," she said as we retraced our steps to the main house. "It came out of the blue. I had no idea Miguel wanted to sell. I've been careful not to say much because I was worried that once word got out, this very thing would happen."

"It's not your fault." I stuck with my talking point. This was out of Valentina's control.

"It's hard not to feel like it is," she admitted softly. "He's my family. I'm guilty by association. I can't help but wonder what my great-grandparents and grandparents would be thinking. We've ruined their legacy."

"That's not true," I insisted. "There still may be a solution."

"Maybe." She sighed.

We made it back to the house to find Sofia Rojas, the woman we met briefly at the Central Market, waiting for us in the entryway. She was sitting in one of the plush chairs in the vast foyer, sipping an iced coffee as if she hadn't a care in the world. A file folder and pen rested on her lap. "Valentina, you're just who I wanted to see." She stood and extended a hand, tucking the file folder under one arm. "We have an important matter to discuss."

Valentina stiffened. She turned to me. "Would you mind checking with the cook to see how dinner preparations are coming?"

"I'd love to." That was the truth. I was eager to see Valentina's kitchen and itching to put my hands to work. Plus, I could tell she wanted to speak with Sofia alone, which was fine with me. Was this the moment she'd been dreading? Was Sofia here to inform her that Miguel had signed a deal with Terra Café International? I hoped not. There had to be another way.

I left them with a deep, internal sigh and wandered through the first floor, following the aromas of simmering beans and peppers until I found the kitchen. It was a chef's dream, with a six-burner gas stove and huge windows offering ample natural light. The pool sparkled below like a little oasis in the middle of a sea of green. A large butcher-block island sat in the middle of the room with an assortment of copper pans hanging above it. Open cupboards and vibrant artwork lined the walls. I could easily get used to working in a kitchen with this view.

A woman I guessed to be the cook greeted me in Spanish.

From living with Carlos and Ramiro, and my time on the ship, I knew enough kitchen terminology in Spanish for her to direct me to the ingredients and supplies I needed to make arroz con leche, a traditional Costa Rican rice pudding I'd seen offered at several of the sodas in the Central Market. Being in the kitchen again instantly grounded me. I just wished my conversational Spanish was stronger. It was much easier for me to understand the romance language, versus speak it. Carlos intended to speak Spanish to the twins once they were born. I loved the thought of having bilingual children and needed to improve my own speaking skills to keep up with them.

I mangled my way through Spanish small talk with the

cook while I boiled white rice in water on the stove with cinnamon sticks and a healthy pat of butter. She excused herself to pick some vegetables outside, leaving me alone with my thoughts.

While the rice boiled, I gathered whole milk, condensed milk, and evaporated milk, as well as salt, lime, cinnamon, and nutmeg. I wished there was a clear solution or specific way I could help Valentina, but my best offering at the moment was adding the creamy, sweet rice dessert to the cook's dinner spread.

Once the water evaporated from the rice, I removed it from the heat and discarded the cinnamon sticks. Then I added the milks, salt, and lime zest; returned the pan to the stove; and brought it back to a boil. I turned the heat to medium and stirred constantly until it began to thicken into a pudding.

Then I took it off the burner and stirred in plump, juicy raisins.

I wondered how Valentina's conversation with Sofia was going. Did she have any sway? Doubtful. But what about the other employees? Alex, Carmen, and Isabel clearly shared Valentina's sentiment about preserving the farm. The same was true for Javier. If he had a successful chain of coffee shops, perhaps there was an opportunity for him to invest in Finca las Nubes.

My phone buzzed with a new text.

Shocker, it was from Lance. "You haven't even been gone a full day, and I'm bored out of my ever-loving mind. Tell me all the wonderful things about Costa Rica. No, scratch that. I'll be bitterly envious. Although, how do you feel about scouting honeymoon locations?"

I walked to the window to snap a photo of the terrace,

pool, and coffee fields and text it to him. "My current view could be a contender."

"Aww, that's absolutely bucolic. I'm sold. Book it!"

I laughed and found a small spoon. Event rentals, weddings, honeymoons, family reunions, holiday parties—this could be another revenue stream for Valentina. She had mentioned it in passing earlier, but maybe that was another area to explore.

The pudding was steaming hot, so I scooped a small bite onto the spoon and blew on it to cool it off. The minute I put it to my lips, I understood why the dish was so popular. It was light and creamy with a spicy cinnamon finish and a bright zest of lime. The recipe called for dusting it with more cinnamon and nutmeg before I served it later.

I scooped it into pretty glass dishes. The pudding could be served warm or cold. I decided a chilled pudding made the most sense for our dinner party.

Carlos showed up as I was getting ready to put the last dish into the fridge. "I thought I would find you here." He wrapped his arms around my waist and nuzzled my neck.

I squeezed his hand and turned to face him. "How did it go with Miguel?"

"Don't ask." He released me and tried to sneak a taste of the pudding with his finger.

I swatted it away and then pointed to the pan, which still needed to be cleaned. "You can lick the pan, but don't disturb my finished product."

He threw his hands up in surrender. "Yes, chef."

I offered him the spatula I'd used to scoop the pudding into the glass bowls. "What did he say?"

"Not much." Carlos dragged the spatula along the

inside of the pan. "He's slick. A smooth talker, but I do not trust him. He says he cares about the farm and only wants to grow his family legacy and improve upon what they've done, but I think he is also greedy and blinded by money."

"I know." I washed my sticky fingers under warm water. "I feel bad for Valentina. I was hoping a little time in the kitchen might clear my head and I'd suddenly be struck with the perfect solution, but I've got nothing."

"You have delicious pudding." Carlos licked the spatula. "This is something."

I grinned. "I'm afraid pudding doesn't solve her issues, though."

He turned serious. "No. No, it does not."

I was about to ask him his thoughts on putting a call out to everyone we knew in the industry. As he'd mentioned on our tour, we had extensive contacts. We could go so far as to reach out to higher-ups on the *Amour of the Seas*. If Valentina could land a partnership with the cruise line, that could bring in a lot of cash, and a farm like hers was a perfect match for the ship. It would be a great story for guests, who would connect with the idea that they were supporting a coffee grower who had gotten her start working on the ship. I could practically have written the press release right then, but before I was able to say more, Andy burst into the kitchen.

His face was splotched with red marks like he'd been stung by wasps. Sweat stains spread across his chest. He gasped for breath, sucking air in big bursts. "I can't believe it—the emergency crew is on their way, but it's just so awful—I can't . . . I can't . . ."

"What? What is it?"

He bent over and grabbed his knees like he was going to pass out.

"Andy, what happened?" I ran to him and rubbed his back instinctively.

"Miguel. It's Miguel." His entire body heaved as the words tumbled from him. "Miguel's dead."

Chapter Nine

"Miguel is dead?" Carlos repeated, sounding stunned. "I was just with him."

Andy stood up, placing his hands on his hips and blowing out air in short bursts. "He's dead, for sure."

I could tell he was on the edge of a panic attack. I ushered him to the island and helped him sit on one of the stools. Then I poured him a cool glass of water and dampened a dish towel. I wrapped it around his neck and continued to rub his shoulders. "It's going to be okay. Take it easy. Nice, slow breathing." I modeled sipping air in through my nose slowly, holding it for a few seconds, and then releasing it. "Can you tell us what happened?"

Andy's breath hitched, but he sat up taller and clenched his jaw like he was forcing himself to push past the shock. "It was horrible. Alex was great. He gave me a step-by-step tutorial on the machines and the process. I've read about it, you know, but seeing how the beans transform in real life is so different. Everything was going fine at first. Alex and I totally hit it off. He's a coffee junkie like me. He knows his stuff. He told me about how he grew up on the farm. His dad was the farm manager before him and taught him everything he knew. The equipment is older, but it's in good shape. He's kept everything running like a well-oiled machine. I doubt there's anything he can't fix. I think he was leery about me at first, but once he realized I knew my stuff, he got super into showing me everything. I learned so much—my mind's kind of blown."

This was good. We needed to keep him talking. I'd been in his shoes before and knew how consuming shock could be. My priority in the short term was keeping him breathing and as calm as possible.

"Miguel came down and started telling Alex how to run the machines. It was like he wanted to be the one to show me. He took over and basically pushed Alex away." Andy rocked back and forth on his heels, his voice growing quieter. "Then it all happened at once. I heard him fall with a horrible thud, but I still can't believe it's real."

"Did they get into a physical altercation?" I asked.

Carlos moved the water glass closer to Andy. "Try drinking this."

Andy nodded, not looking at him, staring at the arched tile entry in a daze. "Yeah, okay." He picked up the water but didn't take a drink. "They didn't get into a fight, but I could tell Alex was irritated with Miguel. He was really upset about Miguel potentially selling his shares of the farm."

I had gotten the same impression from Alex.

"What happened next?" I asked, trying to steer the conversation back to poor Miguel.

Andy clutched the glass with one hand and rubbed the side of his head like he was trying to erase the image from his mind. "The woman we met at the market showed up—Sofia."

"Sofia was there?"

"Yeah, that's when Miguel really leaned into I'm-the-boss energy." He gulped and looked at his feet, shaking his head like he wanted to shake off the memory. "He was showboating for her and I think for me, although I don't know why. Alex warned him to be careful and cautioned him about operating the equipment properly, but Miguel wouldn't listen."

I didn't like where this was going or that Andy's cheeks had lost all their color.

"Then Carmen and Isabel showed up. Isabel was screaming at him—I couldn't make out what she was saying, it was all in Spanish, and Carmen tried to hold her back, but they both raced over to us, and then . . . then . . . Well, uh, it just happened so fast." Andy's voice was distant as if he were in another world. "Miguel turned on the machine, and then he slipped. I don't know how. One minute he was fine. The next thing I knew, he fell and landed on the ground twenty feet below. It was bad, and it was so fast. So fast. And he hit the concrete hard. It was instant." He stopped and shuddered, closing his eyes and covering his mouth with one hand like he was about to be sick. "I don't think there's anything we could have done. He was gone in an instant."

Valentina had shown us earlier that the machine was used to separate the coffee cherries from the beans. It had a large rotating drum with razor-sharp blades designed to strip the pulp from the beans. All of the machinery was located on tight catwalks twenty feet above large concrete containers that took the beans on to their next phase of processing. A hard fall would be fatal for sure. I couldn't fathom what Andy had seen.

Andy nodded, his eyes still glued to the other side of the kitchen. "The emergency shutoff valve failed. Alex tried to stop the machine. He tried to override the switch manually, but the blades kept rotating faster and faster. It was like it suddenly shot into warp speed or something."

"Oh, Andy, I'm so sorry." I placed my hand on his shoulder, knowing that my words were little comfort.

"Alex and Sofia are still there. Carmen and Isabel, too. Someone called the police. I don't know who. It's all a weird blur, like did it really happen?" Andy clutched the glass so hard I was worried it might break in his hands. "I said I would come tell you and get Valentina. I can't believe he's dead. The irony is he was telling Sofia that the machinery and equipment were one of the first things he wanted to upgrade. He said it's been in operation since the 1990s."

"Why don't I go find Valentina?" I suggested, catching Carlos's eye.

He nodded and clapped Andy's knee. "I'll stay with you. Can you eat something?"

Andy shook his head. "I don't think so. I feel pretty shaky and kind of weird."

"That's normal. That's fine," Carlos assured him. "We'll sit and rest for a while."

I didn't want to be the one to have to break the news to Valentina that her cousin was dead, but I refused to put Andy through that. It would be better to hear it from me than have her wander up to the processing area and see it firsthand.

"Valentina, are you here?" I called, leaving the kitchen and checking the living room first. She wasn't there, so I continued to the dining room and checked outside. She wasn't in the courtyard, so I peered out onto the terrace. At first I thought the terrace was empty, too, but I heard a soft whimper and stepped outside to get a better look. "Valentina, is that you? It's Jules."

"Yes, I'm here." She gestured from the farthest corner.

I approached her slowly, trying to think of what in the world I was going to say.

She was already crying.

Had she heard?

This end of the long deck wasn't far from the kitchen. The windows were open. Maybe she'd overheard our conversation.

She used both hands to wipe tears from her face. "I'm a mess. Sorry. This weekend is not at all what I had hoped for you."

I sank into the seat next to her, twisting my fingers together as I worked up the courage to tell her. My stomach churned as I tried to find the right words.

"It's everything." She wiped tears from her eyes and then met my gaze. "I think Miguel might have made a deal behind my back. Sofia tried to convince me yet again that I should give up my shares and take the money." She broke out into more tears. "I can't say for sure, but the rumors are swirling, and if they are true, I'm going to be gutted. The farm as we know it is done. How could he do this to me—sell our family legacy right out from under me?" Valentina's big brown eyes locked onto mine, burning with frustration.

I swallowed hard. There was no easy way to say this or soften the blow. But she had to hear it. "Valentina . . . there's been an accident."

Her expression flicked with confusion. "An accident?"

She blinked, her voice growing softer. "What do you mean?"

"It's Miguel. He's had a fall." I reached for her hand. Was it better to rip the Band-Aid off or ease into telling her the truth?

"What? Where?" She glanced around and started to get up. Her chest rose and fell in sharp uneven bursts.

I squeezed her arm. "There's no easy way to say this." As the words tumbled out of my mouth, sirens wailed outside. "He had an accident when he was demonstrating the machinery. I'm afraid he's dead."

"No! Not Miguel." She jumped to her feet and ran to the window. Her wide eyes darted from one side of the room like she was searching for an escape. "You're sure? Was anyone there?"

I nodded. "Alex, Sofia, Carmen, Isabel, and Andy. They all saw it."

"Oh no. Oh no. This is terrible." She took a staggering step backward and threw her hands to her cheeks as her mouth fell open. "Do you know what this means?"

I shook my head.

"He was murdered. Someone killed him, Jules."

Chapter Ten

"It sounds like it was an accident," I told Valentina as the wailing sirens grew louder. "He slipped and fell, and the emergency shutoff switch failed. Is that right?"

She shook her head, waving her finger back and forth like a metronome. "No, no, no. You don't understand. I was worried this was going to happen. I planned to speak with him after dinner tonight because I found something." She power-walked inside like she was in a race.

I assumed she wanted me to follow her, so I hurried after her to the foyer.

The emergency vehicles were close. The police would be here any minute. I could see flashing lights as an off-road ambulance bumped along the gravel road.

Valentina went straight to an antique walnut desk near the door. A large, cracked tile vase filled with birds of paradise rattled slightly as she yanked the top drawer open and handed me a folded sheet of paper with Miguel's name written in bold black ink. "Read this."

I opened the paper and read the note. It was written in Spanish but only two sentences long. My skills were decent enough to interpret the message. "'End the deal

now, or I end you'?" I looked at Valentina to clarify I had
the gist.

"Sí." She tapped the desk. "I found it here after I talked
to Sophia. I have no idea who could have left it. It's another reason I believe he must have gone behind my back.
'End the deal,' what does that mean? Did he already sign
the paperwork?"

I inspected the note. The handwriting was almost
childlike with frantic brushstrokes, like it had been written in a hurry. "I wonder if it was here earlier," I said
aloud, thinking back to returning to the house. I hadn't
noticed the note either. Although it wasn't as if I had paid
close attention to the details in the foyer, so it was possible the letter had been on the desk.

"No. I don't think so." Valentina shook her head, twisting her hair into braids like she was trying to hold herself
together.

"Do you have any idea who could have written it?" I
handed it back to her. "Do you recognize the handwriting?"

She folded the letter in half and tucked it in the front
pocket of her overalls. "No, but Miguel made so many
people angry with his plans. It could have been anyone."

The ambulance pulled in front of the house. I stuffed
a finger in my ear to block out the piercing sirens as we
went outside to greet them. The sound was painful, but
my body flooded with relief, knowing that the authorities
were on the scene.

"He's up in the production area," Valentina shouted
over the wailing. She reminded me of a skittish rabbit.
Her eyes couldn't focus on any one thing. They darted

from the fountain in the courtyard to the ceiling and then back to me like she was rapidly trying to process too much information at once.

The paramedic killed the siren.

They had an exchange in Spanish that I couldn't keep up with.

"Would you come with us, Jules?" Valentina asked, motioning to the off-road vehicle and pressing her hand to her eye as if that might help keep the tears in. "It would be nice to have a friend. I understand if it's asking too much."

"Of course." I didn't hesitate. The paramedic helped me into the backseat and expertly navigated the rough road. It only took us a few minutes to get to the scene of the accident. Sofia flagged us down. Alex was sitting on a concrete slab with his head buried in his hands. Carmen and Isabel must have heard the commotion. They were huddled together, crying.

The paramedics moved everyone away from the machinery. "El poli está en camino."

I caught that meaning—the police were on their way.

"They want us to give them space," Valentina explained, motioning to a covered structure nearby. "Let's move this way."

We all shuffled to the wooden A-frame where stacks and stacks of burlap bags packed with dried beans ready for roasting waited to be distributed to coffee shops around the world.

"Alex, how did this happen? You checked the equipment like always, sí?" Valentina asked. There was a hint of accusation in her tone.

My mind flashed to our tour. I wondered if she had

asked because Alex had been servicing the machine. Was he aware that the emergency shutoff switch was malfunctioning?

"Yes, of course. It's my job. You know that. I do it every day. I checked every knob and dial. It's part of my everyday routine. I don't know why Miguel turned on the machine." He sounded distraught and defensive. He removed his hat and clenched it in his fists. "He was showing off for her." His bloodshot eyes landed on Sofia.

Sofia stood near large wooden troughs containing dried coffee beans that had yet to be packed. Valentina had explained earlier that they used the old beans for tours and education. They hosted a variety of school field trips and small private tours and taught their guests the process of procuring and roasting beans, just like she was doing for us. She scooped up a handful of beans and massaged them between her fingers. "Me? What? I didn't have anything to do with this. I'm as horrified as you by this tragic accident."

"Yeah, sure," Alex scoffed, glaring at her with a dark hardness to his gaze that made me want to take a step away from him.

Carmen slowly loosened her grip on Isabel, her fingers lingering on the younger woman's shoulders like she was afraid to fully let go. The two women had been wrapped in each other's arms since we arrived. Isabel's face was buried in Carmen's shoulder. Her quiet sobs were muffled by the soft fabric of Carmen's blouse. "We will need to inform the workers, our vendor partners, and suppliers. The news will spread quickly, and you will want to be out in front of it, Valentina." Carmen's eyes were glassy and unfocused, as if she were trying to take in the weight of what had happened. She pulled away from Isabel, giving the younger woman a look I couldn't quite decipher.

I appreciated that she was concerned about Valentina and taking a practical approach, but I couldn't help but wonder if she had another motive for wanting to control the narrative.

Isabel folded her arms around her chest and rubbed her shoulders like she was trying to soothe herself. She had the same greenish tint to her face that I got during the first trimester when I was sick every morning. "Has anyone seen Javier? Do you know where he could be? He was here, but he vanished after, after—Miguel . . ." She trailed off, glancing at Carmen for help.

Carmen clutched Isabel's hand, her knuckles turning white as she squeezed the younger woman as if letting go might pull her under, clasping her like a lifeline in a raging storm.

"Javier was here?" Valentina perked up. "He was with Miguel earlier, but I assumed he left the farm. Now that I think about it, I realize his car was still in front of the house when the ambulance arrived. I didn't even consider it because everything feels like a bad dream."

"I know. This can't be real. He can't be dead." Isabel released her grip on Carmen and shook her head. "He was fine. He was fine. And then he tried to operate the machine, but he didn't know . . . he didn't know . . ." She stopped, scrubbing her arms with intensity as she fought to speak through the emotion. "Javier was furious. He was screaming at Miguel too, but then Miguel fell, and it was so awful."

"His car was still in front of the house when the

ambulance arrived," Valentina repeated, like she was trying to work out who had been on-site during the accident.

I was piecing together the same thought. Alex, Sofia, Isabel, Carmen, and Javier were all nearby when the accident occurred. Could there be another explanation for Miguel's fall? Had one of them pushed him?

Was Valentina right? But how could someone have killed him?

Or what if Javier had slipped him something to make him unsteady on his feet during their argument?

That's a stretch, Jules.

I furrowed my brow. If, and it was a big if, at the moment, Miguel's accident was a homicide, that logic didn't work. How could Javier possibly have predicted what Miguel would do next?

Although the warning note did have me on high alert.

It would be quite a coincidence that Miguel suddenly had a fatal fall, and I couldn't argue that everyone around me had a motive for wanting him dead.

I sighed.

If only the Professor were here now. He would take charge and get to the bottom of whether Miguel had slipped or someone else had orchestrated his fall.

Carmen attempted to console Isabel, but Isabel dropped to the ground, hugged her knees to her chest, and wrapped herself into a tight ball. She was taking the news the hardest. Not that I blamed her. It was a terrible way to die, but something about her reaction gnawed at me. Her grief was raw and almost overwhelming, but was that all it was? Could she and Miguel have been closer than it appeared? Or was she panicking for an entirely different reason? Her hands trembled as she pressed them to her cheeks. Her breathing was shallow and unsteady, like she couldn't suck in air fast enough. And then there was the way she kept glancing at the machinery. Was she trying to work out how it happened, or was she afraid of what someone might find there?

And why was Alex equally focused on the machinery? He refused to tear his eyes away from the control panel, studying every switch and dial with an intense focus, as if he were committing every detail to memory. He didn't so much as blink or even glance away as the conversation continued around him. Had the machinery been a distraction to pull everyone's attention away from Miguel's fall?

The police arrived before I had time to ponder the possibilities. They directed us to stay where we were until they had a chance to secure the scene, speak with the paramedics, and gather evidence.

Time moved in a weird, fuzzy blur. I wasn't sure if an hour or fifteen minutes had passed when two uniformed officers returned to take our statements. Sweat dripped down my neck as I waited for my turn. The late afternoon heat was palpable, pressing down on me like a vise. The concrete patio radiated the heat it had absorbed all day, making me wonder how Isabel was sitting on the hot pavement without burning herself.

Humidity clung to my skin as I watched Carmen continue to try and soothe Isabel by leaning over to speak to her in hushed tones. Whatever she was saying wasn't working because Isabel buried her face farther into her hands and rocked harder.

Sofia dabbed her forehead with a silky cloth. She looked the most out of place in her floral sundress and strappy sandals. I thought back to Valentina's warning about not traipsing around the fields with exposed skin. Why was she here? Had she gotten the paperwork signed right before Miguel died?

Even the birds and insects seemed subdued by the heat and heavy energy. Their calls and chirps were mere whispers in the warm wind.

The police made their rounds, speaking with each of us individually. Fortunately, the officer in charge spoke perfect English, so nothing was lost in translation as I shared my perspective.

"Do you think there's a chance it wasn't an accident?" I asked after giving him a complete rundown of everything I'd witnessed. Sweat beaded on my forehead and trickled down my cheek. I wiped it with my sleeve, wishing I could jump in the pool and wash away the sticky feeling on my skin.

He showed me pictures on his phone of the panel of dials attached to the machinery. "Someone tampered with the safety mechanisms. The machine's settings were adjusted to the highest level, making it incredibly dangerous. This machine has double protections," he explained, scrolling through the close-up pictures he'd taken. "There's an automatic safety switch that should have shut off the machine immediately upon Miguel's fall. It failed, and so did the emergency stop button, which Sofia claimed to have hit multiple times. It would have stopped the machine instantly. Both safety measures failed. No, I do not think it was an accident. Highly unlikely. In this line of work, we don't believe in coincidences. We are ruling this a homicide and taking Alex into custody."

"Alex?" I gasped.

"The killer had to have extensive knowledge and understanding of how to operate the machinery. There's only one person here with that knowledge—Alex Vargas."

Chapter Eleven

The police continued to question Andy, their expressions unreadable. Surely, they couldn't seriously consider him an accomplice. The thought sent a cold wave through me as I imagined having to call his grandmother to break the news that he was sitting in a Costa Rican jail. My stomach twisted at the idea, dreading the heartbreak that would surely come if he was arrested.

Who could I speak with?

Should I call the Professor?

Or was I overreacting? The more likely explanation was that they were taking their time, simply being thorough, getting the details of his statement since he'd been at the scene when Miguel's fatal accident had occurred.

Fortunately I didn't have to worry for too long because we all stood in frozen silence as the police snapped handcuffs around Alex's wrists and led him away. His protest rang out sharp and desperate, cutting through the tension in the thick, humid air. "It wasn't me. It wasn't me. I checked the safety switches. I fixed them. They were working. Someone else must have done it. It wasn't me." He twisted against their grip, his voice growing more frantic, but the officers remained stoic as they escorted him out of sight.

Valentina fell to the ground. I knelt to console her.

"Alex? I can't believe Alex would do this. He and Miguel were like brothers. He would never hurt him. Never." She pressed her fingers to her temples and closed her eyes, rocking on the concrete floor, dusty from coffee husks. "He's like a little brother to me. He grew up on the farm. He loves this land. He loves us. He's been so loyal. Jules, you have to do something. You have to help him. Your 'Professor,' as you call him, has taught you many things about crime and investigations. The police will want this to be easy and done. Alex doesn't have a chance." Her cheeks were flushed with color, and her speech came in breathless bursts as she scanned the patio, her voice softer but laced with an intense urgency. "It must be someone else. Not Alex."

I breathed the humid air in through my nose and stood up, careful not to move too quickly. I'd learned the hard way that it was easy to get lightheaded with my growing belly, especially at elevation and in this heat. I understood why the police had zeroed in on Alex. There were many signs pointing to him being the killer—he and Miguel had been at odds on selling the farm. I'd witnessed them arguing earlier and had to assume that many other people had seen similar exchanges. Alex was the expert when it came to equipment and machinery, and he had a strong motive for not wanting the sale to go through—his livelihood would be directly affected. Even his house was slotted for demolition with the sale. Yet I agreed with Valentina. It was almost too convenient. Everything pointed to him as if he'd been set up.

I wondered about the note. Did it match Alex's handwriting? Was there any way we could compare it to a sample of his writing?

I also needed to get a closer look at the emergency shutoff button and the processing equipment. I wouldn't be able to do that until the authorities finished their investigation and removed the body, but that was first on my list.

The other thing I wanted to do was speak with each of the suspects. I wasn't sure how much they would tell me, but I did have one potential advantage—I was an outsider, a tourist, Valentina's personal friend. That gave me the ability to ask plenty of questions under the guise of wanting to learn everything I could about the farm before we returned home to Ashland.

It didn't guarantee that anyone would open up to me. The other reality of being an outsider though was that they might not be willing to spill their secrets to a stranger, but it was worth a shot. Frankly, it was the only shot I had at the moment. "It sounds like the police are going to be here for a while," I said to Valentina as a plan started to take shape. "There's not much we can do for Alex now. Why don't you have everyone come to the house for dinner? The cook has already prepared a meal. I made a dessert. It would be a good opportunity to talk with everyone while the details of Miguel's death are still fresh."

"Yes, sí, I like this idea." Valentina smiled up at me in relief. "Thank you, Jules. I knew you would help. You know about these things because you have an expert detective in your family."

"I'm not a professional," I corrected her. It was true that I had learned quite a bit about detective work due to my relationship with the Professor and Thomas and Kerry (Ashland's top-notch detective squad). Some of their knowledge had likely rubbed off on me by osmosis. In a moment like this, the Professor would have a perfect Shakespearean quote to summarize his initial observations. The only quote running through my head was "This is the air—that is the glorious sun." It was a line Sebastian recited when repeatedly questioning his identity as a sane person in Shakespeare's *Twelfth Night*. Lance had produced the play a few summers ago. I was surprised I even remembered the reference. Did that mean something?

I was no Shakespeare aficionado, but an identity crisis and questioning sanity both tied in to our current situation.

"I know. I understand, but at least you have ideas of where to start." She brushed debris from her hands. "I refuse to believe Alex killed Miguel, and I'm the closest thing to family he has; we have to find a way to prove his innocence."

"I'll do whatever I can to help," I said sincerely. I wasn't sure I was as qualified for the task as she believed, but I would do everything possible and use all the techniques I'd learned from the Professor to get to the truth.

With the all-clear from the police to return to the house, we made a solemn parade through the coffee fields. The puffy white clouds clinging to the top of the volcanic ridgeline in the distance, the cornflower blue skies, and the dewy humidity suddenly felt oppressive. No one spoke as we traipsed under banana trees heavy with bundles of fruit and swarms of butterflies.

Miguel's death cast a dark pall over the exotic, lush landscape.

At the house, I was surprised to see Javier waiting for us. He was leaning against his candy apple red sports car, tossing his keys with one hand and catching them again.

"You're still here, good," Valentina said. "We're having dinner on the terrace and discussing what happened. You should join us."

"I have dinner plans," Javier replied. He gave off dashing explorer vibes from an era long gone. He was bold and confident, with a hint of danger and intrigue hiding behind his steely eyes and thin mustache. Like Sofia, he was dressed for business, not manual farm labor, which made his presence in the fields all the more suspicious. What was he really doing roaming through the fields in his well-cut suit? Sure, as a business owner, his formal attire made sense for a meeting—but not for wandering through the coffee plantation. And then there was the other glaring issue: he vanished right after arguing with Miguel. Where had he gone, and why had he stayed out of sight for so long?

He smoothed his crisp white shirt and glanced over his shoulder toward the police vehicles. "But the police informed me I must stay until they release us. I'll have a drink. I could use a shot of guaro."

"Fine, good." Valentina kept her hand in her pocket as she sent everyone outside. I wondered if it was because she was worried about losing the note. "Go sit. I'll be out with drinks in a moment."

I hung back to help her. After everyone was out of earshot, I asked about the note. "Did you give it to the police?"

She winced and gnawed on the inside of her cheek as she removed it from her pocket and handed it to me. "I didn't. Don't be angry with me. I realized something while we were waiting to give them our statements. Did you notice the whiteboard on the wall above the coffee sacks?"

I shook my head. I'd been so distracted thinking about how Miguel had died and observing everyone's behavior that I hadn't paid much attention to anything else. But I didn't like that she hadn't shared the note with the authorities. They needed to know everything. No detail was too small to overlook at this point. It raised a red flag for me. Not that I suspected her, but it was odd. Could she know more than she was telling me?

I thought about her conversation with Sofia. Had she learned that Miguel had indeed signed the deal, and she wanted to keep it quiet? This wasn't the time to hold anything back from the authorities.

"Alex updates our daily totals on the board. I added those numbers into our computer system, but it's a good glance at how much stock we have ready for wholesale clients. No one else writes on the whiteboard, only Alex, and I'm sure the handwriting is a match." She ran her finger over the writing like she wanted to erase it away.

The paper felt hot in my hands, like it might spontaneously burst into flames. "Valentina, that is withholding evidence. The police need to see this."

"I know. I want you to keep it safe." She folded the note, pressing it into my hand. "Put it in your room. Tomorrow, we can look at the whiteboard and compare it. I can tell the police that I was so upset and frazzled that I forgot about it. I will give it to them, but I want to try and find proof that Alex isn't the killer before I do. You must trust me on this. We've been friends for how many years, now? Ten? I promise I will turn the note over to the police, but we need to buy a little extra time to find proof ourselves."

I hesitated. I didn't like the idea of keeping evidence from the authorities, especially knowing that someone had tampered with the machinery.

She leaned in closer, her voice barely audible. Her eyes flickered toward the courtyard and then the doorway as if she was concerned someone was eavesdropping. "The more I've been thinking about it, the more I believe the killer is trying to pin this on Alex. I think he's being set up."

"Okay," I replied, not feeling confident I was making the best choice. "But we show this to the police tomorrow, agreed?"

She crossed her heart with her index finger. "I promise."

"Is there anything else I should know?" I asked with a touch of caution.

"No, nothing. Why?" Her eyes grew wide, a flicker of surprise crossing her face. "Like what?"

"About Miguel—do you think he signed the deal?" I kept my tone measured.

She hesitated for half a second before shrugging. "I have no idea. I don't know who to trust or believe right now." Her eyes welled with tears as she reached for my arm and squeezed my wrist. "That's why I'm so glad you're here. I don't know what I would do without you. We must get to the bottom of this and clear Alex."

I nodded, wanting to say more, but I wrapped her in a half hug instead. "We'll get through this."

She forced a sad smile as we went to the kitchen. There was no sign of Andy or Carlos. The cook reported that another police officer had interviewed them, and they had gone upstairs to change before dinner. I left to find them and store the note in a safe location.

Carlos was sitting on the balcony gazing over the fields when I entered our room. The plantation looked as if it had been painted by one of the greats in vibrant green and pastel brushstrokes. He got to his feet and greeted me with a long hug, letting his lips linger on my forehead. "Julieta, how are you? I've been worried."

He smelled like a comforting combination of coffee and coconut. I stayed in his arms momentarily, allowing him to hold me in a tight embrace as tears spilled. The reality of Miguel's tragedy was starting to fully sink in.

When we finally broke apart, I brushed a tear from my face. "Sorry, it's a lot, isn't it?"

"Sí, it's unthinkable."

I showed him the note and filled him in on everything Valentina had shared.

He scowled as he studied the note and handed it back to me. "I don't like this either. It could be that Alex *is* the killer, and we're withholding critical evidence from the police."

"I've been trying to think about what the Professor would do." I set the note on my nightstand.

"I know what Lance would do." Carlos raised his eyebrows and made a face.

"Does this make me Lance?" I winced and bit my bottom lip. Not that I didn't love and adore Lance, but he had a certain penchant for meddling.

His face softened. "No, mi querida. You want to help our friend. I do as well. I want you to be careful. One of the people we're about to share a meal with likely killed Miguel, whether it's Alex or not. We cannot take any chances."

"You're right." I reached for the note and read it one more time, wondering if there could be another meaning behind the message. If Alex was being set up, had the killer somehow convinced him to write the threatening note? Or could they have studied his penmanship on the whiteboard and plagiarized the note to make it look like Alex's handwriting? That was probably more likely and would explain the scribbled nature of the wording. I hid the note inside my book and tucked them both in the nightstand, then I freshened up in the bathroom. "How's Andy doing?"

"Better," Carlos said, changing into a long-sleeved button-down shirt and jeans. He tossed a lightweight sweater around his shoulders.

Sunset was only an hour away. Since Costa Rica was located at the equator, the sun rose and set consistently every twelve hours with little variation between the seasons. Since we were at elevation the temps would dip at night. I grabbed a sweater in case it got cool as the evening wore on.

"Do you think he'll join us for dinner?" I asked.

"Yes, I told him I'd knock on his door when I went downstairs. He was much calmer when I left him. I believe speaking with the police helped. They were very thankful for his detailed report and how he handled himself in an emergency. I'm sure, like us, he'll be very motivated to help bring the killer to justice. When you witness a crime firsthand, it changes you."

He didn't have to tell me twice. I'd seen death close up on a few occasions, and I wanted to support Andy however I could in the days ahead. For me, having a focus helped. I had a feeling the same might be true for him. He could continue to focus on his coffee education and help us interview suspects.

Andy came to the door immediately when Carlos knocked softly. "Hey, I'm ready." He darted out of the room like he'd been waiting by the door for us. Carlos was right. He looked better. The usual touch of color had returned to his freckled cheeks. He had showered and changed into a pair of shorts and a T-shirt. His overeagerness was the only clue that something was bothering him.

"Before we go down, I want you to know the police and paramedics took control of the scene of the crime," I said. For me, having more information was helpful at times of high stress. "I'm not sure if the police officer who took your statement shared that they're investigating Miguel's death as a homicide."

Andy ran his fingers through his shaggy auburn hair and tucked his notebook under one arm. "Really? No. The officer I spoke with didn't say anything, but in a weird way, I'm glad to hear that. I've been replaying it over and over again in my head and wondering if there was something I could have done to stop the machine."

"Not at all. It's not your fault, Andy." I went into protective mom mode again.

Carlos clapped him around the shoulder, pulling Andy

into a half hug in a show of comfort. "You are not responsible, understood?"

Andy smashed his lips together like he was fighting back his emotions. "Yeah, I know. It's just hard. I was right there. I keep thinking if only I had reached out, I could have grabbed him. It happened so fast."

Carlos squeezed his shoulder. "There was nothing you could have done. The killer planned his death. Tell him what you learned, Julieta."

"The police found evidence that the machine had been tampered with—maybe it was Miguel or maybe it was a way for the killer to distract him. Both emergency stop mechanisms were altered. They've arrested Alex."

"Alex—no!" Andy pulled away from Carlos, his jaw dropping in shock. "They think Alex killed him? No way. No chance. He's a good guy."

I nodded and held out a hand to try and pacify him. "Yes, but right now the evidence points in Alex's direction. He is the most knowledgeable person on the farm when it comes to the machinery. Multiple people—including us—saw him servicing the equipment shortly before Miguel was killed. He was right there when it happened. He could have easily distracted you and everyone else while knocking Miguel into the concrete tank, but Valentina agrees with you. There's a possibility he was set up."

Andy winced and pressed his fingers to his eyes like a migraine was coming on. "Yeah, that's got to be it. I don't believe it—he couldn't have done it. I mean, I get that I just met him, but he wouldn't do this. The way he talks about the farm is the way I feel about Torte. He told me he was upset with Miguel about the sale. He was honest about it and how it was going to be hard to accept. He even shared that he's been considering other offers. His level of experience and knowledge is highly sought after. He's had quite a few regional farms reach out to him about coming to work with them. There are a ton of people who want to hire him. He told me a few offers are very lucrative, but his heart is here."

That was an interesting piece of information. If Alex had other work opportunities lined up, that could potentially weaken his motive for killing Miguel.

"And, for the record, Alex didn't distract Miguel—Javier did."

Chapter Twelve

"Javier?" Carlos asked. "We saw him on the trail before I left to check on Miguel. They were arguing. I stayed with Miguel for a few minutes afterward to make sure he was okay. He didn't say much. He claimed it was 'just business,' but he was rattled and it was certainly more than 'just business.'"

I interrupted before Andy could respond. "What did he say then? And how long were you with him?" I needed to put together a timeline. That was one of the first things the Professor, Thomas, and Kerry did when beginning their initial investigation. I considered calling them, but what could they do from Ashland? Not to mention, I knew the Professor was helping at Torte, and Thomas and Kerry had their hands full. Kerry had discovered she was expecting shortly after me, but she was more tight-lipped about her pregnancy. I wasn't going to spill the beans until she was ready to share the news broadly, although we had a fun text thread going with potential baby names and the cutest gear.

"Not much," Carlos said, shaking me back into the moment. "He was upset by Javier's reaction. He mentioned

Javier was a longtime friend, and he seemed to be convinced he could smooth things over. I asked if he was hurt. He said he was fine and that he needed to go check on something of the utmost urgency. Those were his exact words—well, roughly translated words."

"How long was your conversation?" I repeated. "Five minutes? Thirty minutes?"

Carlos looked at the ceiling, searching his memory. "Not long. Five minutes. Maybe less. I took the long route to see the workers' housing. He must have gone straight to the production area after that."

Andy considered this for a moment. "Okay, so from my perspective, Alex was giving me the full tour, showing me every step of the process and how each of the machines worked."

"And Sofia was also there?" I asked.

"Yeah, Miguel was already there when Sofia showed up, but it didn't take long for tensions to flare. It was clear from the start that something was off. They were arguing in low voices. I couldn't hear what they were saying, but when they realized we were listening, they clammed up immediately. Miguel turned on the charm. His demeanor shifted in an instant. It was like he wanted to impress everyone, even me." Andy tapped his chest. "Why me? It doesn't make sense."

"Why you? Good question." I felt myself drifting into the Professor's mindset. That was exactly the type of response I would expect from him. Maybe I was channeling him across oceans.

"No clue." Andy shrugged and flipped through his notebook like he was hoping his sketches and notes might jog his memory. "Maybe it was for Alex's sake? Like he was trying to prove he was as knowledgeable as Alex. But I don't think he was. He fumbled around with the dials and levers. Alex kept saying, 'Don't touch that. You're going to break that.' He also claimed that Miguel was constantly messing with the settings, turning them to the highest speed to try and crank up production. He was irritated about that, but this was long before Miguel died. Alex was complaining about how dated some of the equipment was when he was giving me the tour. That's when he mentioned Miguel trying to force the machines to work faster. According to him, it had the opposite effect—anytime Miguel touched them, they broke."

"What about Javier?" I thought he had disappeared and wasn't on the scene, but Andy's revelation changed that. My timeline was growing tighter as we spoke. I also couldn't rule out the possibility that Miguel had accidentally tampered with the machine while trying to show off. If he had a history of tinkering with the machines, that could point to his death being an accident. However, that didn't explain the note.

"He appeared out of nowhere right after Carmen and Isabel. They were upset too, but everyone was speaking in Spanish, so I couldn't track what they were saying. I got the impression they were trying to get Miguel to leave with them. Maybe because of Sofia? I don't know. Anyway, Javier showed up right after that. He was super angry, but again, I don't know about what. I caught a few Spanish words, but I could tell he was threatening Miguel. He tossed a handful of beans at him. Maybe it was him. Like, was that a distraction?" Andy asked, growing more attached to his theory. "Yeah, it had to be him, now that I think about it. It's like little details are springing back into my mind. He was furious. He threw the beans on the dirt and started screaming at Miguel."

"Where was he?" I asked. This was an important piece of the puzzle. The killer must have put a lot of thought and planning into the murder. I couldn't imagine they would risk someone else falling into the concrete tank. Miguel's death had to be meticulously timed.

"He was off to the side, spewing insults at Miguel. I remember exactly what he said when he slipped into English briefly, 'You are an idiot. This is what you're giving up. You're throwing away your golden beans and the Espinoza legacy.' It distracted Miguel. That's when he slipped and fell—" Andy trailed off like he didn't want to remember what happened next.

"Did you see him after that?" I asked.

Andy shook his head. "No. We all sprang into action, trying to do something—anything—to save Miguel, but it was too late. It happened so fast."

"Who's all of you?" I wanted to clarify exactly who was on the scene at the time of death and take his mind off the crime scene.

"Me, Alex, Sofia, Carmen, and Isabel." He counted everyone out on one hand and clutched his notebook under his arm.

"What about Carmen and Isabel? What were they doing?" They had been practically latched on to each other while we waited to give our statements to the police. I got the impression Carmen had taken on a motherly role with Isabel. Was that out of the goodness of her heart, or could there be another reason?

"You mean after he fell? Uh, it's kind of fuzzy. They were

right there, but then everyone scattered. Carmen called the police, I remember that." Andy sounded sure of that point.

"Okay, this is good, Andy. It's very helpful to have a picture of exactly what happened." I heard a dinner bell chime on the terrace. That was our cue. "We should probably get moving."

"You don't think Alex did it, do you?" Andy asked as we went downstairs.

"There's a note," I said, using the dark wood banister to make sure I was steady on my feet. "Valentina found it earlier today."

"What kind of a note?" Andy stayed two steps behind me to give me a wide berth. I wasn't sure if I would ever get used to being treated so gingerly while pregnant.

"The note was threatening, warning Miguel to put an end to the sale or else—"

"Or *else*." Andy whistled, shaking his head. "I knew it. It was planned."

"There's one problem: the note appears to be written in Alex's handwriting," I explained, watching my footing. It felt good to have changed into clean clothes and flip-flops for my swelling feet. This time of day was typically when my feet would start to ache and swell. It would be good to prop them up during dinner.

"Seriously?" Andy punched his fist into his palm. "That's why they arrested him."

Carlos cleared his throat. We made it to the landing on the first floor. I lowered my voice. "This is just between us. The police don't know about the note yet. Valentina agrees with you. She doesn't believe Alex is the killer, and she asked me to hold on to the note tonight so that tomorrow we can compare it with Alex's handwriting before we pass it over to the authorities."

Relief washed over Andy's youthful face. "See? It's not just me. Valentina knows him even better, and she agrees. I'm helping, okay? We have to help figure out who killed him. It's the only way I'm going to feel normal again."

I understood his urgency. Witnessing Miguel's murder tethered Andy to him. "For sure," I whispered. "But tonight, let's try to lay low. Dinner will be a good opportunity to observe everyone."

"Got it, boss." Andy gave me a two-finger salute.

The terrace was washed in shades of pink honeysuckle. Tea lights flickered in hanging lanterns. Strings of golden lights stretched from the house to the deck railing, creating a canopy of shimmery, dazzling electric stars. Everyone had gathered around a long teak table.

"Come join us," Valentina called, patting the empty seats beside her. She had also changed out of her overalls into a halter dress with light blue polka dots. Her hair was tied in a long braid, and her cheeks were dusted with just a touch of shimmery blush. I was glad to see her in better spirits, too.

Andy took photos of the terrace and dimly lit coffee fields on his phone and sketched out a few notes before taking a seat. I knew he was likely sending pictures to everyone back home, which made my heart happy. It would be good for him to have a touch of normalcy even in the form of a text from Torte.

The mood was definitely subdued. Bottles of wine and sparkling water were passed around, along with platters of yucca fries, chicken empanadas, black bean dip, and corn pancakes.

I loaded a plate and sipped my bubbly water while trying to get a read on the suspects. Carmen and Isabel sat directly across from me. Javier and Sofia were seated at the far end of the table.

"It's a shame Alex has thrown his life away," Javier said, addressing the table. He swirled the rich, burgundy wine in his glass and leaned his other arm on the edge of the table, maintaining intense eye contact with Valentina. His mustache twitched with almost smug amusement as he hardened his gaze. "I would have thought that after everything your family has done for him, he would be in your debt."

Valentina frowned and cut into a corn pancake with her fork. "We don't know if he did it yet."

"The police arrested him, sí?" Javier let out a short laugh as if he was enjoying pushing Valentina to the edge. "That's good enough for me. I hate to speak ill of the dead, but you should have kept your cousin in line. It never needed to come to this, but Miguel was cocky and refused to listen to reason. You realize he did this to himself. He sealed his fate by signing the contract with Terra Café International—if it's true. I have my doubts, but his death now makes me wonder." He shifted his body, turning to face Sofia. "You do a deal with the devil, and look what it gets you."

Sofia choked on her wine, not exactly confirming or denying whether the deal was done. "I don't think it's fair to say we are the devil. We have grand ideas for this farm. Ideas that will bring money and prosperity to the family and the staff. Miguel was a visionary. He saw that. He understood what Finca las Nubes could become with our financial support and backing. Terra Café International is a brand recognized around the world."

That was the most I'd heard her speak in hours. She had to be uncomfortable as the only guest at the dinner table who wasn't particularly welcome. Come to think of it, was she sticking around at Valentina's request?

"You can't be serious." Javier shook his head slowly and twisted his lips into a thin smile as if waiting for the punch line.

"Javier, that's enough. This isn't the time or place," Carmen scolded. "Miguel is dead. I think we all need to take a moment and put things in perspective. It's time to set aside our squabbles. Regardless of Miguel's choices, he was family."

Tears fell from Valentina's eyes. "I can't believe he's dead."

Carmen handed her a napkin across the table. "I think this would be a good time to go around the table and share the things we loved about Miguel. I'll start first. Miguel had an impish personality. No matter the situation, he could make me laugh. He liked to play pranks on me, leaving plastic snakes on my porch and slipping into ridiculous fake American accents when vendors would call. He did so many extra things for our workers' families that went unnoticed. He sent flower bouquets for worker birthdays and ensured that I gave him receipts for parties and that there were always new toys and clothes waiting for the children when they arrived. He had a big heart." Carmen lifted her glass in a toast.

Everyone followed suit.

The tender moment eroded when Javier stroked his mustache, glancing around the table before his eyes landed on Carmen. "Interesting tribute. When I saw you with Miguel earlier, you had a much different sentiment, didn't you?"

Carmen pressed her lips together and seethed quietly, ignoring his comment and looking at Isabel. "Do you want to share next?"

Isabel offered similar glowing praise about Miguel's support of her efforts to make the farm more sustainable. She was timid as she spoke, gnawing on her nails like she was on the verge of tears again. "He was a complicated man, but there's no denying he cared about the people he loved."

Was that a not-so-subtle clue?

Again, I wondered about Isabel and Miguel's relationship. Her commitment to preserving the land seemed to be in direct opposition to his dreams of expansion. Were the tears for show? Was it all an act, or was she truly distraught at his death?

As everyone recounted stories of Miguel, more food arrived, but I couldn't take my eyes off Javier.

He presented himself as overly confident, but his small telltale gestures, like constantly fidgeting with his mustache, betrayed his nerves. Why had he singled out Carmen? Did he know something? Or was he trying to manipulate the conversation so as not to draw any more attention to himself?

Chapter Thirteen

Dinner turned into an impromptu wake for Miguel. The more I heard about him from those who knew him best, the more I came to realize he was complicated. It was obvious from everyone's recollections and stories that Miguel had cared deeply about the farm and the people attached to it while also being singularly focused on its expansion. Regret hung heavy in the air as we shared my rice pudding.

"I wish I had told him how much I love him," Valentina confessed, wiping her puffy eyes.

"He knew," Carmen responded instantly. "He knew we all loved and adored him, even when he got under our skin. This is what family does, sí?"

The conversation continued long after dark. The day was finally starting to catch up with me. My eyes felt heavy as coffee and after-dinner drinks were passed around.

"Is it bedtime, Julieta?" Carlos leaned close and whispered, rubbing my back.

"I'm fading," I admitted. Between the long hours of

travel and Miguel's death, it felt like I'd been awake for days.

"You must all be exhausted," Valentina replied apologetically. "I'm sorry. We've been going on and on for hours."

"No, it's been wonderful to hear so many happy stories about Miguel," I replied truthfully. "But I might excuse myself to head up to bed. I have a feeling I'll be up early. My baker's hours are programmed into me at this point."

"Yes, yes, please." Valentina stood to hug us. "Help yourself to anything in the kitchen if you're up before me."

"Julieta will take that to heart," Carlos cautioned with a little wink. "She'll have a five-course breakfast waiting for all of us before the sun has even come up."

"I won't complain about that." Valentina kissed both my cheeks and squeezed me tight. "Thank you for everything. We'll speak more in the morning."

I caught her meaning.

Andy stayed behind, patting his notebook. "I have to sample the after-dinner coffee in the name of 'research,' of course. I'm just getting started with documenting everything I've heard and seen. I have so many notes I can probably write an entire book when we get home, and I can't pass up another tasting opportunity," he said with a sheepish grin, waving good night.

Carlos ushered me to our guest room and began making us tea.

I'd missed a new voicemail from Lance:

"It's curtains-up here shortly. I can't believe you're missing opening night of *Perfect Crime*. The cast is going to smash this. Their energy is intoxicating. Speaking of intoxicating, what are your thoughts on a cocktail hour before the reception? We'll serve Uva at dinner, of course, but who doesn't love a celebratory cocktail? A Diamond Royale with rare, vintage cognac, Madagascar vanilla bean syrup, and a single edible diamond floating on the foam. Or perhaps champagne infused with twenty-four-k gold flakes?

"I'll be imbibing post-show drinks with the cast into the wee hours of the morning. We're taking over Puck's Pub for the after-party. Murder always calls for a stiff drink, yes?

"No need to text back. I'm going into airplane mode as I must take the stage to introduce the show. I'll save you and Carlos the best seats in the house when you return. Truly, you're going to swoon over this show. Ta ta!"

I couldn't resist texting back with a "Break a leg!"

Lance's fall production of *Perfect Crime* was already receiving rave reviews. He was staging it at the Thomas Theatre, which gave audience members a more intimate experience. His vision for the Broadway show was to center it in a New York apartment during a fall storm. It was the perfect show to kick off the last portion of OSF's long-running season.

The company was one of the largest and most critically acclaimed repertory theaters in the United States. The season began in March and ran until November. Some of the bigger shows, like *Twelfth Night* or *Romeo and Juliet*, ran for the duration of the season. It wasn't a stretch to say that lead actors might perform Shakespeare's soliloquies over one hundred times between evening and matinees. Small plays were peppered in with short runs—two or three months.

Perfect Crime was debuting in late summer and would close out the season after Halloween. I was eager to see Lance's version. His take on material and staging always left me feeling a bit starstruck. It was hard to articulate exactly what made his style stand out. I'd seen plenty of plays and musicals over the years with incredible choreography and talented casts, but Lance had that touch of ethereal magic that only he could capture. He drew his audiences into every production, making us feel like we were as much a part of the performance as the actors on stage.

His visions rarely lined up with budgets. I didn't envy Arlo—as managing director of the theater, he had the daunting task of reining in Lance's spending.

Carlos brought me my tea. We enjoyed the calming sound of crickets in the fields as we sipped the relaxing tea and recounted the strange and unsettling turn of events. When we finally turned out the lights, I wondered, for the briefest moment, if I would have trouble falling asleep, but those fears abated when my head hit the pillow. Maybe it was the tropical breeze blowing in through the arabica trees, but I fell into a deep, restorative sleep.

I woke the next morning to the melody of a thousand birds chirping, warbling, cooing, chattering, and twittering. Purplish light signaled that it was still early, but like the birds, the day was calling. I padded out of bed and got dressed quietly, not wanting to disturb Carlos.

The entire house was in a sleepy slumber. It was just me and the birds at this hour. That was fine with me. I wanted to clear my head and come up with a solid strategy for looking into Miguel's murder today, and the best way for me to do that was in the kitchen.

I tiptoed downstairs and turned on the lights. Valentina had left out a variety of coffee blends and a note encouraging me to make myself at home. I did exactly that. I started by brewing a pot of their house decaf, which they processed naturally so as not to taint it with any chemicals. Then I searched the pantry for baking supplies. I decided to try my hand at a recipe I'd had years ago on my last visit to Costa Rica—torta chilena. The flaky pastry was layered with rich dulce de leche and was typically served with a strong cup of coffee.

For the dough, I combined flour, sugar, and salt. Next, I cubed cold butter and used a pastry cutter to mix it in with the dry ingredients. Once I had a crumbly texture, I added eggs, cold water, and vanilla. I sprinkled flour on the island and rolled up my sleeves to begin working the dough. Mom has always said that the best time to work out life's big issues is while kneading dough.

I reviewed each of my potential suspects as I turned the dough onto the floured surface and put my weight into kneading it. Alex had already been arrested. He had a clear motive, he had the means and opportunity, as the Professor would say, but like Andy and Valentina, I wasn't convinced he had killed Miguel. Maybe it was wishful thinking, but Alex felt like the scapegoat. That didn't mean I was willing to rule him out completely, but I was eager to explore whether he could have been set up.

The dough began taking shape. I brushed more flour on my hands and divided it into eight equal portions. I wrapped each portion in plastic wrap and set them aside for thirty minutes.

While the dough rested, I turned my attention to making the dulce de leche filling. For that I added sweetened condensed milk and a touch of sea salt to a saucepan. In a larger pan, I started water boiling. Once the water came to a rolling boil, I placed the smaller saucepan inside so the water covered the base. I turned the heat down and left it to simmer for a while. It would take at least an hour or two to thicken, but that gave me time to let the dough rise, savor my coffee, and consider everything I knew about Miguel's death thus far.

I needed more information about the remaining suspects. Sofia had been at the scene of the crime and standing near Miguel when he was pushed. However, what would her motive be for killing him? If she was close to inking out their contract, it would seem like she needed him alive to move forward with the sale. Unless I was missing something. But I didn't think I was. Valentina was adamant that she had no interest in selling. If Sofia wanted to finalize the deal, she needed Miguel.

My coffee was ready, so I poured myself a cup, taking a minute to savor the sunlight starting to trickle in through the windows and the aroma of the rich coffee beans.

I wanted to learn the specific details of the Terra Café International buyout. That might give us a hint as to who else could have killed Miguel. Carmen, Isabel, and Javier had all expressed their displeasure with the deal. Carmen's deep concern for the workers and their families could have led her to murder. It was plausible that she had knowledge of the machine, given how long she'd been employed at Finca las Nubes. Javier had been in the business long enough that it was equally likely he had at least a basic understanding of the coffee processing equipment.

Isabel had a clear motive for wanting to put an immediate

end to the sale—her passion for preserving the land. But how could she have tampered with the machine without being noticed? According to Andy, she and Carmen had shown up right before Miguel's fatal fall. Physically, how would she have done it? Was there enough time? And with Andy right there, wouldn't he have seen her? Or was it possible she adjusted the equipment in plain sight, so subtly that no one even questioned it?

Unless two or more of the suspects were working together.

I considered the possibility, enjoying my coffee and the cacophony of birds. It wasn't a surprise that everyone connected to the farm and, subsequently, Miguel's death wanted to protect their way of life. It was impossible not to be captivated by the bucolic views as the sun rose over the coffee fields.

My timer dinged, reminding me the dough was ready for the next step. I took another long, slow sip of my coffee, wondering if the police had found any other firm evidence linking Alex to the crime.

As soon as Valentina was awake, our first task would be to compare the writing samples and inform the authorities that we had the note.

I sighed as I dusted the island with more flour and began rolling out the first batch of dough. I rolled it into a thin eight-inch circle and transferred it to a parchment-lined baking sheet. I slid it into the oven to bake for ten minutes or until it turned golden brown. I repeated the process with the remaining portions of dough.

Andy stumbled into the kitchen, looking less than refreshed as I removed the last round of dough. His movements were sluggish like he was still half-asleep.

"Morning, boss. I followed the scent of coffee downstairs." He set his backpack and notebook on the island and rubbed his face, blinking as if trying to chase away the exhaustion. He was dressed for the elements again in his hiking boots, shorts, and a long-sleeved shirt, but I noticed dark circles shadowing his bloodshot eyes. I had a feeling he hadn't had a great night of sleep.

"I'm afraid that's decaf." I nodded to the coffee maker. "Valentina left an assortment of their roasts, so feel free to brew a new pot."

He brushed an uneven tuft of hair back into place and held the last of my decaf. "Do you want me to top you off first?"

"Sure." I motioned to my cup and set the hot baking sheet on the counter. "I'm about to assemble my torta. How do you feel about dulce de leche?"

"Good. I feel real good about that." He smiled and filled my cup. "Did you have an epiphany last night? I barely slept. I kept dreaming about Miguel."

"Sadly, no." I shook my head and placed the first layer of pastry on the bottom of a cake stand. "But I've been up for a while, and I've been trying to run through everyone's potential motives and where they were when the incident occurred. Can you hand me the dulce de leche? It's cooling over by the stove."

Andy stuck his finger in the thick, creamy, dark caramel sauce. "I should taste it, right?"

"Always. Have I taught you nothing? A chef must sample everything before it leaves the kitchen." I repeated the mantra I'd told my team at least a thousand times.

"No notes." Andy licked his finger and handed me

the pot. "You better take this. I could eat the entire pan. Sugar is a healthy coping mechanism, right?"

"Oh, Andy." I pressed my hands together. "I'm so sorry that you had to witness something so awful. I'm glad you like the dulce de leche, but I'm worried about you."

"Nah, I'll be fine. It's okay. I think focusing on finding out who killed him and on getting the most out of our remaining time here will help." He watched me spread the silky caramel sauce over the first pastry layer and then stack the next one. "What's this called?"

"A torta chilena."

"It looks delicious." He reached into his pocket for his phone. "How early is too early to text the team? They're only an hour behind us, which means Torte's open, right?"

"Oh yeah, they're probably already crafting lattes and serving hot-from-the-oven peach scones by now, for sure." That reminded me I wanted to check in with Mom soon. I continued stacking layers.

Andy read the descriptions of the various coffee options Valentina had left out. "So, nothing on the murder?"

"Not yet." I finished the torta with a dusting of powdered sugar and cinnamon. "After breakfast I'd like to take the note and compare it with Alex's handwriting. That's a first step."

Andy scooped aromatic coffee into a gold filter. "Did you pick up on the tension between Carmen and Javier last night? What did you think of his comment? He made it sound like he'd seen something between her and Miguel. Maybe she did it."

"I have quite a few questions for Javier, too." I wasn't ready to commit to one suspect at this point. "Like why did he vanish? That seems like the behavior of someone who's guilty, and he made it abundantly clear he did not approve of the sale."

"Yeah, he's shady. Smooth. Like what's he hiding behind the 'stache?" Andy ran a finger along his upper lip, mimicking the curve of Javier's thin mustache and slipping back into his more lighthearted personality. I hoped that was a sign he really was ready to tackle the day and not that he was masking his emotions on my account.

I laughed and wiped a dribble of dulce de leche from the rim of the cake stand.

"Hey, I'm going to grab a few shots of this sunrise. The light is amazing right now, and I promised Bethany and the team that I'd bombard them with pictures—I'm behind after everything that happened last night."

"Go for it." I wasn't surprised Andy had specifically mentioned Bethany. They had been casually dating for a while now. I tried to stay out of my staff's love lives, but I was secretly rooting for the two of them. They were so well matched in personality and worldview. Hopefully reaching out to her would give him a soft place to land right now and someone else he could talk to about what he'd seen. I knew that just hearing Mom's voice when I was upset was enough to bring my blood pressure down.

As if she had read my mind, a voicemail from Mom came in.

"Morning, honey. Sorry for the long message, but I know you'll want to hear all of the news. Here's my Torte update with photos. Bethany's book brownies are my new favorite. Can you believe the detail she captured? And I'm happy to report they taste as good as they look. She went with romantic flavors—dark chocolate and strawberry and raspberry and white chocolate. The next photo is of Doug on his bread delivery route. He begged Marty to borrow a white chef coat. To tell the truth, he didn't have to beg, Marty offered. He asked me to tell you that with every delivery, he's been sharing a pun: 'The crust of true loaf never did run smooth.'

"Let's just say he's having too much fun with this. Marty may never get his route back. Things are running smoothly. Sequoia wants me to pass on that the espresso special yesterday was a rainbow matcha, and it sold out by noon. She's quite pleased with herself and possibly ready for another coffee competition with Andy.

"Lance is like a lost puppy without you. He's dropped by twice with tickets for *Perfect Crime*, offering them to the team, Doug, and me. It's quite thoughtful. Doug and I are going tonight, so I'll keep you posted. I stopped into A Rose by Any Other Name to order some flowers for book club. Bethany thought it would be fun to have some little romantic bouquets of roses to accompany the book. According to Janet, Lance instructed her to order three dozen flower samples for the wedding. He wants her to make a variety of test arrangements before he decides on a final design. Janet is more than happy to oblige. She quoted him a price that most people might spend on a small party or event due to the fact that many of the flowers he's requesting are exotic and expensive to ship to Ashland. No surprise, he didn't bat an eye.

"I hope you're all having a wonderful, relaxing getaway. I'll send book club pics and my report on the play tomorrow."

I couldn't decide whether to tell her about Miguel. I didn't want to worry her, and there wasn't anything she could do from Ashland. If I didn't tell her, I knew she would be upset when we got home, so I shot her a text.

"We're all okay, but there was an accident on the farm yesterday. Valentina's cousin died." I figured the best idea was the truth without a lot of extra details. I could fill her in on the gory specifics in person.

"Juliet, I'm so sorry to hear that. Do you need anything?"

She replied immediately. "We're fine. We're having breakfast soon and making a plan for the day. Thanks for the pictures and update. Give everyone my love, and I'll check in soon."

I polished off my coffee and a plate of leftovers from last night. I was about to head outside when Carmen came into the kitchen looking disheveled and out of sorts. Her glossy white bob had lost its sheen. It was matted to her cheeks, like she'd just rolled out of bed. She was dressed in a pair of wrinkled linen pants and a crumpled T-shirt.

Maybe she *had* just gotten out of bed.

Or slept in her clothes?

"Oh, hi, sorry to barge in. Is Valentina here?" She scanned the kitchen as if expecting Valentina might be hiding under the farmhouse sink.

"No, I haven't seen her yet. There's coffee brewing, though." I gestured to the counter.

She drew in a breath and blew it out again. "I don't know what to do. I've been up all night. I couldn't sleep."

"Do you want to talk about it?" I pulled out a bar stool.

Carmen dragged her fingers through her hair, wringing them out nervously. "I don't want to bother you."

"It's no bother," I insisted, not mentioning that I had been hoping for an opportunity to speak with her alone.

Without asking, I poured a cup of Andy's coffee and set it in front of her. "Coffee might help, but I guess I don't need to tell you that."

"Coffee is the root of our problems." She cradled the mug in her hands and stared into the mug like a tea-leaf reader. Was there an equivalent for coffee? Could she use the coffee for divination—predict the future based on the acidity or depth of the brew? "Coffee is the reason Miguel is dead."

Chapter Fourteen

"From your stories last night, it sounded like you and Miguel were close," I said, sitting on the stool beside Carmen.

She kept the coffee clutched in her hands like a security blanket. "He was like a son to me. The same is true for Valentina and Alex. Alex is younger, of course. He could be my grandson, but we're all family. It's a double tragedy. Miguel is gone too soon, and Alex is in danger of having his freedom snatched away. He's a gentle soul. I refuse to believe he killed Miguel."

This seemed to be a recurring theme.

"So you're close with Alex too?" I asked.

She brought the cup to her lips, but her hands trembled so violently that the hot liquid inside sloshed against the rim, sending droplets onto the island. I dabbed it with a napkin. Her pale, stiff fingers clenched the dainty handle with such force I thought she might snap it. It was a strange reaction. She tried to take another sip, but the cup rattled against her teeth, forcing her to set it down before she could take a drink.

Watching her shaky hands attempt to lift the ceramic

mug to her lips made me wonder if her physical reaction was due to grief or if she could be hiding something.

"Alex is wonderful. He takes care of me. Our houses are near each other, and every night, he checks on me. He does so many little things—clearing the walkway and weeding my garden. This farm is as much a part of him as it is the Espinozas."

"Could that be why he snapped? I've heard talk that his cabin is slotted for demolition with the renovations and that he might be out of a job. Do you think that could have made him do something rash? It sounds like there's a possibility he loved the farm too much." My eyes drifted to the arched windows, where tangerine sunlight seemed to illuminate the gently sloping rows of coffee plants. It was no wonder someone would have killed to protect this space. Not that I condoned murder, but being here and feeling the deep connection to the land made me understand why everyone was so passionate about saving Finca las Nubes.

"Is there such a concept as too much love?" Carmen's eyes were clear and earnest. "I don't believe so. Yes, he loved this land, as we all do. He wanted to protect it. He wanted to keep our old ways, but would he kill for that? No. Impossible." She shifted her stool to avoid the direct sunlight beaming in through the windows. "Alex had other options. He would have been sad to leave the farm if it came to that, but he's a good worker. He would have had every farm in Costa Rica begging him to come work for them. He has a highly valued skill set. He knows and understands the mechanics of the equipment better than anyone. It's a lost art these days with technology. Alex can fix anything without a manual or special equipment."

Everything I heard about Alex was consistent, no matter whom I spoke with. That had to mean something.

"What about you? What will happen if Miguel's shares go through?" I asked.

"Miguel's shares won't be sold." She lifted the coffee cup again, this time without trembling. "I made sure of that." She reported this news in a direct, matter-of-fact manner, like a reporter reading the news on camera.

I gasped, sharper than I intended, but Carmen's tone left no room for doubt. Why was she so sure of this?

"No, you don't need to worry about me. I didn't kill him." She rested the coffee on the island and tucked her hair behind her ears. "I had a heart-to-heart with Miguel shortly before he died. It was my last-ditch effort to talk some sense into him. As you heard last night, Miguel was a charmer and a big dreamer, but he wasn't a monster. He's an Espinoza. His family's legacy of caring for the land and the people who tend it is in his blood. I reminded him of that fact, and I showed him proof of what Terra Café International would do to our workers and their families if he proceeded with the sale."

"What kind of proof?" I was curious to hear whether Carmen had succeeded in getting Miguel to call off the deal. If that was true, it would change the entire scope of the investigation.

"I showed him documentation of what they've done with other buyouts. I don't think he realized how destructive the deal would be for our workers. Their housing would be obliterated in favor of expanding the fields. They'd end up living in temporary shacks. There's no history of the corporation providing the benefits we do—only the basics of water and electricity. Not even Wi-Fi. My programming, childcare, healthcare, and education would all be eliminated. He listened to everything I had to say with an open mind, and at the end of our conversation, he had come around. He said there was another offer he was considering and that with the pushback he'd had from Valentina, Alex, and Isabel, he was going to look into a new deal."

"A new deal," I repeated. "Do you know with who?"

She frowned and ran her tanned finger along the rim of her coffee mug. "He didn't say. I didn't ask because I was glad I had gotten through to him, but then shortly after our conversation, he was dead."

"When was this?" Could that explain the note?

"What?" She knocked the cup, tipping it partway and spilling the liquid onto the island. "Oh, dear, I'm such a shaky mess today."

"Don't worry. It's obviously a very upsetting time." I wiped it with my napkin and washed my hands in the sink.

"Thank you for the coffee and the chat." Carmen stood. "If Valentina isn't awake yet, I'll find her later. I have a long task list for the day."

"Can I ask you one more thing?"

She glanced at the clock like she had somewhere to be but nodded. "Yes, go ahead."

"What about Isabel and Miguel? What was their relationship like?" I couldn't shake the feeling that maybe I was missing something about their connection. But what? And Carmen had been so protective of Isabel that I wasn't sure she'd be willing to tell me anything, even if I was missing something major. By all accounts, she and Miguel were polar opposites in terms of their vision for the farm, but she'd been visibly upset by his death, almost distraught. It didn't add up.

"They had a fine working relationship," she said, emphasizing "working."

"Were they close? Isabel seems so upset by his death. I wondered if maybe they were closer than people realized."

"Why would you suggest that? Everyone is upset by his death," she snapped, her tone turning bitter. "It's a tragedy. We're all heartbroken."

With that, she turned and exited the kitchen, bringing an abrupt end to our conversation. Was it because I asked her where she and Miguel had been? I wanted to believe her. Mainly because I wanted to believe that Miguel had changed his mind about the sale, but I wasn't convinced she was telling me the truth. Her unyielding support for the farmworkers was admirable, but what if that was what ultimately prompted her to kill Miguel? Their conversation could have gone differently. Perhaps he refused to review the documents she showed him about Terra Café International. Or maybe he read them and didn't care.

Was she covering up for Isabel? Did she know that Isabel was involved in killing Miguel somehow and was protecting her?

I knew for sure she was nervous. The multiple coffee spills on my stained napkin were proof of that.

I needed to figure out exactly where she had been at the time of the murder. I also wondered what I could learn about Sofia's employer. Did the corporate coffee giant have a history of treating workers poorly? What would Carmen stand to gain with the sale going through?

Another possibility was that Carmen was telling me the truth. Maybe she had succeeded in convincing Miguel to keep the farm in his family's hands.

I tossed the napkin into a laundry basket in the pantry and washed our coffee cups. Our conversation left me with more questions than answers. I knew from the Professor that was normal, but it didn't make me feel any better.

How could I figure out whether Miguel had another deal in the works?

And was Carmen the sweet grandmother she portrayed, or a cold-blooded killer? As much as I would have loved to cross her off my suspect list, it was too soon.

Chapter Fifteen

The kitchen buzzed with a strange energy when Andy returned, followed by Carlos and Valentina. It was an odd mixture of delectable aromas and flavors mingling with the backdrop of murder.

We congregated around the island. Valentina brought fresh fruit and sweet bread to accompany my dulce de leche torta. Carlos fried eggs, beans, and plantains while Andy hand-crafted cinnamon lattes on Valentina's espresso machine. There was no shortage of food, coffee, or theories as to who may have killed Miguel.

I told them what I had learned from Carmen. "Do you think he could have been negotiating another deal? Maybe he was juggling multiple offers? Trying to ignite a bidding war for the farm?"

Valentina cut into her slice of the buttery pastry with a fork. "I wouldn't put it past him. Miguel was always working on new deals and investments. He would constantly text me when I was on the ship with a new idea, a new business partner, and a huge plan for renovations. He'd be excited about it for a few days, and then the idea would vanish and slip away into nothing. I think he liked the thrill of it. It was like dating for him. Investors would invite him to expensive wine dinners in the city and court him. He would return eager to implement sweeping changes, but it was rare that any of his plans came to fruition. I was surprised when Sofia actually made him an offer. I didn't believe it at first. I thought it was another one of his big dreams. I can't tell you how many 'sure deals' and 'buyers' he's had over the years. He got excited about possibilities, but offers never materialized from his long lunches and fancy dinners. I suspect this is because of several things—the red tape to buy a Costa Rican farm, the expense of expansion compared with the reality of how much potential that would bring in, and many other factors we can go into."

"Maybe another buyer came through when they heard Terra Café International was interested?" I suggested, tasting my final product. The soft layers of pastry dough blended beautifully with the luscious dulce de leche. Each bite practically melted in my mouth. The sweetness of the breakfast pastry balanced nicely with Andy's rich and spicy latte.

"Sí, this happens often in business negotiations," Carlos agreed. "Jules raises a good point. Could Miguel have started a bidding war for the farm?"

She considered his question for a minute. "I suppose it's possible, but he didn't include me in those conversations if they happened. There were so many rumors circulating, I don't know what to believe anymore." Valentina paused to swallow a bite. "Jules, this is absolutely delicious. It reminds me of my grandmother's."

I pressed my hand to my heart. "That's the highest compliment you can pay me."

"It's true. It brings me back to my childhood. I wish Miguel were here to taste this." She grew quiet as she closed her eyes and savored the flavors, getting lost in her memories and her sadness. After a second, she shook her shoulders and refocused. "Sorry. It's still not real, but I didn't answer your question. It could be possible Miguel had another buyer lined up, but if he did, he didn't tell me anything about it."

"What about Javier?" I asked, thinking about his behavior at dinner last night. Maybe he'd been trying to deflect attention from himself by bringing up Carmen's argument with Miguel.

"Javier? A buyer?" Valentina blinked hard as if she was trying to process the question. "I don't know. Dulce Coffee, as you know, is very popular. It's probably the most recognized chain in all of Costa Rica. His business continues to expand. He's opening a number of new stores this year and growing his line of coffee products. He puts coffee in everything—literally. His shops sell a skin-care line infused with coffee—coffee soap, shampoo, and body lotion. He's never expressed interest in owning the farm, though." She paused. "But he has been very upset about the deal. We've had an exclusive partnership for decades. He doesn't want to go with an inferior bean. Quality matters to him, as does the story of keeping Costa Rican farms in the possession of Costa Rican families. He's built his brand on that. We've had several conversations about how detrimental the sale would be to his businesses."

Andy caught my eye. "Sounds like a motive to me."

"Sí," Carlos agreed, nodding to Andy. "You told us last night that Javier intentionally distracted Miguel at the machine, and we all saw them arguing. It seems possible to me."

"Javier? I don't know." Valentina ran her teeth along her bottom lip. "Why wouldn't he have spoken to me about a partnership? I would have been much more receptive to working with him over Terra Café. Dulce Coffee has been our steadfast supporter. If he was considering going into business with us, I can't imagine why he wouldn't have come to me first."

"There's one way to find out. You could ask him," I said, licking caramel from my lips. "This could be important. Do you think you could call him?"

"I don't need to call him. He'll be here soon. He told me last night he would come by in the morning to formulate a joint statement for the press." Valentina glanced at an antique clock hanging above the rustic cupboards. "He should be here in forty-five minutes or an hour."

"That gives us just enough time to compare the note with Alex's handwriting on the whiteboard," I said, gathering my dishes.

"Can I tag along?" Andy asked, picking up his backpack and notebook.

"Sure. I need to run up to the room and grab the note," I said.

Carlos motioned for me to stay put. "I'll get it. I want to put on hiking shoes anyway. While you look into the handwriting samples, I'd like to wander up to the workers' housing again."

"Yes, feel free," Valentina said. "Did you notice something in there?"

"No. I'd like to retrace my movements to understand the timing better, and the view from the hillside might give me a new perspective." Carlos took my dishes to the sink and went upstairs. He was clearly as invested in figuring out who killed Miguel as the rest of us. It warmed my heart to know that I had a partner in this. Between Valentina, Andy, Carlos, and me, surely we would be able to at least uncover more about each of the suspects.

A wave of wistfulness washed over me. Should I reach out to the Professor, Thomas, or Kerry? But what could they do? If anything, they'd likely tell me to leave it alone and hand the note over to the local authorities.

Carlos returned promptly with the note. "Should we meet back here?"

"Sounds good." I left him with a brief kiss.

"Be careful, Julieta," he whispered in my ear. "There could be a killer on the farm."

"I will be, I promise." That wasn't lip service. I wouldn't take any chances, and I wasn't doing this alone. Andy and Valentina would both be with me. There was safety in numbers.

On our way to the drying patio and coffee storage area, my phone buzzed, alerting me to a new voicemail. I was surprised cell service was this strong in the coffee fields.

The message was from Lance.

"The play was a smashing success. Thanks for your well-wishes. The cast received a ten-minute standing ovation and three curtain calls. We may have celebrated a bit too hard if my throbbing headache is any indication. I'm off to Torte soon for a double latte. Scratch that. Make it a triple.

"But, darling, details. Details. Where are they? I'm dying of boredom here without you. I need the gossip on your romantic getaway. How's our wide-eyed coffee protégé? Is he in love with the coffee jungle and vowing never to return home? Hit me up with the deets. Ashland isn't the same without you. Arlo is refusing my best wedding ideas. No real swans! Why? I hate to say it, but I'm almost missing Richard Lord. There is a serious lack of drama around here. Please tell me something interesting. Anything interesting."

Classic Lance.

I chuckled to myself. If he was missing Richard Lord, he really was desperate. Valentina had paused to point out a budding coffee cherry to Andy, so I texted him back.

"So glad *Perfect Crime* is a hit! I can't wait to see it. Unfortunately, we have more drama than I'd ever want."

I went on to give him a brief rundown of Miguel's murder.

"Wait—full stop! What? You're investigating without me? I want a minute-by-minute update. Should I book a flight? I can be there in a flash, just say the word." He texted back immediately.

The last thing I needed was for Lance to insert himself into our investigation. I knew his flippant response was for show. Lance cared deeply for me and everyone around him.

As if reading my mind, my phone vibrated again.

"In all honesty, Jules. Do take care of yourself and don't do anything I would. Love you. Kiss. Kiss."

In a strange way, hearing from Lance gave me an extra boost. Yes, Miguel's death was a tragedy, but I was in a unique position to see that justice was served. I fell into step with Andy and Valentina. We only had a couple of days left on the farm, and I was going to use the time we had remaining to do everything in my power to find his killer.

Chapter Sixteen

It didn't take us long to reach the drying patio. The sun was already warm on my back, and the air tinged with humidity. Sweat pooled on my neck. I used the thin sweatshirt tied around my waist to mop my brow. I was glad for my sunhat and protective clothing.

"It's a scorcher already," Andy said, patting his cheeks, which were the color of the hibiscus flowers. His freckles spread out like sprinkles of cinnamon on sun-ripened fruit.

Valentina pointed to the mountains. She appeared unfazed by the heat. She wore a new pair of Finca las Nubes overalls with a long-sleeved shirt underneath. Her hair was tied in a ponytail, showing her heart-shaped face. "See the clouds already building on the horizon? That means the day will be humid. It's good we're out early."

We navigated past the rows of drying beans. Large racks were stacked against the side of the storage structure, ready for distribution.

"Yesterday, Alex mentioned you typically rake the beans every thirty to sixty minutes," Andy said, motioning to the rakes and flipping through his notes. "I'd love to give it a try at some point today."

"Of course. These are here for practice. We use them to teach the seasonal workers how to rotate the beans. Then we'll move them out and make space after the harvest for the fresh beans," Valentina said. "I'm glad Alex talked you through each stage. This process is critical. Regular raking ensures that the beans dry evenly. Otherwise, we run the risk of pockets of moisture, especially with this humidity, which can lead to mold." She paused long enough to allow us a good look at the tidy rows. "We spread the beans out in a thin layer like this and rotate them so they are exposed to sun and air on all sides. It takes about seven to ten days for the beans to dry completely."

"One of the things I'm most excited about is to share these kinds of details with our customers," Andy said, snapping a few pictures and scribbling something in his notebook. "I don't think the average coffee drinker has any idea of the amount of work and time that goes into brewing a single cup."

"Yes, and there are still more steps after this." Valentina moved to the A-frame storage structure. "Once the beans are dried, they need to be hulled. We send them through the hulling machine to remove the thin, papery husk to get to a lovely green bean. We manually sort our beans by size, weight, and quality. Some of the bigger producers use machines for that, but I prefer having our trained eyes on that step before we bag them in our sisal sacks and store them here." She swept her hand toward the stacks of burlap bags.

As she did, someone jumped out from behind the pile.

"Oh my God!" Isabel threw her arms up, letting a spiral-bound journal drop on the ground with a thud. "You startled me. I didn't know anyone was here."

"Isabel, what are you doing?" Valentina asked, a touch of irritation creeping into her voice. "Why are you hiding out in here?"

Isabel reached down and scooped up her notebook, hiding it behind her back. "Checking inventory. I figured I should do something to help. Alex usually takes care of inventory, but since he's in jail—" She didn't finish her sentence.

Valentina brushed past her and walked to the white-board. "Did you erase this?"

"Huh?" Isabel's doe-like eyes grew wide, like she'd been caught in a lie. She nibbled on her fingernails, her eyes darting around the storage barn as if trying to figure out the fastest escape route. "What?"

"Alex's chart and notes. Where are they?" Valentina tapped the dry-erase board. It was completely blank. Everything had been wiped clean. The coffee sack tallies, bean counts, Alex's wholesale client notes. Only white space remained. "All of Alex's notes were here. They're gone."

"What?" Isabel took a step backward. Her short dark hair was pinned with two green barrettes, and her ears were dotted with matching green studded earrings.

"Did you erase this?" Valentina repeated, her voice rising in pitch.

"Yeah. Uh, sorry. Why, is there a problem?" Isabel pulled the notebook from behind her back. "I told you, I took a new inventory count this morning. I was planning to update the board when you showed up. I figured

I could do something—anything to help, since Alex is in
jail. He normally updates the numbers. I don't get it. You
seem mad."

I noticed black smudges on her fingers. Was that why
she'd been hiding?

Valentina wasn't just mad—she was livid. I could almost see the heat radiating from her like the humidity
clinging to the tropical trees in the coffee fields, simmering with an intensity that warned Isabel to keep her
distance. "What would possibly compel you to erase
everything? Alex had columns, wholesale client notes,
and a complete inventory count. There was no need to
destroy that. You could have updated the numbers."

"I didn't realize I was *destroying* anything." Isabel
sounded defensive. She chomped on her fingernail like it
was an ear of corn. "I thought I was helping."

"Don't help again," Valentina said sharply. Then she
motioned behind us. "We need a minute alone."

Isabel tucked the notebook under her arm and hung
her head as she scooted around us. "I'm so sorry. I didn't
know what to do. It's all just so horrible. Miguel. Alex. I
only wanted to help."

Valentina waited until she was gone and waved us
closer to the board. "What do you think, Jules? It's odd
she erased everything. Do you agree?"

I took a closer look at the board, hoping there might be
a remnant of Alex's writing, but it had been wiped clean.
"She seemed skittish. I feel like we're missing something."

"That's an understatement," Andy added. "Super
jumpy. Defensive. And did you notice she took off with
her notebook? Did she actually update numbers in it, or is
she hiding something?"

"I'm not sure what she achieves by erasing the board," I pondered out loud. "Let's assume she's trying to frame Alex. Wouldn't she want us to see Alex's handwriting?"

"Not if it wasn't an exact match," Valentina said, unfolding the note. "This is close to his handwriting, but if she forged this note, she could have realized that his real handwriting would give away the fact that the note was faked. I think she could have done it. She had access to this area. She's often here alone, and it's been bothering me that she claims she's practicing her raking skills to relate to the workers—that doesn't make sense. Raking isn't that hard. It doesn't require hours of practice."

"Do you think she was hiding something?"

Andy inspected the stacks of coffee sacks. "Yeah, but she showed up at the processing area right before he fell. She seemed like she was trying to get him away from the equipment. Carmen too."

That was a sticking point for me. How had the killer pulled it off with everyone nearby? But then again, a quick push could go unnoticed.

"She's been acting odd for a while now," Valentina continued, picking up a dry-erase pen and examining it carefully. "I've been worried she's up to something since even before Miguel's death."

"Like what?" I asked, glancing around the storage area. The coffee sacks stretched to the roofline. If Isabel had stashed evidence in any of the burlap bags, it would take hours and hours to search them all. Plus, what would she be hiding?

Valentina took the cap off the pen and smelled it, quickly regretting her decision, waving her hand over her face, and replacing it quickly. The intense chemical aroma drifted toward me. "She's been the most vocal about the sale, which I understand. Her entire job is preservation. Terra Café International's plans were in complete opposition to hers, but lately, I've been wondering if she could be considering more drastic measures to protect the farm."

"Drastic like murder?" Andy asked, waving his hand in front of his face to get rid of the smell.

The same question came to my mind.

"This certainly points in that direction." Valentina tapped the board with the pen and then put it away. "Carmen and Alex have both reported seeing Isabel sneaking around the property late at night, taking photos like she's an undercover spy."

"Hmm." I considered the possibilities. What could she be up to at night? If Isabel had been doing night reconnaissance, could she have plotted how to kill Miguel? Was there something I was missing in terms of the murder method?

How could the killer have guaranteed that Miguel would fall into the concrete tank?

It seemed like a huge risk to tamper with the safety shutoffs and assume Miguel would be in the right place at the right time—or the wrong place at the wrong time, in this case. Unless the killer didn't care who fell victim to their diabolical plans?

No. I sighed.

That was the kind of theory Lance would immediately become attached to. I didn't think that we were dealing with someone who would kill at random. The murder seemed calculated and targeted. And there was still the problem of the note.

If Isabel had been involved, could she have had an accomplice?

Or was it possible she had jerry-rigged the machine so that only Miguel could have fallen in?

That also felt impossible.

I was about to abandon the idea when a new thought surfaced.

Miguel had shown up out of the blue and taken over Alex's demonstration. What if he'd been sent to do so? Sent by his killer?

Could Isabel have concocted a reason for Miguel to inspect the machinery, knowing that the safety protections had been disabled, and then pushed him, ultimately sending him to his death?

Chapter Seventeen

"What do we do?" Valentina asked, staring at the note and frowning. She smoothed it with her hand and held it up to the empty board, looking for any trace of his writing that might be left behind, just like I already had. "I thought for sure the whiteboard would give us a good idea whether Alex wrote this or not."

"Would his handwriting be in other places?" I asked. "Maybe invoices or other paperwork?"

"Miguel handled that side of the business." Valentina twisted her mouth and tugged a keychain from her pocket as she thought about something. "I do have master keys to all the houses on the property. Would it be wrong to go into la Casita de los Abuelos, Alex's cottage?"

We were already this far in. I wanted to know if Alex had written the note, but I didn't want to interfere with the investigation. "Did the police cordon off his cottage or say anything about areas to stay away from?"

"No. They only told me to keep staff away from the processing area." She dangled the keys and lifted her eyebrows. "What do you think?"

"As long as we're careful and don't disturb anything." I

sounded like the Professor, but in this case, I didn't think that was a bad thing. We needed to act as professionally as possible.

Andy gave me a sheepish shrug. "I'm game if you two are. I'll be the muscles in case we run into any trouble." He flexed his arm. "No, but seriously, finding a writing sample seems important. I'm still convinced Alex didn't do it."

"Me too. Let's hurry to make it back in time to speak with Javier." Valentina took us on a shortcut along a small trail that wound above the processing area. The narrow pressed-dirt pathway took us through a heavily tree-lined section of the farm. "Watch for snakes overhead, just in case."

I kept my eyes glued to the skyline, not wanting to be surprised by a boa constrictor dropping onto my head.

Alex's cottage appeared empty when we arrived, and there was no sign of police activity. No caution tape on the door or signage warning us to keep out. The exterior was built out of stone and dark wood. The red-clay roof was slightly weathered but otherwise in good shape. Hand-carved wooden shutters were painted with colorful patterns, giving the space a welcoming charm.

I thought back to the argument Carlos and I had overheard between Miguel and Alex. Miguel had referred to Alex's house as a "shack," making it sound like he lived in squalor. Nothing could be further from the truth. It was clear Alex took care of the house. The cottage was in immaculate condition. Vibrant flowers had been lovingly tended, as had the oversized terra-cotta pots bursting with fresh herbs that flanked the front door. Two wooden rocking chairs placed next to a wine barrel provided a shady spot to read or curl up with an iced coffee on a warm afternoon.

Valentina opened the door—it wasn't locked.

Was that important?

Could it mean someone else had beaten us here?

My body pulsed with nervous energy—I was on high alert as we stepped inside.

A small stone fireplace dominated the main room. Family photos and pictures of the farm throughout the years were framed on the walls. The air held a faint hint of coffee and homemade bread.

"It's a sweet space," I said to Valentina, admiring the long wood beams that ran the length of the ceiling and the hardwood floors. Alex had made it his own with handwoven rugs, pottery, and a collection of painted ceramic coffee mugs on display. Each had unique Costa Rican designs and family monograms.

The kitchen was exactly what I pictured when I thought of a farm-style space, complete with a cast-iron stove and a long table that served as centerpieces for the room. Nothing about the cozy kitchen gave off killer vibes. Vintage hand-cranked coffee grinders from different eras took up an entire cupboard. Some had wooden bodies and brass mechanisms. Others were well-worn from years of use. A chorreador, a traditional Costa Rican coffee maker, rested on the counter.

"Is this a chorreador?" Andy asked, moving to get a better look at the wooden stand and cloth filter.

"Yes, Alex prefers to keep things old-school," Valentina said. "He brews his coffee using the traditional method every day." She gestured to ceramic canisters painted with delicate floral patterns. "It's no wonder the two of you hit it off. Alex is constantly testing new roasts and inviting me, Carmen, Miguel, or the workers to sit outside on the porch and enjoy a cup."

"Where do you think we might find a sample of his writing?" I asked, wanting to make sure we stayed on task. I felt bad invading his privacy, but if we could find proof that he didn't write the note, it might help his case.

Valentina opened a drawer at the end of the counter. "He keeps notes about his coffee."

I nudged Andy in the waist. "Sounds familiar."

"This is why I'm telling you there's no chance Alex did it." Andy opened one of the canisters and smelled the beans. "No one who puts this much care and attention into his craft could be a killer."

I wasn't entirely sure I agreed. I wanted to prove Alex's innocence as much as Valentina and Andy, but his passion for his craft could have been the very thing that sent him over the edge.

Alex had explicitly stated how much he loved the farm—his home and the only way of life he'd known. That, unfortunately, gave him a strong motive for murder.

"Here!" Valentina exclaimed, finding a leather journal mixed in amongst pens, scissors, tape, and other supplies. She shut the drawer and brought the journal and note to the table, spreading them in the center. "Can you turn the overhead light on?"

I flipped on the light and leaned next to her to compare the two writing samples.

"They look very similar." Valentina ran her finger along the ink in the journal and then did the same to the note. "I don't see a clear difference, what do you both think?"

Andy tore himself away from the chorreador. I studied the solid, bold brushstrokes in the journal. Alex's handwriting mirrored his personality: strong but composed. His handwriting was neat and clean and level on the page.

"Look at this," I pointed to the note. "Do you see how the sentence slopes down? None of Alex's writing in his journal does that."

Andy reached for the journal. "You're right, Jules, and there's more. Look at his *t*. He crosses his *t* perfectly in the middle. See?"

Valentina huddled closer. "Yes, but not in the note. The *t* is crossed much lower. Almost to the bottom. These are not the same."

"I think you should bring the journal with us," I said. "The police likely have handwriting experts who can analyze these samples professionally." The Professor had used handwriting analysis in previous investigations, and I remember him explaining that it was rarely enough alone to prove a case. He shared that the analysis relied heavily upon the examiner's expertise and that interpretations could vary widely between experts. He also mentioned that handwriting can change based on a number of factors like stress, age, and health, making it even harder to present it as conclusive evidence. But it was better than nothing and more than we'd had when we started the day.

Valentina flipped off the light and stuffed the note inside Alex's journal. "I'm convinced Isabel must be the killer. We caught her erasing the evidence. Now I understand why. She didn't want anyone to be able to compare Alex's handwriting to the note because she *forged* it. She's trying to have Alex take the fall for what she did, and I'm not going to let her get away with it."

Chapter Eighteen

Valentina broke into a full sprint on our way back to the main house. She was on a mission now that we had something tangible to show the police. She breezed down the hillside, bushwhacking with her hand as she barreled toward the house. It was hard to keep pace with her. I did my best, but finally told her to go ahead and I'd meet up with her later. Andy hung back. "Are you okay, Jules?"

"I'm fine. Just slow." I pointed to a bench near the coffee rakes. "I might sit for a minute."

"I'll wait with you." He gave me a once-over, trying to decide whether he needed to call reinforcements.

"I promise I'm fine, but I don't want to overdo it." I took a seat on the bench. "Hey, if you're hanging with me, you should give raking the beans a try."

"Don't tempt me. Do you think I can?" He was already reaching for a rake. "Alex showed me how they do it yesterday. It's an art form. You want to go slowly and push the beans in one direction and then slowly rake them in the other direction." He demonstrated his new skill.

"Well done. You look like a pro to me." I fanned my face. I wondered if I would ever get used to my body not performing like it had pre-pregnancy. A little hike in the sun and humidity wouldn't have bothered me a few months ago. Typically, I take long runs at elevation through the network of trails that wind through Lithia Park. But carrying twins was changing my stamina. I needed to remember my body wasn't only my own right now. I was more than happy to share it, but I did need to adopt that as my new mantra.

I breathed slowly, watching Andy rake the drying coffee beans.

Could Isabel have orchestrated Miguel's death?

My pocket vibrated, causing me to startle. It was another text from Lance. "Um, update? It's been nearly an hour. Have you solved it yet? Is the coffee killer behind bars? I'm at Torte with a front-row view of the plaza and a rainbow matcha, and now I need the murder update."

"Nothing much to report. We're checking writing samples and interviewing suspects. Andy is convinced Alex isn't the killer, and I'm starting to agree with him."

"Excellent. That's progress. Put on your sleuthing cap, darling."

My sleuthing cap was failing me at the moment.

I was glad Valentina was handing the note over to the authorities. I doubted that they would share much with us, though. Having a detective in the family came with some benefits, like getting insider information.

We were on our own here.

The Professor often said that the most likely suspect tended to be the one who did it. Unlike how crimes were portrayed in the movies and on television, in the real world, if solid evidence pointed to one person, it was usually them.

Unfortunately for Alex, at the moment, everything pointed to him. Even if a handwriting expert was able to prove that the handwriting samples didn't match, would it be enough for the police to release him? Doubtful.

He was standing next to Miguel when he fell. He was seen servicing the pulping machine. He was familiar with all the equipment on the farm, and he had a motive. It was too many strikes against him. I was worried time was running out. No wonder Valentina was in a rush. She must have felt the same way. Unless we could find tangible evidence linking someone else to the crime, I had a sinking feeling Alex would remain behind bars.

"Jules, this is very cathartic," Andy said, sweeping a row with gentle force. "I could get used to this. I could get used to Costa Rica. I could actually imagine living here, which kind of surprises me. I never thought I'd say that."

My heart pounded wildly against my chest, and not because of being overheated. If Andy wanted to make a permanent move to the coffee capital of the world, I would never stop him. Of course I would encourage him to pursue his passion. But after Steph and Sterling had left, I wasn't sure I could take losing another staff member.

I plastered on a smile. "It's incredibly beautiful, isn't it?"

"Amazing," he gushed, seemingly unaware that I was doing my best to hold it together and be upbeat for him. I had zero doubts that Valentina would hire him in an instant if he wanted to stay.

"I mean, you're really part of it here, you know? I understand why everyone feels connected to the land. I do, too, and we've only been here for two days." He stretched his lanky arms long as he carefully dragged the beans over the ground.

"I had a feeling you would fall in love with this place." I smiled genuinely. If Andy's path was here at Finca las Nubes, it was my job as his boss, his mentor, and his friend to help guide him in the right direction.

"Yeah, I knew I would love it, but I didn't realize I would love it this much. The smell of the air, the sun looks different, the volcanoes on the ridgeline, the food, and we're surrounded by coffee. So much coffee." He dragged the rake in the other direction, his eyes glazing over slightly at the awe of the experience.

"Do you want me to speak to Valentina?" I forced the growing lump in my throat away with a hard swallow. "She's short on staff, and I'm sure she wouldn't hesitate to scoop you up."

He dropped the rake and gaped at me. "What? Are you trying to get rid of me? Pass me off to Valentina? Wait, did you book me a one-way ticket? Am I Costa Rican now? Do I live here?"

I chuckled. "Check your ticket. I promise we booked you a return flight. And, no, I would never do anything to get rid of you. Carlos and I have bigger plans for you at Torte, but I refuse to hold you back, either. If you want to spend some time here in Costa Rica, I'll be sad, but I'll also be your biggest cheerleader."

"Aww, Jules. You're going to make me blush." He reached for the rake. "My answer is no. I don't want you to speak with Valentina. I could never leave Ashland— my grandma, my friends, Bethany, Torte, and don't even get me started on skiing. I can't live without mountains in my life. I mean the snowy kind of mountains like

Mount A. There's definitely no skiing here unless you can shred on the volcanic ash." He winked. "Although, if you need a coffee liaison, I wouldn't mind having to come visit every once in a while."

I exhaled deeply. Whew. Thank goodness.

"I'd love to hear more about your ideas for me, though. I'm up for anything you and Carlos want to discuss." He gave me a thumbs-up. "As long it involves coffee, I'm your guy."

"Good." I blew another breath and allowed a smile to tug at my lips. "Let's chat with Carlos later. He's the mastermind behind the plan."

Andy propped the rake against his shoulder and rubbed his hands together. "I like the sound of that—a coffee mastermind."

There was so much more I wanted to discuss, but it could wait. Our priority right now was figuring out who had killed Miguel. "Before we head back to the house, I want to take a quick look at the crime scene. Why don't you wait here? I don't think it's a good idea to subject you to that again."

"I'm cool with that, Jules. I'll keep going with my Zen raking. You know where to find me." He returned to his practice, cultivating neat, long rows of beans slowly as if doing a meditation.

I resisted the urge to hug him. Andy was almost like a younger brother to me. Knowing he was attached to Ashland and Torte made me more than happy. He was ready for more responsibility. He had proven his work ethic and his talent. I couldn't wait to fill him in on our vision and see his reaction.

I stood up slowly, feeling calmer. My heart rate had

slowed, and my body felt more centered. I wasn't sure if it was from taking a rest or hearing that Andy intended to stay at Torte. I was lost in my thoughts as I headed toward the processing area.

I rounded the corner, watching my footing as the sturdy metal framing came into my view. The machine was made of cast iron to withstand the humid, rugged environment. It was about eight feet high, with a large hopper (a funnel-like container) standing out at the top like our hand-rolled waffle cones at Scoops.

Unlike the rest of the farm, caution tape was strung around the equipment, walkways, and tanks, barricading it to preserve the crime scene. Every piece of the machinery was roped off, from the hopper to the drum and chute and the motorized gears, belts, and levers.

I was about to approach the area and get a closer look at the blades where Miguel had fallen when I spotted motion out of the corner of my eye. I wasn't alone.

Chapter Nineteen

I threw my hand over my chest and jumped back. "Javier, what are you doing?"

Javier stuffed something in his pocket and smoothed his mustache. Then he pretended to fiddle with the police caution tape, tugging it to determine if it was tightly secured. He ducked under the yellow plastic barrier and moved toward me with slow, lanky steps. Lance had the same catlike walk, but I never found his practiced movements intimidating. Javier was a different beast. He reminded me of a panther on the prowl.

Instinctively, I took another step back. "I thought you were meeting Valentina."

"Yes, I'm on my way to the house as we speak." He glanced at an expensive watch on his wrist. "Shall we walk together?"

I was torn. I wanted to look closer at the processing area and the crime scene, but this was also an opportunity to speak with Javier alone. I hesitated. Was it a bad idea to head out on the trail with him?

He was currently high on my suspect list. But it was broad daylight. Workers were already in the fields. I wasn't going to take any risks. I could tell Andy where I was going.

"That would be great," I said to Javier. "Would you mind if we walk past the drying patio so I can let Andy know? He's in the coffee raking zone."

Javier smiled knowingly. "Ah, yes. The raking can be addictive. Miguel used to say it was his morning meditation."

He had lined up the perfect segue for me. "Were you and Miguel close?"

"Very." He coughed and pounded on his chest. "It's hard to speak of him without becoming emotional. Miguel was family."

Was it an attempt to pretend like he was broken up over Miguel's death?

"You've been working with the Espinozas for a long time?" I asked as we rounded the corner, and the drying patio came into view.

"Yes, since before Miguel and Valentina took over from their parents. This farm and Dulce Coffee have been a team since the very beginning, when I only owned one store in San José. You wouldn't believe how much has changed in the last few decades. The rise of coffee tourism has been highly impactful to our business and our culture. When I opened my first coffee cart almost thirty years ago, I never would have imagined visitors would travel from all around the globe to come to taste our coffee and learn about cultivation and processing. We have become known as one of the top ecotourist destinations in the world, but as I told Miguel, we can't take that for granted. With climate change, we must work even harder to adapt and preserve these fields. There are many threats from diseases like coffee rust to giant corporations like Terra Café International that could put a permanent end to our way of life." He paused and lifted his hand to give Andy a formal greeting.

"Hey, boss. What do you think of my rows?" Andy moved to the side to show off his handiwork.

"Well done." I clapped twice. "You're a natural and a pro."

"I'm not done. I have, uh, let's see—" He counted the rows with his fingers. "At least fourteen more to go. I guess technically, it doesn't matter, but I want them to look like a professional did this."

"Javier offered to escort me to the house, so I'll see you later?" I raised my eyebrows, hoping he caught my drift.

"Good plan. It's back to the grind for me." Andy raised the rake and gave me a lopsided grin. "Get it? Grind, because these will eventually end up as coffee grounds?"

I rolled my eyes. "Where's Bethany when we need her?"

"Oh, thanks for the reminder." Andy propped the rake against the fence that enclosed the drying patio. "I'm slacking on my picture-taking duties." He lifted his phone and snapped a selfie.

"See you at the house later." I left with Javier, taking the main path through the coffee fields. It was a relief to see Andy more like himself. Raking was probably the ideal task for him to recenter and ease some of the trauma. "How many shops do you own now?" I asked Javier, wanting to keep him talking.

He was careful not to ruin his leather loafers, stepping on his toes to avoid getting his shoes too dusty. Whatever he was doing at the processing area must not have been planned, because otherwise, he would have dressed accordingly. "We currently have twenty stores in operation with expansion plans for another dozen in the next few years."

Twenty was a substantial number. Carlos and I had our hands full with Torte, Uva, and Scoops in the summer. Lance had grand plans for a Torte franchise. He would often slip the idea into casual conversation, saying things like, "Imagine a Torte on every street corner, beckoning customers in with the scent of coffee and cardamom."

He knew cardamom was my favorite spice, but his pitch for total global coffee domination (his words, not mine) didn't sway me.

"Will you be able to continue working with Finca las Nubes as you grow, or will your needs outpace production?" I asked.

"The only option is extending our partnership," Javier huffed, sounding almost offended by my question.

"Wouldn't Miguel's deal with Terra Café International benefit your business, I mean assuming it was a go? There's no denying his vision would have dramatically increased production." A warm breeze wafted over us, making the waxy green banana leaves appear to be waving us onward. I kept one eye open for snakes.

"Miguel's deal would have killed our partnership." Javier was only a couple of feet behind me, but I could feel the hot anger in his words. "He was irrational. He had many talents, but his biggest flaw was that he could never see the larger picture. He wanted instant success. Instant cash. I explained growth takes time and nurturing, just like these coffee plants."

I turned around to see him massaging one of the plants and then plucking a coffee cherry from it.

"Our Costa Rican heritage is extremely important to Dulce Coffee and me. I've built a brand to support our farmers. I promised Miguel I would do the same for him and Valentina. There are many opportunities to improve workflow and output at Finca las Nubes without having a huge corporation take over and destroy our natural way of growing. You should stop by one of my shops. You'll see that we educate tourists and guests about the importance of preserving our land and our coffee culture while serving the highest quality product."

His impassioned speech was heartfelt. I had to give him that.

"Have you ever considered investing in the farm?" I hoped my question sounded innocent enough.

"It's a possibility, but our partnership contract is enough for me. I have plenty of work on my plate without adding the stress of owning a piece of the farm." Javier gave no indication that my question had rattled him.

"But you weren't happy about the potential that Terra Café International was interested in buying Miguel out?" I tried another direction, hoping he might say more.

"No. How could I be? They're a soulless corporation. They have no care or concern for our people or our land. Miguel knew this. He knew it was wrong, but he got swept up in the money and the dazzling dinners. This is the problem with the next generation. They want everything immediately, and they don't want to have to put in the hard labor." He sighed heavily. "I sound like an old man. I suppose I am an old man."

I wouldn't have pegged him as old. Maybe mature.

"What would you have done if the sale went through?" Brittle leaves crisped from the unrelenting sun crunched under my feet.

"It wouldn't have gone through." He didn't mince his words.

I stopped and turned around again. This was new insight and backed up what Carmen had said. I wished there was a way to know for sure whether Miguel had signed a contract with the corporate coffee chain. "You don't think it would have gone through? I was under the impression it was basically a done deal."

Javier waved his index finger at me and scoffed. "Miguel wanted people to think that, but I've been working other channels. The deal was dead."

I didn't like his choice of words. This was his second reference to death. Was it subliminal messaging?

"How can you be so sure?" I brushed a mosquito from my face as we continued along the trail. The foliage thickened, dense with greenery that almost seemed to hum. Farther out in the fields, the sounds of chatter and singing floated toward us as work crews tended to the coffee plants. Violet patches of trumpet vine and clusters of pink bougainvillea were scattered across the landscape, their blooms standing out against the rich green, adding bursts of color.

Javier let out a low laugh that lacked any warmth or humor. "There are many groups and entities committed to keeping acreage like this in the hands of Costa Ricans."

I tried to weed through his meaning. "Like environmental groups?"

"This must be true in America, too, yes? Farms are under attack by big businesses across the globe."

That didn't exactly answer my question.

"And you believe Miguel would have been swayed not to sell?" I pressed. I was inclined to believe him, given my conversation with Carmen. She had basically said the same thing, but I had no idea who was lying at this point.

"No, Miguel would have sold to the highest bidder. I have no doubts about that. What I'm sure of is that the deal would have been stopped legally. The courts would not have allowed it through." He didn't waver. "We have strict laws prohibiting corporations from taking advantage of local farmers, and we have many connections here that will find ways to stop progress." He had to be hinting at Isabel.

We were almost back to the house. The maize walls and red tile roof appeared above the green canopy.

I decided there was no point in not asking the questions. I had a short amount of time left and little to lose. "As the farm's agronomist, Isabel must have connections in environmental protection."

"Sí, you understand." He curled the edge of his mustache and considered me with new interest. "I figured you must, as a small business owner yourself." He didn't expand on this.

Could he and Isabel have plotted Miguel's murder together? Or was there another possibility I hadn't yet considered? What if Javier wasn't being honest about his interest in buying the farm? Something about the timing didn't sit right. What if he and Miguel had struck a secret deal *before* Miguel ever entered negotiations with Sofia? Maybe Miguel used Sofia as leverage, making her think she had the upper hand, while keeping his real buyer under wraps? Or he intended to try to start a bidding war between them. But if a deal with Javier was already signed, Miguel's death would seal it—ensuring Javier got what he wanted without any competition.

I wondered if there was any chance Valentina had access to Miguel's files or whether the police had confiscated his computer as evidence. I also wondered what Javier had been doing at the processing area before I interrupted him. By all accounts, it appeared he'd been up to nothing good. If he had been involved in Miguel's death, could he have returned to the processing area this morning to destroy any remaining evidence?

Chapter Twenty

When Javier and I arrived at the house, police cars lined the driveway. There was a frenzy of activity. Officers were posted at the front door and flanked out into the field. Were they looking for someone? Was there new evidence that had come to light?

Javier and I were allowed inside and directed to the terrace.

Everyone was congregated outside, aside from Carlos and Andy, who hadn't returned yet. Police officers were interviewing Carmen, Isabel, and Sofia in different areas of the large deck.

"What's happening?" Javier asked Valentina, who was pacing in front of the railing, looking out into the fields nervously.

"The detectives have follow-up questions for each of us. I'm glad you're here." She caught my eye, looking flustered as she nodded toward the fields.

Was I missing something?

The police must have discovered new information; otherwise, why the sudden show of such a large presence?

"Juliet Capshaw." One of the uniformed officers called my name. "Over here, please."

I left Valentina and Javier.

The officer directed me to a grouping of chairs on the far end of the deck. "According to your statement, you were here at the house when Miguel died?"

"That's correct."

He made a note on a clipboard. "Did you notice anything unusual in the house?"

"*In* the house? No." I shook my head, slightly surprised by the question.

"Did you see anyone moving through the house?" He pursued the same line of questions. His accent was thick, but his English was immaculate. He constantly scanned our surroundings, taking notes without looking at his clipboard. He was obviously on high alert.

Why?

I shook my head again. "No, not until Andy, my staff member, showed up to tell me about the accident."

He scribbled something else on the paper. Then he lifted the pages on his clipboard and removed the note Valentina had found, offering it to me for examination. "Have you seen this? Go ahead. You can open it and read it."

I nodded. "I already know what it says."

"When did you see the note?" He tore his eyes away from the far side of the deck and stared at me.

Was I in trouble?

Was that why Valentina seemed nervous?

My stomach fluttered.

"Last night," I replied truthfully, explaining that Valentina had shown it to me, intending to inform the police about it as soon as possible.

"You accompanied Valentina to compare the writing samples?" the officer asked.

Valentina must have told him everything.

"Yes." It wasn't my proudest moment, but he didn't seem fazed by my responses.

"Is there anything else you can share?" he asked pointedly, as if he suspected I was holding more information back.

"Yes, I'll share everything I know." I launched into what I'd learned about the suspects thus far. "Is there a way to look into potential sales to see if Javier might have secured a deal with Miguel before he died or if Sofia successfully got Miguel to sign with her? Have you found a contract or any paperwork? If there's proof of a deal, that might help point to who killed him, right?" I asked after I finished relaying what I knew.

"I can't answer those questions." The officer clipped the note onto the board.

"I understand." I started to stand. "Has anyone mentioned the possibility that the sale of the farm wouldn't be legal?"

I figured he wouldn't be able to answer that either, but to my surprise, he bobbed his head in agreement. "Sí, this is true. We have very strict laws in Costa Rica. We are a small, small country, and yet we hold six percent of the world's biodiversity. This farm is an ecologically sensitive area and part of a fair-trade agreement. There are many factors involved in selling a family farm like this, but the combination of environmental regulations, community resistance, and local agricultural policies is a significant barrier to such a buyout."

"You don't believe the sale is viable?"

"I believe the sale, or attempt to convince him to sell, led to Miguel's murder." He stood, tucking the clipboard under his arm. "Thank you for your time. I hope you enjoy the remainder of your stay in our beautiful country."

Our conversation reminded me of how the Professor interviewed suspects and witnesses. He was open and receptive yet gave very little away. I tried to glean as much meaning as I could from his words, but I didn't come up with anything revolutionary.

I wasn't sure what to do next.

Every new piece of information I learned seemed to lead to dozens of new questions. I had hoped that as the day wore on, I might start answering questions instead of constantly coming up with new ones.

Valentina scooted over to me, carrying a tray of fruit-infused waters. Pretty glass pitchers were filled with ice and slices of fresh lemons, limes, and oranges. "Would you like a cool drink?"

"Yes, thank you." My mouth was parched from the walk and being out in the heat.

Valentina poured me a glass of citrus water and sat down. "What did you learn?"

"I found Javier at the processing area. He was behind the caution tape. I don't know what he was doing. I startled him, and he played it off as if it were no big deal. I think he put something in his pocket. Maybe evidence he left behind?"

"Did you see what it was?" Valentina's foot bounced on the floor, causing the chair to shake.

"He was too fast. He's very smooth. I tried asking him several questions that he didn't exactly answer." I sucked on a piece of ice, wishing I had gotten a better look. Whatever Javier found was small enough to hide in his pocket.

"That's Javier." Valentina poured herself a glass of water and stared in his direction. Another police officer was still interviewing him.

The Professor would have been impressed with their diligence. They were clearly taking the situation seriously and were committed to either proving or disproving Alex had killed Miguel.

"Did you know he was an actor before he got into the coffee business?" Valentina arched her eyebrow toward her forehead as she glanced at Javier.

"Was he?" It made sense. "That fits. He gives off old-school Hollywood vibes. But the question is, do you trust him? I'm stuck on the theory that he and Miguel could have been planning a deal that went south."

"Went south?" Valentina scrunched her brow.

"Sorry, that's an American saying. A deal that went bad. If Miguel realized he could make much more money with Terra Café International, he might have called it off with Javier."

Valentina interrupted with a gasp. "And Javier killed him to stop Miguel from moving forward with Sofia."

"Maybe?" I swirled my glass, considering the possibilities. "Do you know if he had any paperwork drawn up with Javier? What if they had planned a secret deal? Carmen seems convinced that Miguel wouldn't sell—at least not to Sofia."

"If he did, he didn't show me. He wouldn't have because

he knew I was angry." Valentina swirled the slices of oranges and lemons in the bottom of her glass. "We could check his house."

"We should probably wait until the police are done." I tipped my head in that direction.

She smiled. "True."

"Were you trying to tell me something about the fields before I spoke with the police officer?" I raised my head to try and see over the railing. Variegated shades of green stretched as far as I could see.

She scooted her chair closer so our knees were practically touching. "It's Isabel. She was out in the field taking pictures and huddling with the workers. You have me questioning Javier now, but I'm still concerned about Isabel. First, she erased the whiteboard, and then she was sneaking around having hushed conversations with the workers. What could she be plotting?"

"Does she normally engage with the workers?" If she was tasked with the farm's sustainability, it stood to reason that she would have cause to speak with the workers about their process.

"Yes. She does a lot of collaboration, training, and education. A lot of it is hands-on. That's one of the reasons I hired her. She is very familiar with every aspect of farming. She teaches specific methods on composting, natural pest control, organic fertilization, crop rotation, and much more. She regularly walks the fields with the workers and encourages them to be involved in decision-making. Her goal is to foster a sense of ownership in the organic process so that the workers not only have pride in what they're doing, but they also offer new ideas that they've learned from working the land. She starts every training session by telling the workers that they know this land better than anyone. If they see areas where the soil quality is poor, or pests are a problem, she asks them to come to her, so they can find an organic solution together."

"Okay, well, that probably explains her behavior," I said, feeling a twinge of disappointment.

"No." Valentina plunged a lemon slice into her glass and shook her head. "This felt different. She was acting strange. She kept glancing up here to the deck, like she knew I was watching her and she didn't want to be seen. Today is a typical workday, so there shouldn't be anything regarding her environmental work she would need to tell them. I feel like I sound paranoid, but Miguel is dead, and I don't want harm to come to anyone else."

"It's completely normal for you to feel paranoid," I said, putting a hand on her knee.

She didn't speak for a minute. She ran her fingers along the side of her neck, stretching on one side and then the other. "It sounds ridiculous, but I keep waiting for something else to happen. I'm so tense and jumpy. This isn't like me."

"You've been through a shock. I promise it's normal to feel—well—anything and everything. Try to be gentle with yourself."

"You're a good friend, Jules. You came for a vacation and ended up taking care of me. This isn't what I intended." Her eyes were wide, round, and filled with emotion.

"That's life." I shrugged and smiled. "I know I sound like a broken record, but none of this is your fault, and I think the police presence is a good sign. It means that they're exploring other suspects. Maybe they've uncovered new evidence that points to someone other than Alex."

"I hope you're right." She gulped down her water. "I should go check on lunch. When the police are done, I'll take you to Miguel's."

"Do you need help with lunch?"

"No, you sit. Relax. I'll bring it to you."

I felt terrible for her. Even though I'd tried to tell her she wasn't ruining my weekend, I would have felt the same if the situation were reversed. My thoughts drifted to Torte. The bakeshop was a space where everyone who came through the front door was welcomed with love and pastries. Mom's gentle way of actively listening had set the tone for years. People wandered in as strangers and left as friends. I knew Valentina cared about the farm in the same way.

I got lost in my thoughts and didn't notice Sofia slip over to me. "Do you mind if I sit? We haven't had a chance to chat and get to know each other very well yet."

"Sure." I motioned to the chair Valentina had vacated.

"Can you believe this? It's a circus." Her thin wrist jingled as her bracelets clinked together. She wore another sundress, this one a bright green halter top with a plunging neckline. Her arms and neck were adorned with gold necklaces and bangles.

Her annoyance seemed odd for someone who had watched Miguel fall to his death.

She strummed her fingers on the edge of the chair and leaned closer to me, lowering her voice in a conspiratorial tone. "I thought the police were competent, but now I'm not sure."

"Really? Why?" I was surprised to hear that and surprised that she was suddenly wanting to be chummy with me. She'd kept to herself most of the day and at dinner last night, only chiming in when Javier had made disparaging comments about her employer.

"They arrested the wrong guy."

Chapter Twenty-one

"You don't think Alex killed Miguel?" I asked Sofia.

She tossed her hair over her shoulder and pursed her lips. She was dressed for a leisurely brunch in her revealing dress and sandals instead of a Saturday on the farm. Come to think of it, what was she doing here?

She held a small gold clutch on her lap. "I wasn't in a clear state of mind after Miguel's death—" She sucked in a gulp of air in a gasp like she'd forgotten to breathe. "I don't need to tell you. You saw the aftermath. It was terrible. Awful. Alex was right there. I thought at the time it had to be him."

I nodded, waiting for her to say more. Did she have an ulterior motive? I couldn't figure out why she was suddenly interested in opening up to me. However, I wasn't going to stop her either.

She swished her mouth like she was trying to get rid of a sour taste. "The police arrested him, and I suppose I was in a daze. But this morning, when I woke, I remembered something important."

Was she intentionally trying to build my anticipation? It was working.

"Carmen. It's Carmen." She unlocked the latch on her purse and locked it again. "It sounds like they might be releasing Alex today."

"What?" This was big news. The officer who had interviewed me gave no indication they were intending to let him go, or that they had found any evidence supporting Carmen as the killer. Why was Sofia singularly focused on Carmen? Could she know something that the police had missed?

She looked over at one of the officers questioning Javier and rolled her eyes. "They're all over the map. Incompetent. I've put in a call to our company's legal team for guidance. I don't trust that the local police can handle a case of this magnitude, and we can't risk a PR scandal."

There were so many threads I wanted to follow up on. Sofia was tossing out clues like candy thrown from a float parade. Each one was tempting me to chase after it, but I didn't want to get tied up in a million threads.

"Can we circle back to Carmen for a minute? What makes you think she's involved?"

Sofia crossed her legs and curled her body so I could see behind her. "Don't look. Don't make it obvious we're talking about her."

"I won't." However, my first reaction had been to look in that direction.

"Play it cool. Do you notice anything strange about her?" Sofia asked, keeping her body tilted toward me.

I casually glanced around the terrace again, letting my eyes land on the police officers, Isabel, Javier, and Carmen. Nothing seemed out of the ordinary to me. She was standing near the railing, drinking a coffee and talking with Isabel. "No. I don't," I said truthfully.

"She and Isabel have been glued at the hip since Miguel fell. They showed up at the processing area together. Basically, right before it happened. Don't you find that odd?"

"They were both working nearby," I said. "From what I've been told, they were trying to get Miguel away from the machine and then attempted to stop it once he fell."

"Not Carmen."

"What?" This was another new piece of information. I wasn't sure how valid it was yet, but I was curious to hear where Sofia was going.

"Me, Alex, your barista Andy, and Isabel, we put our entire weight into trying to shut the machine off. Alex tried to grab him at the last minute but it was too late. It happened fast. He fell, smacked his head on the concrete, and was dead instantly." She stuck her tongue out and shivered, pressing her purse closer to her body. "Carmen stood there and watched. She did nothing."

There were plenty of explanations for Carmen's lack of action. She could have been in shock, or there might not have been space for her to try and help. The narrow passageway above the rotating drums was only three or four feet wide and maybe ten feet long. She could have been worried the walkway wouldn't support another body.

"There's more. I saw them fighting shortly before Miguel was killed," Sofia continued. Her bracelets dangled together, clinking like champagne glasses as her gestures became more animated. "Carmen was screaming at him. Miguel blew it off, but I could tell he was upset. I tried to speak with him, but he was in a hurry."

"When was this?" I asked.

She shrugged and checked the gold and diamond

watch on her wrist as if it might give her a specific time. "Minutes before he died, I would say. Five? I'm not sure, but it was right before the fall."

That was odd. Andy had made it sound like Miguel had been talking with them for more than a few minutes before his death. But then again, everyone had likely been in shock seeing such a tragic accident. It wasn't a complete surprise that the timing didn't add up, but I made a mental note to check with Andy again.

"Why were you at the processing area?" I reached for my water, trying to get a read on Sofia. She was more polished than Isabel or Carmen. That likely came from her corporate background, but it was also hard to tell if her emotional reactions were authentic or practiced. Everything sounded rehearsed.

"I was looking for him. Andy, that's his name, right? Your employee?"

I nodded.

"He'll tell you. He saw me there. I had been here at the house, speaking with Valentina. She told me Miguel was in the processing area. I had a few last things for him to sign before our contract was finalized."

"Did he sign them?" I reached for my water glass. The ice had melted, but the citrus flavor remained strong. "I've heard varying accounts of whether Miguel had sold his farm shares."

Her attempt at a demure smile faltered for the briefest second before she recovered, her polished exterior snapping back into place. But in that instant, I caught something in her chestnut eyes—something sharp and fleeting. Triumph? Satisfaction? "He did." She smoothed her hands down her sleeves as if adjusting an invisible wrinkle. "We successfully signed the paperwork, which means the sale can progress as planned, and Miguel's legacy will live on in a much broader and bolder way with Terra Café International. I'm already in discussions with our team about naming a coffee blend after him as well as setting up a scholarship fund in his name."

Miguel had signed the paperwork before he died?

This changed everything. Did that mean the killer's plan had failed?

"Does Valentina know?"

Sofia traced the stitching on her clutch. "I've been waiting for the right opportunity to speak with her, but we haven't had a chance, what with so many people around. I need to give her a copy of the contract for her lawyers to review."

Valentina was going to be devastated. First, she lost her cousin, and now she was losing half the farm.

"What will this mean for the staff and workers?"

"Better benefits, better working conditions, better everything. We get painted to be the bad guy—the big corporation that comes in and ruins family farms," Sofia said with a touch of sarcasm. "But it's simply not true. Terra Café International is the most reputable coffee company in the world. We do business on every continent and with coffee shops of all sizes. This will exponentially grow Finca las Nubes's profit margins and expand their production. It's a huge opportunity for everyone. I don't understand the hate we get. We're here to improve upon an already great product and get it into more customers' hands. How can that be a bad thing?"

I got the sense it was a rhetorical question, but I had to ask about the farmworkers. "Will the workers lose their housing?"

"You sound like Carmen." She twisted her necklace, a hint of irritation creeping into her tone. "That woman is obsessed. It's sad. This is the only thing she has, and it shows. We'll be making some moderate changes as we expand the coffee fields, but it's not as dire as she likes to pretend. No one is going hungry. The workers will have a roof over their heads, and their housing will be up to industry standards."

I understood the subtext. Carmen was right to be concerned. The question was, had her concern led to murder? And was there a chance that Miguel wasn't the intended victim? Could the killer have been trying to target Sofia instead?

Chapter Twenty-two

Sofia touched up her lipstick and stood, smoothing down her skirt. "I need to find Valentina. She can't avoid me forever."

Was Valentina avoiding her? I got the impression Valentina was trying to speak with everyone who'd been at the scene. But maybe Valentina knew the truth at her core—that Miguel had sold his shares of her beloved family farm. That might explain why she wanted to hold out on sharing the note with the authorities and had been avoiding a conversation with Sofia.

Sofia excused herself and drifted inside.

My new theory started to take hold. What if Sofia had been the intended victim? She was at the processing area. No one was pleased about Terra Café International taking over the farm. Had Miguel spilled the news that the contract had been finalized? What if the killer had tried to take out Sofia to stop the sale from going through and missed?

I wondered if the police were exploring the possibility. It wouldn't hurt to at least raise the idea with them.

"Everyone, lunch is ready," Valentina announced,

balancing two trays of sandwiches, fruit, and salads. "Please come help yourselves." She set the food on the table and encouraged everyone to join her.

Sofia seized the opportunity. While the police and Javier filled their plates, she whispered something to Valentina. I could tell whatever she said rattled my friend, because Valentina shook her head to stop Sofia from saying more and then grabbed her wrist to escort her inside.

Carlos and Andy were still out in the fields, so I made myself a plate and returned to the cozy, shady spot to enjoy my lunch and ponder the case.

"Would you like company?" a voice asked.

I looked up to see Carmen standing over me. She set her plate on the side table. She was wearing the same wrinkled outfit as earlier, but her cheeks had more color and she seemed a bit more composed. "I hate to see you sitting alone. It's not in our Costa Rican nature to leave guests unattended."

"I appreciate that. These are not exactly normal circumstances."

She pressed her hand to her chest and left it there, closing her eyes like she was desperately trying to remain centered. "This is not the pura vida way. I hope you realize that."

"I do." I patted Sofia's vacant seat. "Please sit; I'd love company."

Carmen reminded me a bit of Mom. They had similar energy—calming, grounded, the kind of personality you wanted to open up to and spill your innermost fears, knowing they'd hold space for you without judgment. She tucked her hair behind her ears, revealing what looked like a bruise on the base of her neck. I hadn't noticed that before.

"Did you hurt yourself?" I asked.

She tossed her hair back in place and covered the injury with her hand. "This? It's nothing. I bruise easily these days. I banged into the side of the door frame. It doesn't even hurt."

"Good." I picked up half of a sandwich, my mouth immediately watering at the sight of the crusty French bread slathered with black beans and salsa and stacked with thinly sliced caramelized onions, skirt steak, and melted Muenster cheese. The sandwich had been grilled in a panini press and served with sliced avocado and fire-roasted jalapeños.

"Have you had a pepito before?" Carmen asked, biting into her sandwich. "Here in Costa Rica, we call it the best sandwich in the world."

"It deserves that billing," I said, tasting the oozing, melting medley of flavors. "We used to have them occasionally on the cruise ship, and they were always a hit."

Carmen lifted her sandwich in a toast. "To the world's best."

The sandwich was just as good as I remembered. I made a mental note to add a pepito to our lunch rotation at Torte when we returned home. I tried not to stare at the purplish bruise on her neck. Had she simply run into the side of the door frame, or could she have gotten into a struggle with Miguel? The mark almost looked like it could have been from a finger or thumb.

"It's even better than I remember," I said through a mouthful. I wanted to bring up Miguel and the contract but didn't want to put her on the defensive. Fortunately, she gave me the opportunity.

"I noticed you speaking with Sofia." Her thin lips

practically disappeared as she scowled. "I don't understand why she's here. Who invited her? She's enemy number one on the farm. I can't imagine that Valentina wants her here."

"The police, maybe?" I suggested. Carmen's reaction made me wonder if maybe I was onto something about the killer making a mistake. Sofia was certainly not well-liked among any of the farm staff. She was there at the time. What if the killer had meant to push her, not Miguel?

Carmen ate her sandwich slowly, contemplating every bite. "Why would the police ask her to return to the farm? She shouldn't have been here yesterday, either. None of this would have happened if it weren't for her. She is the cause of all our problems and Miguel's death."

"Do you think she killed Miguel?" I couldn't tell if she was speaking metaphorically.

"It's possible. I leave that to the police. My concern is for the farm and our future. How will we proceed without Miguel? There are so many unanswered questions, and harvest will begin in October. There is much work to do before then. The coffee plants are in their maturation phase right now. The cherries are steadily growing, but they aren't ripe enough to be picked. We have a small permanent crew of workers currently living on the property. That's who you see out in the fields now." She paused, her eyes moving in that direction. "This crew is responsible for pruning, checking for pests, weeding and clearing, fertilizing, trimming the shade trees so the coffee plants receive enough sunlight, and prepping for harvest. By October, we'll hire an additional hundred workers to keep up with the demand. All the picking is done by hand here at Finca las Nubes. The influx of workers is essential for the season, but it's a huge task."

"I can only imagine. Are you responsible for managing all of the workers and their families?"

She nodded. "Miguel was very helpful. We were a team, but yes, now it will fall on my shoulders. Our permanent crew will assist in preharvest training and preparing the seasonal workers for the rigorous handpicking process, but there are many, many details that need to be taken care of now. I'm concerned about overwhelming Valentina. Miguel was her cousin, after all, but work and preparations can't come to a halt if we're to have a successful harvest season."

"It lasts for a few months, correct?" I dabbed my chin with a napkin. The sandwich oozed with flavors.

"Yes, it depends on weather conditions and when the cherries ripen, but typically, harvest lasts from late October until March, with peak times being November to January. The seasonal workers and their families will live here for the duration of the season. That's why it's critical we have childcare, transportation, health care, and all the supports and services we offer our staff ready to go by the end of next month."

I felt a headache coming on just imagining all the moving parts Carmen had to juggle. It gave me a fresh perspective on Torte, Scoops, and Uva. Suddenly, our staff schedules didn't seem quite as daunting.

"I don't envy you. I'm guessing, though, since you've been with the farm for so long, you probably have historical data and plans to use as a base for this year." I finished the first half of my sandwich and went for the second half. It was too good not to eat the entire thing.

"Yes, although each year brings a new round of changes and challenges." Carmen folded her hands together and stole a brief look at the fields. "Pests, disease, too much rain, not enough rain. It goes on and on."

"Especially with Terra Café International in the mix now, right?" I brought up the topic to see how she would react.

The skin around her eyes tightened in sharp creases as her frown deepened. "If I never hear that name again, it will be fine with me. They don't care about us or the land. They only care about their profits. I'm glad to be done with them for good."

"You mentioned seeing me speaking with Sofia. She made it sound like Miguel signed the contract and that the deal is proceeding."

Carmen dropped her sandwich on her lap. "What?"

"That's what she said." I glanced at the house. "She's been trying to get a minute alone with Valentina to tell her."

"No. That's a lie." Carmen picked up her sandwich. She put pieces of the gooey bread on her plate and dabbed her pants with a napkin. "The sale is done. It's finished."

"Not according to Sofia."

She wouldn't back down. "She's wrong. Or she's lying. I know without a doubt that the sale did not go through."

Why was she so confident?

Because she'd put an end to the sale by killing Miguel? Or because she knew that he was going to sign with Sofia, and she accidentally killed him instead of her target. Ultimately, either way, if she was the killer, she'd succeeded in ending any impending sale and thereby saving the farm.

Chapter Twenty-three

"Why is she spreading such lies? This woman is a menace." Carmen pushed her plate away like she was ready to confront Sofia.

"Do you think she would lie about something as important as the contract?" I asked. Carmen's demeanor had shifted radically. Gone was any pretense of calm. I felt the tiny hairs on my arms spike and my back stiffen in response to the shift.

She balled her napkin in her hands and steamed with anger. "Your guess is as good as mine. I have no idea why she would be claiming something that is not true. It's completely false. Miguel did not sell the farm. He did not. He would not. He promised me."

I took another bite of the cheesy, spicy sandwich. She sounded convinced, but every indication pointed the other way. "I understand you're upset," I said, choosing my words carefully. "It seems like Miguel was ready to cash out. Sofia was here with paperwork yesterday. It's not out of the realm of possibility that he signed the contract shortly before he was killed."

I watched Carmen grow redder and redder.

Could she have killed Miguel because she learned the truth, and now she was struggling to keep the news under wraps?

Where was the contract?

If there were physical proof, it would answer so many questions.

"No, I'm sorry if I sound rude, but it is you who doesn't understand." She tilted her head and looked at me from the corner of her eye like she was scolding me. "Miguel did not sign the contract. I know because I convinced him. I gave him another path forward."

I didn't think she was rude, but I was very curious about what she meant by "another path forward."

She twisted the napkin tighter and kept looking around as if she expected Sophia to pounce on her at any minute. "Miguel did want to sell. This is true. He and I had many discussions about the pros and cons. You've likely heard many stories about him, and you were able to meet him yourself. He wasn't a villain. He was hungry for money and wanted to grow the farm into a name and a brand that people would know across the world. He was a dreamer. But he was also an Espinoza. You can't take his family legacy out of his blood. This is what I finally told him. He wouldn't want his workers to suffer only so that he could profit." Her gaze drifted to the far side of the terrace where the police were finishing their inquiries. "He was naïve. He believed the best about people. Even people who didn't have his best interest at heart."

"You mean Sofia?"

She'd managed to tie the napkin into a tight spiral. "Sofia cares about profits and making the sale. She stands to receive a large commission if the sale goes through.

Miguel believed her story because he wanted it to be true. He wanted to make money, expand the Finca las Nubes name, and continue to care for the workers."

Everything she was saying was a repeat of what I'd already heard. "Isn't that why everyone was upset with him?" I asked. My sandwich had satiated my appetite, but I couldn't resist a suspiro, a light-as-a-feather meringue cookie.

"I believe many people misunderstood his motives and desires. That's why I'm saying he wasn't a villain. He did care deeply about people and the farm. He was dazzled by Sofia's lies. Once I was able to show him proof about Terra Café International and how they've destroyed other family farms, he changed his mind. I know he didn't sign the contract, because I convinced him not to, and I told him I would offer my life savings to help with farm expansions."

I crunched the cookie, which immediately melted in my mouth with a tangy, bright zing from the whipped egg whites and lemon juice.

Carmen intended to invest in the farm.

She was the secret investor?

I hadn't anticipated that.

"I've lived a very modest lifestyle," she continued. "My expenses are covered, and the Espinoza family has always been generous. I don't travel. I don't have a family. This is my home, and I've saved a substantial amount. Enough to purchase a small portion of the farm. That's what Miguel and I discussed. He would retain forty percent. I would purchase ten percent of his shares. I provided him with documentation of what Terra Café International has done to other family farms. They do not keep their promises. They are notorious for treating seasonal workers poorly. I showed him pictures of some of the living conditions of Terra Café's workers, and he was horrified. He had no idea what Sofia and her corporate bosses intended to do with the farm either. He believed we could keep our Rainforest Alliance certification, but I also found evidence of their unecological farming practices. They use heavy, toxic pesticides and nasty chemicals in the treatment process."

"And that changed his mind?" I savored the sweet cookie and took a second one. They were mainly air, after all.

"Yes." She tossed the napkin over her uneaten plate of food. "He couldn't believe it. He admitted he had done little research because he was so captivated by Sofia and her vision for the farm. Once he learned the truth, he was furious."

I brushed cookie crumbs from my hands and tried to take in everything Carmen had shared. If she was telling the truth, why was Sofia claiming the contract was a done deal? Could she have killed him after he signed the contract? But would that even matter? If he'd already signed the paperwork, it would seem things would continue to proceed.

Or what if Miguel had signed the contract *before* his conversation with Carmen?

I wasn't sure yet how this new piece of information played into the case, but it was a huge revelation.

"Would you like to walk up to my house with me?" Carmen asked. "I have the documentation I shared with Miguel. I'll show it to you and bring it for the police to see."

"Sure." Having solid evidence would help back up her claim and potentially remove her from my suspect list, although there was still no way to prove that Miguel agreed with her. He could have seen the documentation and proceeded with the sale anyway. All I had to go on was her word.

She motioned to the side stairwell. "Come, we can take the back route."

I didn't hesitate, but once we were a few hundred yards away from the house, the thought crossed my mind that it might have been a mistake to leave with Carmen without letting anyone know where I was or where I was going.

I wanted to believe her story. She sounded sincere, and her energy mirrored Mom's to the point that they could be long-lost sisters, but I needed to stay alert and aware. There was still an outside chance that she had killed Miguel.

What if she had realized I knew too much during our conversation?

Was she intentionally luring me away to silence me before I could tell anyone what I knew?

You're being ridiculous, Jules.

I matched Carmen's pace as we traversed the rolling switchbacks. The workers had broken for a siesta and a long lunch.

"We don't like for them to work during the peak heat of the day," Carmen explained as we passed a group enjoying cold drinks and sandwiches under the shade of a clump of banana trees. "These are the kinds of things that make us the best farm in Costa Rica."

I continued to be impressed with her dedication to the staff.

The walk to her hacienda took us about fifteen minutes. Situated on one of the higher points of the farm, the house commanded an expansive view of the patchwork fields and was surrounded by coffee plants. The white stucco walls and red tile roof stood out in striking contrast amongst the deep, lush greenery.

"Please, come inside." Carmen opened the door for me. I noted it wasn't locked. That had to be a good sign. If she was concerned about people finding out her secrets, surely she would lock the door.

The inside was exactly how I imagined it: a small living room, open dining room, and kitchen. The red tile floors, tall ceilings, and wooden fans kept the space naturally cool. The walls were painted in earth tones to match the landscape. Worn but comfortable furniture had faded over time from the natural light that spilled in from the large windows.

"Have a seat," Carmen said as if she were inviting me in for high tea, not to show me evidence in a murder investigation. "Would you like a coffee or a tea?"

"I'm fine, thanks." Not only had I just eaten lunch, but I'd seen enough murder mystery productions at OSF to know you should never accept any food or drink from a potential suspect. I could hear Lance screaming at me from Ashland. "Do not drink the tea! The killer always spikes the tea with poison!"

I was still relatively confident Carmen wasn't the killer, but I wasn't going to take a chance.

"I'll be right back." She went down a small hallway off the dining room.

I sat in one of the wooden chairs with faded yellow cushions. Bundles of dried herbs—rosemary, thyme, and lavender—hung from the windows in the kitchen. Photos of Carmen with Miguel, Valentina, and the Espinoza family hung on the living room walls. The pictures dated back to the farm's earlier days—images of harvests, family gatherings, parties, and celebrations.

It was no wonder Carmen considered herself family. From the pictures, it was obvious that the Espinozas reciprocated her feelings. She'd been around for births and graduations, weddings and anniversaries. I wouldn't have guessed that she *wasn't* part of the family.

The same warning thought crept into my head.

What if she had been so desperate to protect the farm and the only family she'd known that she'd killed for it?

What was taking her so long? I surveyed the living room and hallway.

A shiver raced down my spine as I leaned to the side, craning my head to listen in. Whatever Carmen was doing, she was quiet about it. Too quiet.

Was she looking for the information about Terra Café International she'd shown Miguel? Or had I been as naïve as him?

Couldn't she have pulled the articles or whatever else she'd collected up on her phone?

Why had she brought me to the house?

My pulse thudded against my neck as a cold sweat broke out.

This was a mistake.

I need to get out of here—fast.

But you're pregnant, Jules.

I couldn't go on a tear, running down the trail at a breakneck pace, but if I could sneak out without Carmen hearing me, I could get a head start. She was fit and strong, but she was at least twenty-five years older than me. I could probably beat her back to the house, even at my pregnancy pace. Or at least make it to the spot where the workers had taken a lunch break.

I stood gingerly, careful not to disturb the chair.

It creaked.

I froze and checked the hallway.

There was no sign of her.

Had she left me here on purpose? Snuck out a back door?

But why?

Nothing was making sense.

Or I was slipping into a deep delusion.

I inched toward the door, grateful for the tile floors. At least they didn't squeak. I reached for the handle and was about to turn it when Carmen's voice sounded behind me.

"What are you doing?"

I'd never had a good poker face. Blame it on my name—Juliet Montague Capshaw. Being named after arguably one of the most famous characters in literature practically destined me for a life where my emotions were always written across my face. I was also a terrible liar.

I let go of the handle, frantically trying to come up with an explanation for my sudden departure. "I realized I was supposed to meet Carlos at the house. I wasn't paying attention to the time." I tapped my wrist. I wasn't wearing a watch, but Carmen would get the point. "I didn't realize it was late, and he's going to be worried about me."

I held my breath, anticipating the worst-case scenario. Would she come after me? Try to assault me physically?

Was that what happened with Miguel?

Was the bruise on her neck from an argument? My

mind splintered with dozens of possibilities, but none stuck. This was the moment where a poker face or a quick, convincing lie might have saved me, but all I could do was stand there, blank and useless.

Carmen's jaw tightened, her eyes flicking toward the door as if trying to figure out how she could make an escape before me. For a moment, I thought she'd fight me on this. Then, just as quickly, she deflated, her shoulders slumping. "Okay," she muttered, a resigned edge in her voice. "I'll come with you."

"What about the documents?" I asked, not giving up my position at the door.

"They're gone." She tossed up her arms. "Someone must have broken in and stolen them."

Chapter Twenty-four

"The documents are gone?" I repeated.

Carmen motioned to the hallway, her arms flailing in distress. "I've searched everywhere. I left them in my bedroom, on the top of the dresser. They were bundled together with a rubber band. There's nowhere else I would have put them, but I searched the bedroom anyway. They're gone. Missing. Who could have done this?" She shivered and rubbed her arms like a cool wind had blown inside. "Someone has been inside my house."

"Are you sure?"

"Absolutely. I showed the papers to Miguel yesterday and brought them home with me. No one has been here. Only me. How can they be gone? There's only one explanation—someone has taken them." She hung her head and stared at the tile floor.

"Should we check the rest of the house, just in case?" I moved away from the door.

"We can, but I know where I left them." She repeated the same sentiment.

"Is the door usually locked?" I asked, motioning to the ornately carved wooden door.

"No. We don't lock our houses on the farm. There's no need." She sounded almost incensed at the suggestion.

"So anyone could have come in."

"But who would? What would they want with the paperwork?" She glanced over her shoulder as if expecting someone to be lurking in the shadows.

My blood pressure had calmed down. I didn't think Carmen was going to hurt me, but she was right: who benefited from taking the documents? Sofia? "Let's sit for a minute and think this through. What exactly was in the documents? Did you find news articles about Terra Café International or social media posts?"

She sank into a leather couch. "I began by searching the internet, but they have a talented marketing team. It's hard to find much about their actual properties. Everything is beautifully styled. Warm, happy, smiling workers, rows of coffee plants, stylized pictures that look like glossy travel brochures. Isabel told me to look at some of the internet forums like Reddit to see what people who had actually worked for the company had to say. I did find a few posts with horrible reports of the living and working conditions. I showed Miguel the forums, but that wasn't enough to convince him. He said everyone has disgruntled former staff."

I'd never considered searching Reddit for posts about Torte, but I could imagine Richard Lord finding a way to troll us there.

"I was out of ideas, but then I happened to have a conversation with Javier. He's here often. We were both discussing how awful it would be to have Terra Café as our new owners, and I told him about the Reddit boards. He mentioned he could get me proof of their business practices."

"Javier?" I readjusted the pillow behind my back.

She picked up a framed photo from the coffee table and ran her finger along the glass. "He has visited a number of their farms under the pretense of partnering with them, and while he had access to their properties, he took photos and documented everything. That's what I showed Miguel. That's what finally convinced him not to sell."

I tried to keep up with the barrage of theories vying for space in my brain. Miguel wasn't going to sell. That could mean Sofia killed him, or it could mean she was the target. What had Javier been doing at the machine earlier this morning? Gathering evidence he'd left behind? Wiping away his fingerprints?

But that wouldn't make sense. When I found him this morning, the police had already searched and secured the area. They would have scanned for fingerprints when they first arrived at the scene.

"I don't know how much the police are aware, but Javier has been working tirelessly to expose the company, and he's had help." Carmen arched her brows like she wanted to say more but wasn't sure she should.

"Help? As in from someone on the farm?"

She returned the photo to the coffee table and folded her hands in her lap. In the picture, she and Isabel posed in front of a massive pile of freshly picked coffee cherries. The mound of sun-ripened fruit towered over both of them. "You've spoken with Isabel. You must have picked up on her passion for the land."

I nodded, not wanting to say anything that might bring a halt to the conversation. I could tell Carmen wanted to share more but was nervous about betraying her friend from the way she folded and unfolded her hands.

"Isabel and Javier partnered together a few months ago when they realized how serious Miguel was about moving forward with Terra Café International. At first, we all thought it was another of his schemes, but once Sofia started coming around more and more, and architectural plans were drawn up, it became clear that this wasn't a joking matter. Isabel was distraught. She's made it her life's work to preserve Costa Rica's natural spaces, and she couldn't stomach the thought of a giant corporation taking over the farm. None of us could . . ." She trailed off, her eyes drifting to the kitchen windows. "She and Javier were unlikely allies. They teamed up to use their connections to try and bring a stop to the buyout."

"Javier must have extensive contacts in the coffee world," I said.

"He does, and Isabel has a . . ." She searched for the right word, pressing her fingers into a steeple. "Well, she has a different kind of contact."

I had a feeling I knew what she was hinting at, but I wasn't clear why she being careful about what she shared. "As in environmental protection groups?"

"That's correct. She used the proper channels first, but that was going to take too long. It's so much paperwork and red tape. They formed a new plan."

"They? You mean Isabel and Javier?" I clarified.

"Yes." She sighed. "They decided to do a full exposé on Terra Café to bring attention to their terrible business practices. Javier began compiling data about their treatment of workers and working conditions on their farms. Isabel got in contact with some environmental groups that use stronger tactics and methods to ensure farms remain intact."

"What kind of methods?"

She pushed her fingers together tighter like it was a challenge to admit whatever she was about to tell me. "I'm not saying I condone these things, you understand?"

I nodded.

"We were at a point of desperation, so there weren't many other options." She was still defending Isabel.

Where was she going with this? I knew there were a variety of climate protection groups in Costa Rica and all over the globe committed to using whatever means necessary to ensure farms and wild spaces weren't bulldozed. While it was a controversial issue, we were at a critical point on the planet. If we wanted a livable environment for future generations, radical tactics might be the only option.

Preservation was near and dear to my heart. We'd had similar issues in southern Oregon from overlogging, development, and forest fires. Climate activists had played a critical role in saving open spaces throughout the Siskiyou Mountains.

I could imagine Isabel recruiting fellow activists to barricade access to the farm, but Carmen's distress made me wonder if they had other plans in mind. Other plans involving violence, perhaps?

"I should have told the police this, but Isabel is family now, too. Whatever she did, it wasn't on purpose. She couldn't have meant to kill him." She massaged her temples like she didn't want to believe it or couldn't face the truth. "I've been trying to protect her, but I realize that was a mistake."

"What?" I sat taller. This wasn't at all what I thought Carmen was going to tell me. "What did Isabel do?"

"She snuck her colleagues onto the farm the night before Miguel died, and they decommissioned all of the processing equipment. Representatives from Terra Café International were supposed to be coming by for a demonstration. They came up with a plan—none of the equipment would be working, which would harm their reputation. Javier was calling the press to attend so he could share the photos and documents he gathered on the company and demonstrate that they couldn't keep their machinery running. It's been bothering me. I've been staying close to her side during the police investigations, but I'm afraid it's getting out of control." She sniffled, her eyes misting. "Whatever Isabel did to the machine caused Miguel's death, and I've been trying to protect her, but now I realize she must be the person who stole the documents. I encouraged her to speak with the police, but she's terrified. She's sure they'll arrest her. Now, she's taken the last of the evidence. I bet she's destroying Javier's documents as we speak. She was skittish this morning. I advised her to tell the truth—it was an accident and unintended consequence of trying to do something positive—saving the farm."

"Surely Isabel knows that Javier will tell the police everything. Destroying the documents doesn't absolve her."

"She's not thinking straight. She's panicking. Part of it is my fault. I told her I wasn't going to lie any longer. The police must know the truth—Isabel and her counterparts tampered with the machinery and accidentally caused Miguel's death."

Chapter Twenty-five

"When do you think Isabel could have broken into your house and stolen the documents?" I asked Carmen.

She stood and walked over to the hearth, picking up a photo of the Espinoza family. She ran her finger along the edge of the silver frame. "Anytime. I was up early. I like to walk the fields in the morning. Then we were at the house for lunch and the police interrogations. I wasn't watching her the entire time. She could have easily slipped away, taken the documents, and returned without anyone noticing she was gone. She and Javier are the only people who know about the documents. It had to be her. I just wish it wasn't. I wish I could protect her. She never meant to hurt anyone. Really, we're all at fault. Each of us would have done the same."

I wasn't sure if that was true.

Disabling the farm machinery and equipment wasn't without risk. Isabel must have known there was a chance someone could have gotten seriously hurt. And Alex was behind bars for a crime he didn't commit. She was letting him take the fall for her.

"You need to tell the police," I said, standing too

quickly. Little black spots clouded my vision. I took a second to breathe deeply, filling my lungs with air and trying to blink the dots away.

Carmen sighed. "I will. Yes, it's time." She returned the photo to the mantel.

I followed her out the door, wondering if her revelation would be enough to free Alex. Sofia had mentioned he was being released. Could the police know about Isabel already?

Javier would back up Carmen's story. While I understood Isabel's motivation, I wasn't impressed that she hadn't come forward after Alex's arrest. That must have been why he was servicing the machine. What other equipment had been impacted? Carmen said everything. Yet another reason to alert the authorities immediately. Someone else could have been seriously injured—or worse.

It also explained Isabel's reaction to Miguel's death. I'd been wrong about thinking they had some kind of connection. Isabel was riddled with guilt and acutely aware that she was responsible, regardless of whether it was accidental. Although the more I considered it, the more I wondered if it had been accidental.

Carmen was quiet on the walk back to the main house. "I'm sorry about my part in this," she said when we arrived at the terrace. "I suppose I've been consumed with wanting to save the farm, but this isn't right. I will speak with the police right away. We tried to stop him. We tried to get him away from the machine, but he wouldn't listen. It was an accident, I'm sure of that."

I didn't respond, but I was glad to have this new information.

Fortunately, an officer was still on the deck, interviewing Carlos. I couldn't believe how much I had to fill them in on. Speaking of Andy, where was my favorite barista? He couldn't still be up on the drying patio, could he?

I'd left him hours ago.

There was no sign of him on the terrace. Everyone else was gone, too—Javier, Sofia, and Isabel had all departed. I signaled to Carlos that I was going inside and went to the kitchen to see if Andy was experimenting with coffee blends, but I only found Valentina.

She was putting away the last of the lunch dishes. A large vase of freshly picked flowers rested on the island, and a fresh pot of coffee was brewing.

"Can I help?" I asked.

"Oh, Jules, no. Please sit. You've been doing too much." She rinsed a plate in the sink. "Are the police still finishing their interviews?"

"Yeah. They're speaking with Carlos now, and Carmen has some news to share." I told her about my conversation and everything Carmen had revealed about Isabel.

She wiped her hands on a dish towel and joined me at the island. "That explains why the workers said the fermentation tanks were jammed. What else did they tamper with?"

"Carmen made it sound like everything. In fact, that's one of the reasons I'm here. You haven't seen Andy lately, by chance?"

"No, I haven't seen him for hours." She looked out into the fields, her face turning ashen. "This is terrible, though. I need to tell the crew. We have to halt production on everything until Isabel can tell us exactly what she's done. One of them could get hurt."

"Exactly. That's why I want to find Andy. He was so excited about trying his hand at all of the machinery." My heart sank. Why had he been gone for so long? That wasn't like him. I tried not to picture every worst-case scenario, but images of Andy in danger flashed through my mind. "You speak with the workers. I'll find Andy."

"What about Isabel? Do you think she's trying to escape if she stole the documents? Someone should check her house."

"I'm already on it. I'll tell the police about Isabel. Carmen should be speaking to them now. Then I'll grab Carlos so we can look for Andy."

"Be careful, Jules." Valentina sounded distraught. "I don't like this at all. If Isabel was willing to risk our safety and has remained silent about Miguel's murder, what else is she capable of? Do you think she did it? Could she have intentionally killed him?"

"Maybe, but the most important thing right now is finding her." I didn't want to worry her more, but I was thinking the same thing. I also couldn't help but wonder if Javier was more involved than he was letting on. Carmen admitted they had intentionally teamed up to stop the sale. Were they partnering now? Protecting each other? Pushing the narrative that Alex had killed Miguel to keep suspicion off of them? It felt like the clues were finally starting to fall together, yet I still wasn't sure who had done it.

"Let's meet back here soon," I said, leaving her with a half hug.

As I had expected, Carlos had finished giving his statement to the police. He was waiting for me near the entryway. "Julieta, how are you? I heard the first part of what Carmen was telling the detective. Isabel is responsible?"

"It seems that way. You haven't seen her?"

He shook his head. "No. Not for a while."

"Let me interrupt them for a minute." I pointed to Carmen, who was tearfully recounting her tale to the officer. "Valentina is alerting the workers, but someone should be looking for Isabel. If she's the killer, she's getting a solid head start. We need to find her before she's gone for good."

"They need to block the exits." Carlos waved his hands in circles as if to signal they needed to hurry up.

I broke into Carmen's confessional, explaining we were off to find Andy.

"I've already radioed to my team," the officer responded, tapping the small radio attached to his chest. "We'll track her down."

I felt better knowing the police were actively searching for Isabel, but my concern for Andy continued to mount. "Should we start at the drying patio?" I asked Carlos.

"Are you sure you're up for this? You can stay and rest, and I'll look for him."

"There's no chance I'm sitting idly by if Andy is in danger." I planted my feet on the tile floor and crossed my arms, preparing for a fight.

"I figured you would say that, but we will take it slow?" He held my gaze, watching to make sure I agreed.

"Fine, let's go." I didn't want to waste another second. Every cell in my body buzzed with nervous energy. I couldn't let anything happen to Andy.

For the third time in a stretch of a few hours, I found myself on the trail nestled by coffee plants and leafy shade trees. But now, nothing about the farm felt calm and welcoming. The air was thick with tension as if danger loomed in the humid breeze, waiting for the right moment to close in and pull us under.

Andy had to be okay.

There must be an explanation for his disappearance.

"Do you think something happened to him?" I asked Carlos.

"He'll be fine. Do not worry. Andy is smart and strong."

I wanted to say that Miguel was too, but I couldn't let myself go down that path.

We made it to the drying patio in record time. The rows of coffee were neatly raked, but Andy was nowhere in sight.

"He's not here." I couldn't disguise the terror in my tone. "Carlos, this is bad."

"It's okay. He wouldn't rake the practice coffee for this long anyway, mi querida. Let's keep looking."

I appreciated that he maintained an outward sense of control for my sake. I had a feeling Carlos was deeply concerned about Andy's whereabouts but was putting on a brave face for me.

"Let's check the processing area," Carlos said, motioning in that direction.

Andy wasn't there either.

A police officer stood guard near the caution tape.

"We're looking for our friend Andy. He's young—in his early twenties, American, with shaggy reddish-brownish hair." The words tumbled out of my mouth.

The officer looked at me with confusion and then to Carlos.

Carlos interpreted for me in perfect Spanish.

The officer responded with a shake of his head. I didn't need Carlos to translate but my heart sank at his response. "I haven't seen Andy, but we are looking for Isabel."

"Can you ask him how long he's been here?" A huge lump swelled in my throat. I tried to swallow, but my mouth was dry and my heart was pounding against my chest like it was trying to break free. I should have paid more attention. I'd been so distracted with Carmen and Isabel that I hadn't realized just how long he'd been gone.

Carlos explained in his lilting Spanish that we were also looking for Isabel, and gave him more details about Andy, and listened to the man's response. "He says he's been posted for twenty minutes with instructions not to leave until his supervisors tell him it's okay. He says they've called in additional officers and are searching the entire property."

My stomach swirled with anxiety.

Where could Andy be?

Why would he have taken off and not told anyone?

I reflected on our last interaction. I'd been with Javier. Andy had clearly said he'd meet me back at the house. At least an hour had passed since then.

People didn't just disappear on farms. Did they?

Apparently they did at Finca las Nubes.

I gulped, feeling bile rise from my stomach.

Carlos pointed to the trail that led to the employee housing. "Should we keep going?"

I nodded, taking off for the path right behind Carlos.

We wound through the switchbacks as my nerves threatened to get the best of me. Could Isabel or Javier have come after Andy?

Maybe they found him snooping at the scene of the crime.

Don't go there, Jules. My fear exploded into full-blown terror when we rounded a bend and discovered a baseball hat lying on the ground, as if it had been tossed away like garbage.

Chapter Twenty-six

Carlos bent over to pick up the hat. "This is Andy's." His words caught in his throat as he flipped the hat over to examine it as if expecting it might contain a clue to where Andy had gone.

"That's his hat, for sure," I confirmed, placing my hand on my stomach to try and settle the sloshing. "He wears that hat all the time. He wouldn't leave it on the trail."

"Unless he wanted it to be found." Carlos looked at me and then back at the hat. "A sign that we're on the right track. We know he came this way. That's good, sí?"

"I guess, but I don't like it. I can't shake the feeling that someone took him. I know that makes it sound like he's a toddler. I understand he's a grown adult, but if Isabel realized that the police are onto her, she might not be acting rationally. If she has a weapon, she could have taken him as a hostage."

If that was the case, then Carlos's theory about Andy intentionally leaving his hat on the trail for us to find was even more plausible.

"So we keep going?" Carlos pointed ahead.

"Yeah."

It took another ten minutes to get to Carmen's hacienda. Two more police officers patrolled the area in front of her house and garden.

Carlos took the lead, explaining what we were doing. "They say the same thing. No sign of Andy or Isabel."

The longer we searched, the more worried I was that Andy was in trouble.

"Can you ask them to radio to the house? Maybe our paths crossed. He could have taken the other trail." My rational brain fought to come up with logical explanations for his disappearance.

They radioed the main house to check.

"He's not there." Carlos shook his head. His attempt to stay positive for me was fading.

"Should we check the other houses?" I motioned to Alex's cottage and the cabin, not waiting for his response.

We scoured each of the dwellings. There were no indicators Andy had been this way. Not so much as a footprint. Why would Isabel come after him? Was it because of the whiteboard and catching her this morning? Had he realized that she was the killer and confronted her?

He wouldn't have done anything rash, but then again, Isabel probably wasn't thinking straight.

"How are you feeling, Julieta?" Carlos studied me carefully, placing the back of his hand on my brow to check my temp. "You look flushed."

"I'm fine. I'm just so worried about Andy. I want to keep going." The stream was only a few hundred feet away. After we crossed the gurgling brook, the path would take us to the workers' quarters. We'd come this far, and I wasn't turning around now.

"Okay," Carlos agreed with a curt nod. He knew it was futile to argue with me.

The trail curved through denser shade trees until it met the small creek. A wood-plank footbridge had been constructed to allow the workers to cross over the gushing stream. The water was so clear I could see the colorful rocks and pebbles at the bottom.

"Watch your footing. It's slippery," Carlos cautioned, crossing first and then offering me his hand.

I took it gladly. His firm grip kept me upright, but I still nearly slipped. Not because the wood was coated in a thin layer of slippery slime, but because I spotted something out of the corner of my eye. "Carlos, look!" I pointed downstream about thirty feet to a pair of tennis shoes sticking out from the underbrush. "I think someone's down there."

Carlos helped me across the creek.

"Is it Andy? Do you think it's Andy?" I forced myself not to start playing out every worst-case scenario.

"I don't know. Wait here. The trees are dense." He forged a path, paralleling the stream.

"Do you see anything?" I called. I couldn't see the shoes from this vantage point. I was too low.

My palms turned sweaty as my heart pounded in my throat.

"It's him. It's him!" Carlos called after a minute. "He's breathing. Can you get help?"

"On my way." I shuffled across the bridge and ran up the small hill until I spotted the police officers. "We need help! Help!" I waved wildly.

They left their post and followed me, asking me dozens of questions in Spanish.

"Herido. Herido!" I repeated. I knew the word for "injured," but not much more. It didn't matter because I wasn't sure about the extent of Andy's injuries. I hadn't waited around long enough to ask Carlos for more specifics.

Was he conscious?

Passed out?

Had someone attacked him, or had he accidentally slipped?

It seemed like an odd place for a fall and it wasn't like Andy to venture off trail, especially when Valentina had warned us about snakes and spiders. Plus, it didn't explain what his hat had been doing farther back on the path.

The police ripped through the dense trees to join up with Carlos. I felt useless waiting by the bridge.

Please let him be okay. I said a silent prayer to the universe.

It felt like hours passed before the officers and Carlos emerged from the shrubbery. Andy was upright, supported by both police officers. Carlos followed behind them, his arms lightly resting on Andy's back, like he was prepared to catch him if Andy suddenly decided to topple over.

Andy looked unsteady on his feet.

His cheeks had lost all their color, and his eyes were two narrow slits like it was painful to look into the light.

What had happened?

I drank in a breath.

Don't overreact. Stay calm.

Easier said than done. Andy wobbled to one side as he took an exaggerated step onto the bridge. Carlos steadied him from behind.

"Andy, how are you?" I asked. "You gave us such a huge scare."

He closed his eyes, squinting at me. "Oh, hey, Jules. I'm good. Kind of wrecked, but good."

"Wrecked and good don't work together." I frowned and hugged him tight.

One of the police officers said something in Spanish so fast that I could only catch two words. "They want to take him to the house. They've called an ambulance," Carlos explained.

I nodded and moved out of the way. Once they were over the bridge, I noticed a bloodstain on the base of Andy's skull. I gasped and clapped my hand over my mouth.

Carlos caught my eye as I walked with them. "He'll be okay," he whispered.

I wasn't as convinced.

The gash on Andy's head looked deep. Blood had dried on the wound and pooled on the back of his shirt.

I didn't want to distract him with questions, but someone must have hit him. How would he have ended up with a wound on the base of his head otherwise? I supposed he could have taken a hard fall, but with Miguel's murder, it was too much of a coincidence.

Andy winced a few times, letting out a whimper of pain on the trek to Carmen's house. The police squad set him upright in one of Carmen's rocking chairs and went inside to get supplies.

"I'll get you a glass of water," Carlos said, lightly tapping his shoulder.

I sat next to him and put my hand on his knee. "I don't even want to tell you where my head went when we couldn't find you."

He clutched the side of the wooden rocking chair so tight his knuckles turned white.

"What happened?" I didn't like the glazed look in his eyes. Even the slightest movement sent a wave of pain over his face.

"I'm not sure. It's fuzzy."

"Do you remember what you were doing out that far? When I saw you last, you were practicing your raking technique." I glanced in front of us to the path that connected to the other houses.

He nodded but stopped partway, flinching in pain. "That's right. You were with Javier. I stayed and raked for a while."

"Did anyone come by?"

"No. Not that I remember." He paused as one of the police officers interrupted us to dab his wound with a clean, wet cloth.

I hated seeing him in pain.

I kept my hand on his knee, sending him all the healing energy I could muster.

The police officer showed Andy how to use the cloth to put pressure on the gash and then turned to Carlos to translate. Carlos set a glass of water on the side table and asked Andy the same questions I'd been asking.

"I remember hearing something. That's right." Andy closed his eyes and rocked gently from side to side. "Screaming. I heard screaming, so I went to check it out. It sounded like someone was hurt down near the creek, but I couldn't see them."

"That's how you ended up next to the stream?" I asked while Carlos simultaneously translated for the police officers.

"Maybe? That's when it gets fuzzy. I remember crossing the bridge and seeing something in the trees. I headed that way, and then the next thing I knew, everything went dark."

The ambulance screeched to a halt in front of us before he could say more. The paramedics bandaged his head and took him through a concussion protocol. When they finished, they recommended we keep an eye on him for the next twenty-four hours, only letting him sleep for four- or five-hour chunks and watching for any signs of a worsening head injury—dizziness, vomiting, disorientation. Otherwise, they deemed him to be in decent shape and suggested icing the bump on his head and taking over-the-counter pain medication.

The police drove us back to the main house. I was relieved we'd found Andy and that his injuries weren't life-threatening, but I was furious and could tell Carlos was too. Once Andy was safely nestled into one of the comfy couches on the terrace with a drink of his choice, I was going to get to the bottom of this once and for all. Now it was personal.

Chapter Twenty-seven

The paramedics attended to Andy one last time before leaving, with another parting reminder of any danger signs to look out for.

Valentina ushered us into the living room and encouraged Andy to sit. "This weekend gets worse and worse. Who would have done this to you?"

Andy rubbed the base of his skull like it hurt to think. "I don't remember. I wish I could, but I didn't see them. Someone smacked me from behind, and then everything went black. I think they might have had a bat or a . . ." He chewed on his lip, searching his memory. "Oh, maybe a rake."

"A rake from the drying patio," Valentina said, pressing her hand to her forehead. "Thank goodness you're okay. Those rakes are heavy."

"Could it have been Isabel, though?" I pondered out loud, wondering what did and didn't make sense. "She's short and petite. Do we think she could lift one of the rakes high enough to knock Andy out?" I was genuinely curious to hear their thoughts. Whoever had hit Andy had to be relatively strong. Andy was a big guy. But then again, if Isabel was panicked and trying to make an escape before she got caught, she might have managed it. His assailant might have used the element of surprise to knock him out.

Carlos couldn't sit. He ran his hand along the stucco wall and paced. "Yes, it's true she doesn't seem like she would have the strength, but I think it's possible if she was desperate."

"And she had the element of surprise," Valentina agreed.

"Good point. Why you, though?" I asked Andy rhetorically. "She was around when Alex was giving you a tour of the farm and machinery. What if she realized you saw something or knew something? That's the only thing I can figure out that makes sense. Otherwise, what's her motive for hurting you?"

"But what do I know? I don't know anything." Andy shrugged. He started to say something else, but he faltered. He froze, then suddenly started patting himself down, checking his pockets and looking around frantically like he'd lost something. His eyes darted around the room, as panic crept into his voice. "They're gone. They're gone."

"What's gone?" I asked.

"My phone and my notebook. My backpack. Everything. All my coffee notes. They're gone." He pulled his pocket inside out as if expecting his phone might be hiding inside. "I didn't even realize it. I guess I'm more out of it than I thought, but I know for a fact that I had my notebook and my phone with me. I've been documenting everything for the team at home and my own research."

"Whoever hit you must have taken them," I reasoned. "Which must mean you captured something the killer didn't want you to see."

"Maybe tampering with the machine? While you've been taking photos around the farm, you could have captured her altering the equipment without noticing. Maybe she's in the background of your photos or videos," Carlos suggested. "Isabel might not have intended to kill Miguel, but once she realized that the safety mechanism failed, she knew she was responsible for his death. She probably wanted to silence anyone who might reveal the truth."

It was a good theory and one I'd been wrestling with, too. I still felt like we were missing something, but I couldn't put my finger on what.

I didn't want to put too much pressure on Andy. I knew he was trying to remember what happened, and forcing it would only make it worse. "We've established that Isabel arrived on the scene shortly before Miguel was killed. You and Alex took the tour before Miguel showed up. I wonder if you might have seen something then that you wouldn't have even registered."

"But because she killed him—albeit accidentally— she was hyperaware," Andy said, massaging his cheeks as he bobbed his head. "Um, let me think about everything I can remember. Alex walked me through the entire farm before we started the demo. We passed Isabel in the drying patio, but she was just raking the beans."

Valentina sucked in a breath and snapped twice. "Is that it?"

Andy scowled, looking at me in confusion.

I was equally perplexed.

"Like I mentioned before, why would she be raking

the beans? It's not drying season. Those are there for training. It doesn't make sense."

"Maybe that was her cover," I suggested. "She was pretending to be raking the beans when she spotted you because she didn't want you to see what she was really doing."

"Practicing Alex's handwriting?" Carlos suggested. He still hadn't sat. I knew he was trying to burn through the same nervous energy that had been pulsing through me.

"Why would she take my phone for that? She was definitely raking when we passed her." Andy checked his empty pockets again, like he was hoping it would magically reappear.

"I don't know," I replied. "It feels like we're close, but we're missing something critical. What if she *did* intend to kill him? Maybe that was her intention all along. Javier could have been in the dark about that part of their plan. He thought she was merely tampering with the equipment, but perhaps she had a fail-safe in mind—to kill Miguel."

Before I could continue, a knock sounded on the door. Two police officers stood in the open doorway, respectfully waiting to be invited in.

"Come in. Come in." Valentina motioned for them to join us.

"We have an update for you." The officer addressed all of us. "We've arrested Isabel Castillo. She is in the car outside. We found her hiding in the workers' quarters. We're taking her to the station for further questioning. We've advised her to wait for her lawyer, but she admitted to sabotaging the farm equipment. However, she claims she had nothing to do with Miguel's death—that it was purely an accident. She's also insisting she was at the workers' quarters when you were attacked." The officer turned to Andy. "We'll see if her story changes once she's been booked and interrogated by our lead detective. You're sure you can't identify the attacker?"

Andy shook his head. "No, I didn't see them."

"Okay. That's fine. We'll proceed with what we have and be in touch." The officer started to leave but stopped in midstride. "Alex will be released. He's free to go but will need a ride."

Valentina exhaled slowly and patted her chest. "What a relief. I'll come pick him up."

"We'll keep you updated." The police officer nodded formally to all of us and left.

Valentina jumped to her feet. "I hate leaving you like this, but I must go to the city. I was planning to make dinner, but with the time and everything that's happened it slipped away from me. I could swing by the Mercado Central and grab food after I get Alex, if that's all right with you?"

Carlos waved his hands. "No, do not go to extra trouble. I will make dinner. I would love to do this if it is okay with you."

"Me too," I chimed in. Being in the kitchen was exactly what I needed to figure out the few last pieces of the puzzle that didn't seem to fit.

"Are you sure?" Valentina asked, fanning her face to fight back the tears. "You've done so much for me, and I can't find any way to repay you."

"Sí, Julieta and I will make dinner and have it ready when you and Alex return. He will be happy to have a nice meal after spending a night in jail, I think."

Valentina pressed her fingers beneath her eyes to try to stop her tears. It didn't work. They spilled down her apple-shaped cheeks. "I can't thank you all enough. I don't know what I would have done if you weren't here. I know I keep saying it, but I didn't intend for your trip to go like this. I'm going to make it up to you——a return visit soon, I hope."

I stood to hug her. "This is what friends do. You would do the same for us if the situation was reversed. Now, go rescue Alex, and we'll see you soon."

She wiped her tears away as she headed outside.

Carlos shifted into dad mode, assessing Andy. "Why don't you stay put here? Get comfortable. I will bring you some snacks and a special drink. I have a shrub in mind for Julieta that will boost your immune system as your head heals."

"A shrub?" Andy glanced at me. "Is that Spanish slang for something?"

"It's a type of mocktail," I explained. Carlos had become well-versed in his mocktail-making skills since discovering I was pregnant. "Shrubs use apple cider vinegar as an alcohol replacement and are good for digestion, among other things."

"You could watch a movie." Carlos pointed to the big-screen TV above the stone fireplace. "I can bring you a book or coffee magazines."

"I'll watch something," Andy said. "I'm not sure I can concentrate on reading yet."

Carlos handed him the remote. "Rest easy. Snacks are coming soon."

Andy grinned at both of us. "Thanks, you two. You're the best."

I squeezed his shoulder on our way to the kitchen. "You're the best, and we're going to pamper you and keep a close eye on you for the rest of the weekend, so get used to it."

He propped his feet on the couch and leaned against the fluffy throw pillows. "I've always wanted to be a coffee king. Too bad it took getting smacked in the head to reach this status, but, hey, I'll take it."

I chuckled as I followed after Carlos. Seeing Andy hurt made me hurt, too. It was a good sign he was laughing and teasing again. It felt like we were on the cusp of solving the investigation. Alex was being released, Isabel was being questioned, and it was clear that Andy must have seen something that put him in harm's way. Now I just needed to figure out what that was.

Chapter Twenty-eight

Carlos surveyed the pantry and fridge, gathering ingredients for snacks and his special shrub. "Does anything sound good for dinner?"

"Actually, I've been craving empanadas all day. The market empanadas were so good, and I'd love to put my spin on them and make a few varieties—sweet and savory."

He spread coconut milk, syrups, fresh fruit, and vinegar on the island. "I'll make the shrub and a snack platter. Then I can marinate some meat to grill, make a salad, and some rice and beans."

"Perfect. I'll start on the empanadas, but first, I need to loop Mom in on the Andy situation."

I pulled out my phone to send her a text: "Now, you're really going to freak out, but I want you to hear this from me first." I knew that if Lance heard the news, he would be at Torte within seconds. I gave her more details about Miguel's death and a brief overview of what happened to Andy, reiterating that he was fine and Carlos and I were going to pamper him for the remainder of the trip.

Three dots appeared instantly but then vanished. A

minute later, a voice message came through. "I had too much to say in a text. Lance beat you to it as far as the murder investigation goes. He swept into the bakeshop a few hours ago, as only Lance can do.

"That's terrible news about Andy, but I have no doubt that he's in the best hands with you and Carlos. I appreciate that you don't want to worry me, but let me remind you that's what I'm here for. Doug wants you to know that he'll happily provide any input or advice should you need it. He also wants you to know that you can handle this. His exact words are 'Let the evidence lead the way.'

"Everything will work out. Take a deep breath. I know this is overwhelming. Don't forget to eat and rest."

Her response calmed me, and the Professor's words resonated.

Let the evidence lead the way.

That was what I would do.

I found everything I needed for the dough. While Carlos carefully crafted his mocktails, I started by adding flour, salt, and a touch of sugar to a mixing bowl. Then I cubed cold butter and added it by hand, working the pieces with my fingers until it turned into a coarse crumb. In a separate bowl, I whisked together cold water, eggs, and white vinegar. I gradually poured the liquid in with the dry ingredients and stirred until a dough formed. Next, I sprinkled more flour on the island and kneaded the dough until it was smooth.

Carlos peeled and diced fresh mangos. "Do you believe Isabel is responsible for Miguel's murder and Andy's attack?"

"I'm not entirely convinced. The Professor is right—

where does the evidence take us?" I returned the dough to the bowl and covered it with a towel. It needed to rest for about thirty minutes. Next, I turned my attention to fillings. For the savory empanadas, I decided on a beef picadillo, a chicken and cheese, and a chorizo and potato. As sweet options, I would do a guava and cream cheese, Nutella and banana, and apple cinnamon. "I believe she and her environmental protection group disabled the equipment, but I'm finding it difficult to believe she intended to kill Miguel. Don't get me wrong, I think what she did is incredibly irresponsible. Many more people could have been hurt. As far as Miguel goes, it could have been an unfortunate accident, but that doesn't explain the note or why someone hit Andy and stole his phone and notebook."

"I agree." Carlos chopped pineapple and added it and the mango to the bottom of cocktail glasses. "It's too easy."

"My thoughts exactly." I brushed flour from my hands and found a cutting board to start dicing onions, peppers, and garlic for the beef filling. "The police said she admitted to trying to sabotage the farm but not the rest—Miguel or Andy. My gut wants to believe her. She doesn't strike me as the violent type."

Carlos poured lime juice, pineapple juice, apple cider vinegar, sugar, and fresh mint leaves into a large pitcher and began muddling it. "She also still had options for stopping the sale. It sounds as if there was going to be plenty of red tape to weed through. She didn't need to kill him."

"What about Javier? I keep thinking how slick and smooth he's seemed this whole time. If they were working together, what if he put her up to this, or what if he is trying to have her take the fall?"

"I've been considering this as well. Where is he? He vanished when the police arrived, but he's been on the farm both times—when Miguel was killed and when Andy was injured. But why would he steal his own files from Carmen's house?" Carlos filled the cocktail glasses halfway with sparkling club soda, then he poured in the lime and pineapple juice mixture and stirred each drink, finishing them with a sprig of mint. "Try this." He offered me the mocktail.

"I know. I'm stuck on that, too. Unless he's just trying to implicate Isabel now, maybe he realized Alex was going to be released, and he had to shift suspicion onto someone else." I took a sip. It was instantly refreshing—fruity and cold, with a nice little zing from the apple cider vinegar. "This is perfect."

He smiled. "Good. I will bring one to Andy and then return to make a snack tray. You could be right about Javier. Isabel is passionate about the farm and land because she wants to preserve it for generations to come. Javier's interest is financial. He claims he also cares deeply for Finca las Nubes, but this could be because he is concerned about his business investment."

I considered the possibility as he left to deliver Andy the drink. The easiest and cleanest solution was Isabel. If she confessed to everything, the case would be closed, but I highly doubted that would happen.

My phone buzzed again. This time with another voice message from Lance. "I heard about Andy. I'm distraught. Absolutely beside myself. Who could do this to our boy wonder? You are the talk of the town, and you're an ocean away. This is a testament to your worldly charms, darling.

"Let me impart some wisdom. In staging this latest production, I've done a deep dive into the mind of a hardened criminal. Let me spell it out for you:

1. In a murder investigation, just like the theater, everyone is playing a part. Pay close attention to how the suspects present themselves—what's rehearsed? What's real?
2. In our debut of *Perfect Crime* last night, we intentionally led the audience astray. Who's leading you in one direction when the truth lies elsewhere?
3. Pace yourself. A good story unfolds gradually. Don't rush to conclusions. Let the story tell itself.
4. It's all in the details—the smallest detail can completely change the narrative. A misplaced prop, a wrong look—and the entire play begins to unravel.
5. Last but certainly not least. Trust your instincts. This is the key piece of advice I give every actor. Let the creative process (or murder insight) flow through you.

"You're welcome in advance. Go solve this and shower Andy with coffee."

Where would I even begin with a response? I opted for short and sweet.

"I'm on it!"

I moved to the stove and warmed olive oil in a pan. Then I added my chopped veggies, ground beef, smoked paprika, cumin, and oregano. I cooked the mixture over medium heat until it browned nicely then I added in a little tomato paste and let it simmer.

For the chicken and cheese empanadas, I cooked chicken breasts until they were juicy and tender, and then I shredded them. Carlos returned as I began combining the shredded chicken with cream cheese, shredded cheddar, hot sauce, and jalapeños.

"It is already smelling wonderful in here." He leaned over the stove and wafted the aromas into his face. "Andy is doing well. He said he's hungry, which is a good sign."

"I agree." I set the chicken mixture to the side and got out a clean cutting board to peel and chop the potatoes for my last savory empanada.

Carlos arranged a large platter of tortilla chips, salsa, guacamole, veggies, cheese, and crackers. "It will be good to hear Alex's perspective. He may be able to shed new light on the situation."

"Yes, I'm eager to see him. He's the key to all of this." I set a pot of water to boil and added the diced potatoes. I would let them cook until they were soft and tender and then mash them with butter, sour cream, and herbs. They would pair beautifully with the spicy chorizo and grilled onions.

"This is a factory," Carlos said. "Can I help?"

"It's controlled chaos." I glanced at the island where I'd arranged stations for each filling. "It looks like I have no idea what I'm doing, but I promise there's a method to my madness."

"I would never doubt you, and as always, your stations are perfectly neat and tidy." Carlos made a plate for the two of us to share. "One more Andy delivery, and then I'll marinate the beef."

"Make sure he doesn't need anything else."

"I will." He lifted the tray. "This should keep him satisfied until dinner."

With the savory fillings simmering, I shifted my attention to the sweet empanadas. The banana and Nutella and cream cheese and guava didn't need much prep work, but the apples needed to be peeled, cored, and chopped. I washed my hands again. Half the time spent in any commercial kitchen is cleaning. It was one of the first lessons I taught new staff. A clean, organized kitchen is essential to producing beautiful, quality baked goods.

My brain hurt trying to figure out what I was missing. It was like the answer was just out of my grasp. I should probably take my own advice and give it a break, but we were flying home tomorrow night. I did not want to get on the plane without knowing who had killed Miguel.

I kept coming back to Sofia. What if we'd all wrongly assumed that Miguel was the intended victim? Sofia had more enemies, so to speak, and she'd been at the scene of the crime, but again, what about the note and Andy's attack?

Was the killer intentionally trying to distract us?

I pushed the thought aside and checked my dough.

It was ready to roll out.

Before I did that, I set the apples on the stove with a generous pat of butter and warming spices.

"Andy is snacking away happily," Carlos announced. "He has more color in his cheeks, and I brought him his iPad, so he's texting with Bethany and the team. I checked with the medical staff, and they said a little screen time was fine. We just need to be mindful of concussion protocol and monitor him closely. They don't think he has a full-blown concussion, but it's always best to be extra cautious."

"That's a much-needed glimmer of good news," I said, flouring my hands and rolling a ball of dough out into a large sheet. I was glad I had given Mom a heads-up and that she, Lance, and the entire team back home were sending Andy all of their well-wishes and healing thoughts.

Once the dough was about an eighth of an inch thick, I cut six-inch circles using the bottom of a bowl. Carlos helped with the assembly process.

We scooped the fillings into the center of the circles, folded them over to create a half-moon shape, and crimped the edges. Then we placed them on parchment-lined baking trays, and I brushed them with an egg wash.

They would bake for twenty minutes or until the dough turned a lovely, glossy golden brown. I sipped my shrub and began cleaning the island. Shortly before the timer dinged on the oven, Valentina rushed into the kitchen with Alex on her arm. "Look who's back. We have great news: the police have dropped all the charges against Alex."

"That's wonderful," I said to both of them. It was true. I was very pleased that Alex had been released, but I was concerned the police still had the wrong person in custody, and I was running out of time to find the real killer.

Chapter Twenty-nine

Alex went to his cottage to freshen up before dinner. Valentina set the table outside and kept Andy company while Carlos and I finished preparations. The empanadas turned out better than I expected. They had baked to a nice, buttery crisp. I plated them as Carlos tossed his salad. We took a couple of trips back and forth between the kitchen, delivering platters of empanadas, bowls of rice and beans, and tender, juicy slices of grilled flank steak.

Carlos made an extra pitcher of the fruity shrub, and Valentina opened bottles of wine. I took a moment to survey the table. The food looked and smelled delicious. The tea lights, votive candles, lanterns, and twinkle lights gave the terrace an almost magical glow. Citronella candles strategically placed throughout the deck repelled any unwanted insects.

"Hey, this looks awesome," Andy said, joining us with an empty glass. "Sweet, I see another pitcher of Carlos's concoction. It's a good thing there's no booze in this, because I'd drink the entire thing. It's seriously addictive. I guess I'm a shrub guy now."

"We should add it to the Torte menu when we get home." I sat next to Valentina.

Alex came up the back steps. He'd showered and changed and looked like a new, free man in jeans, sandals, and a powder blue button-down shirt.

"Hey, man, good to see you." Andy clapped him around the shoulder.

"You too." Alex grinned, his relief unmistakable. "I thought I was going to be stuck in a San José prison for a while."

Carmen appeared from the living room. "Alex, is it you?" She raced to him and clutched him in a long hug, rubbing his shoulder and refusing to let go. "Thank goodness," she murmured, finally releasing him. The tension in her voice melted away with her words. "We've been so worried."

"They were decent to me." Alex took a seat next to Andy. "The food was nothing like this, though."

"Please, eat, eat." Valentina picked up a platter of the chicken and cheese empanadas and passed them to Alex. "Jules and Carlos have prepared a welcome home feast for you."

Color spread across Alex's cheeks. "Thank you. That wasn't necessary. You are the guests for the weekend."

"It's nothing," Carlos said, reaching for a bottle of wine. "The kitchen is our happy space."

"That's how I feel about the farm." Alex loaded his plate with empanadas.

I was glad I had made plenty. Although between Andy and Alex, it looked like we just might go through all of them tonight.

"What did the police say?" Valentina held her glass out for Carlos to fill.

"Not a lot." Alex took a bite of the empanada. Steam erupted from the end like a volcano. "They mainly asked me questions. They wanted to know exactly where I had been, what I had been doing, how each of the machines operated, who else had access to the equipment, and they made me write dozens of weird sentences over and over again."

"Handwriting analysis," I said, scooping beans and rice and a slice of Carlos's seared steak onto my plate.

"What? Why?" Alex asked, brushing a strand of wavy hair from his eye.

I'd forgotten that he hadn't been part of our conversations since he'd been in police custody. We needed to get him up to speed. I gave him a quick overview, and the others jumped in to add anything I missed.

"You got attacked?" Alex shook his head in disbelief and looked at Andy. "I'm so sorry that happened."

"It's not your fault." Andy held his glass in a toast and winked at Carlos. "My head feels like I skied into a tree, but on the flip side, Carlos has been delivering me festive drinks and snacks all afternoon."

"They stole your phone and notebook." Alex blew on the empanada. "What could I have shown you? We did the loop so you could see the entire farm. Then I was going to take you through each machine, starting with the pulping machine. Obviously we didn't get far after that."

"Did you notice an issue with the machinery right away?" Carmen asked. She had been quieter, sipping her wine and listening in.

"Yeah, right away. The settings were wrong. They were cranked up to the highest level," Alex said without hesitation. It was clear he was an expert when it came to the equipment. "I didn't think about it at the time because Miguel liked to mess with the settings." He looked at Valentina, who gave him a quick nod of confirmation.

"Why would he mess with the settings?" I asked.

"He liked to tinker. He thought faster was better, and I would always have to explain that wasn't true, especially with older equipment. My first task before I send coffee cherries through any of the machinery is to check it, and five times out of ten, I need to readjust the settings because of Miguel. I explained this to the police, but they didn't want to hear it. Now I understand if they found the note in handwriting that looked like mine. I can see why that would be bad."

Carmen's natural nurturing came through as she pressed her hands together and maintained eye contact with Alex as he explained his responsibilities. "I told Miguel a million times to leave the machines alone."

Alex shrugged. "What could I do? He was the boss. He was also like a brother to me. I would never hurt him." His voice cracked with emotion.

"We know. We told the police the same thing," Valentina said.

"I don't understand why Isabel would do something so drastic," Alex continued. "She knows enough about the farm to understand someone could have been—well, was—seriously hurt. It doesn't seem like a risk she would take."

"Did you see her or anyone else before Miguel fell?" I asked as I cut my steak with my fork. The tender meat practically fell apart. It was infused with a trio of herbs and slightly charred, giving it a rich, smoky quality. The meat had simmered with peppers, garlic, onions, and cilantro. Carlos finished it with a bright squeeze of lime juice. The salad married all the flavors together with its crisp lettuce, sun-ripened tomatoes, grilled peppers, and cotija cheese.

Alex swallowed a bite of empanada before answering. "We saw Isabel at the drying patio. Javier was there. So was Sofia. She was trying to show Miguel paperwork, and he and Javier were arguing, but that doesn't explain why you would be attacked," he said to Andy.

"No clue." Andy rolled his shoulders up.

"It all has to be connected," I said. "The documentation about Terra Café International was stolen from your house, Carmen, not long before Andy was attacked. I've been running different scenarios in my mind, and I have a couple of potential ideas. One is that Javier orchestrated everything. He tried to pin the murder on Alex, and then when he realized the police didn't have enough evidence to keep Alex, he quickly made it look like Isabel acted alone. What if she didn't? Was she close enough to push him?"

"Maybe. I wasn't really paying attention, I was focused on trying to fix the machine." Alex took a chorizo and potato empanada as Valentina passed the platters around again.

"You think Javier broke into my house and took the documents?" Carmen asked, buttering a slice of bread.

"Possibly. If he's trying to implicate Isabel, there won't be any proof to back up her story now. Surely, she'll tell the police that the two of them were working together to expose Terra Café International."

"Jules, this is a very interesting theory," Valentina

said, glancing over the rim of her wine and watching the liquid with intent.

"It's only a theory." I tried to keep the Professor's advice (and even Lance's lengthy murder monologue) in my mind. I didn't want to jump to conclusions, but I was growing more and more convinced that Isabel, if nothing else, hadn't acted alone. Or that the killer had missed their target.

Carmen stabbed her salad with her fork. "Now that I'm remembering, I saw him on the path near my house. You could be right."

"What's your other theory?" Alex asked.

I glanced around at everyone again. "That Miguel wasn't supposed to be pushed into the concrete tank. Sofia was."

Chapter Thirty

"She's good, isn't she?" Andy nudged Alex. "Jules sleuthing out a mystery is top-notch, but it's the worst if we're trying to sneak something past her at the bakeshop. Forget about it. No chance." He made a slicing motion over his neck.

"What are you trying to sneak by me?"

"You'll never know." He rubbed his hands together mysteriously. "No, but Sofia as the victim makes sense to me."

"She is not well-liked around here," Carmen agreed.

"That's an understatement," Valentina said. "Do you think Javier planned to kill her and it went wrong?"

"I'm not sure," I admitted, glancing toward the fields. The sun had sunk completely, casting a darkness over the rolling landscape. "I keep wondering why they both were there. What if Javier made sure Sofia was near the processing area, intending to kill her, and then something happened, either by accident or . . ." I wasn't sure where I was going with this trail of thought.

"He was here at the house." Valentina reached for the

dessert empanadas and sent them around the table. "He could have left the forged note."

Carlos took a banana Nutella and a guava and cheese empanada from the tray. "To play Devil's advocate, couldn't he find a new coffee wholesale partner?"

"It's not as easy as you think," Carmen said. "Yes, there are many local farms that would love his business, but it takes time, and we're the largest producer of our size and caliber. He would have to use a number of other farms in order to stock his retail stores."

"He's expanding, too," Alex added. "His new line of stores is set to open next month. Switching suppliers and beans would be a big headache, especially because we custom blend for him. A new coffee grower would have to get that dialed in. Javier's marketing focus is about consistency in a cup."

"That's his official tagline." Valentina stood. "Speaking of consistency in a cup, I'll brew a pot. Decaf for you, Jules?"

"Thank you, yes." I couldn't choose between my three sweet empanada options, so I went for one of each, knowing that Andy or Carlos would finish my leftovers.

"I wonder if the police have thought about a mistaken victim?" Andy asked.

"They're professionals. I'm sure they're exploring every possibility." I broke the guava and cheese empanada in half. The sweet filling oozed out. I tasted it with my finger and then took a bite. The buttery pastry crust paired with the sweet and bright tropical flavor made my taste buds sing.

Valentina returned with coffee, and the conversation drifted to everyone's memory of what had happened prior to Miguel's death. We tossed around other theories and pondered whether the police would be able to get a confession from Isabel if she was the killer.

My eyelids grew heavy as the night wore on.

Andy excused himself first. "I'm ready for rest."

"Okay, but I'm checking on you every few hours," I reminded him of the paramedic's instructions.

"I feel okay, Jules," he protested, standing and stretching.

"It's nonnegotiable," I replied in my best mom voice. "They said to check on you a couple of times, and as Carlos can attest, I'm up a few times throughout the night anyway."

"Fine." Andy pretended to be upset. "Then I'm really heading up now so I can get some z's in before I'm rudely awakened by my pregnant boss."

"Watch out. She might beg you for a midnight snack or a bedtime latte," Carlos teased.

I took his cue and headed to bed as well. Carlos stayed to help Valentina clean up. I tucked myself in and tried to release my thoughts about the murder, but visions of Miguel and Sofia both tumbling into giant vats of coffee haunted my dreams.

When my alarm buzzed at one o'clock to wake Andy, I had no trouble rolling out of bed. I knocked gently on his door. "Andy, it's Jules. Checking to see how you're feeling. Can I get you anything? Tea? A snack?"

He shuffled to the door, rubbing sleep from his eyes. "Jules, you're the best, seriously. Thanks for taking such good care of me, but I swear I'm feeling fine. It's just a dull headache now. I'm going to take more pain meds and go back to bed."

"Sounds good. Get some rest." I had to resist the urge to hug. He looked so young and vulnerable. If Ramiro or the twins were ever in Andy's situation, I would want them to be cared for and loved.

Returning to bed in hopes of sleeping was likely a losing battle, but a cup of tea and a banana and Nutella empanada sounded tempting. I crept downstairs, not wanting to wake the rest of the house.

I turned on the kitchen lights, filled the teakettle, and set it on the stove to boil. Then I rummaged through the refrigerator until I found the dessert empanadas. I warmed my middle-of-the-night snack in the microwave and waited for the water to heat.

Valentina had an impressive selection of teas. I chose an orange blossom with a hint of mint. I took my empanada and tea to the living room, curled on the couch, and tucked my feet under one of the throw blankets.

Drat, I should have grabbed a book.

I didn't want to risk scaring Carlos if I went upstairs to find it.

For the moment, I would savor my tea, treat, and the stillness of the night.

The house was peacefully calm. I blew on the tea, cradling it in my hands and listening to the gurgling sound of the fountain in the courtyard. I might have drifted back to sleep if it weren't for the heat of the tea and my mind playing tricks on me.

Were those footsteps?

I lifted my head and glanced from one side to the other, surrounded by the glowing lanterns and the soft golden lights in the entryway.

It's nothing.

You're just jumpy, Jules.

I raised the cup to my lips, but the tea was still too hot to drink.

The front door handle rattled. A faint metallic sound echoed unnervingly, cutting through the silence. It jiggled again, this time harder, as if someone was testing it from the other side.

Someone was at the front door.

Then with a slow, agonizing creak, the door inched open, the sound slicing like a warning, shattering my peaceful calm.

I set my tea on the coffee table, sprang up, and glanced around me.

Why was someone else awake at this hour?

My heart skipped a beat.

Is it the killer?

You're overreacting, Jules. It's probably the wind.

I tossed off the covers, picked up my tea, and inched toward the foyer.

My internal warning system fired on all cylinders, causing my heart to spike and my skin to grow cold.

I stayed in the shadows.

Over the years, I've learned to never go against my gut feelings.

Something felt wrong—dangerous.

It wasn't the wind. Someone was up and moving carefully, quietly through the dark house.

I made it to the arched doorway connecting the living room and entryway and peered around the corner.

A hooded figure dressed in black was digging through the drawer.

This was bad.

The person looked too small to be Javier. Their body size was closer to Isabel's or Sofia's. Had the police let Isabel go? Had she returned to destroy any last piece of evidence linking her to Miguel's murder?

Maybe she had an innocent excuse.

For sneaking around the house, dressed in black, in the middle of the night?

Yeah, right.

I considered my options.

I could yell and wake everyone.

But was that the right move?

Should I at least let this person explain themself before sounding the alarm?

I clutched my tea tighter and stepped into the light. "What are you doing?"

Sofia swiveled around and glared at me with so much intensity I nearly dropped my tea. "What are *you* doing? Why are you sneaking up on me?"

"You don't live here. Does Valentina know you're here?" I tried to make my body as tall as possible. I already had a good four inches on her, but it wouldn't hurt to appear as intimidating as possible.

Sure, Jules. A pregnant woman with a cup of tea— terrifying.

Sofia clutched something to her body, too. I blinked, letting my eyes adjust to the light, and realized what she had in her arms—Andy's notebook.

I gulped.

Sofia!

Suddenly, it all made sense. Carmen's revelation that she'd talked Miguel out of selling, Sofia's proximity to him at the time of death, Andy's notebook and photos, the note. Why had it taken me until this very moment to put it all together? Andy had been very vocal at dinner after Miguel died about this extensive research—the notes, sketches, photos. Sofia must have realized that he had seen something or captured something—something that clearly incriminated her.

"I couldn't sleep," I said with as much control as I could muster. I couldn't let her know that I knew she had to be the killer.

Play it cool, Jules.

"Ha! You're following me." Her voice was laced with fury.

"Following you? I'm staying here." I pointed upstairs.

She pressed Andy's notebook against her chest. "You should have let it go. Same for your staff. Why are you Americans so into other people's business? You're so ridiculously sentimental, too, just like Miguel. He should have done the smart thing and sold the farm to me. Terra Café International will take over this land one way or another. He could have had a fat paycheck, but no, no, no, he decided to keep the farm and the workers in the family. Well, he made that choice too late. He was so naïve—so swayed by sentiment. He believed he could get out of our partnership and keep the farm in his name. Wrong. The deal must go through. It will go through."

"I don't know what you're talking about." That was only half true. She admitted everything to me and validated Carmen's revelation that she and Miguel had made a new deal.

Her eyes burned with fury. Her narrow lips pulled tight as she leaned in, trembling with barely restrained anger. "Yes, you do," she snarled, her voice low and dangerous.

Her chest rose and fell with each heated breath as she jabbed a finger at the notebook. "Your barista, Andy—he saw me push Miguel. It was a perfect twist of fate. I simply needed to forge his signature and then put an end to him before he could contest the contract. Isabel gave me the perfect opportunity—I saw her disabling the safety mechanisms. It was like a gift from the gods. What a fool, but honestly, I do have to thank her. I seized the chance once I realized what she'd done."

How did this connect to Andy and his research? Did she think he'd captured photos of her or Isabel? If that were the case, it made sense she was back to find the rest of his notes.

Her hand curled into a fist. Then she unclenched it and tapped her fingers on the notebook with an erratic, nervous rhythm, struggling to keep herself from snapping. "I've been trying to figure out if he has proof," she hissed through clenched teeth.

So that was why she had attacked him? She believed Andy had seen her push him.

The irony is, he hadn't.

If she had let it go, she might have gotten away with murder.

"He's been watching me and Isabel. Taking photos, videos, snooping everywhere. I know he has proof. I have to find it." Her entire body coiled like a snake, ready to strike at the slightest provocation.

I didn't like the wild desperation in her eyes.

"He hasn't been watching you." I hoped that taking a rational approach might calm her down.

It didn't.

My words only inflamed her more.

Her nostrils flared like a racehorse chomping at the bit to get out of the gate.

"I should have finished the job when I had a chance earlier. He was already knocked out cold. One more hard hit with the rake would have done it." She sighed in disgust. "I'm not going to make that mistake again. Sorry it has to end like this, but I'm cleaning up all my loose ends tonight."

In a flash, she dropped the notebook, reached for a heavy vase on the table, and lifted it over her head, preparing to launch it at me.

Without thinking, I used my only weapon on hand and tossed my scalding tea in her face.

Chapter Thirty-one

Sofia screamed loud enough to wake the entire house. She recoiled and buried her face in her hands. "You burned me! You burned me!"

Everything happened in a blur. Carlos, Valentina, and Andy were upon us in seconds. Carlos held Sofia back.

Valentina called the police.

I couldn't tell how badly she'd been burned. I felt terrible, but the alternative would have been her smashing the vase on my head. I slumped against the wall, my entire body trembling with a mix of nerves and relief.

"Jules, let's go sit." Andy pulled me gently toward the living room.

"I'm supposed to be taking care of you," I protested.

"Uh, yeah, I'd say you succeeded. You took down the killer. Not bad." He patted my arm.

I held out my shaky hands. "I hope I didn't hurt her."

"Jules, she tried to kill you, and she successfully attacked me earlier. I'm pretty sure that's textbook self-defense." Andy scowled. "Oh, and she plotted and premeditated Miguel's murder—or at least got lucky. I bet she figured out that the machines had been disabled and used that to her advantage. Either way, she's the bad guy. Not you."

I forced a smile.

It was sweet of him to try and cheer me up.

"You're right. She admitted it—she told me that she caught Isabel tampering with the equipment and seized the opportunity. She was planning to forge Miguel's signature and proceed with the sale as if nothing had happened."

"That's cold. Ice cold." Andy shuddered.

Time moved like honey, thick, every second stretching out in slow drips. The air in the room felt heavy. I hadn't meant to injure her. I didn't like the idea of hurting someone else, even if she was a killer.

I wasn't sure how long we had been sitting on the couch, side by side but not exactly together. It could have been minutes or hours. When the police finally arrived, the world outside felt like a faraway place. The entire house lit up as officers traipsed in, arrested Sofia, and took each of our statements.

Carlos brought me a fresh cup of tea at some point.

"Is she badly burned?" I asked the officer after I'd finished relaying what had happened.

He shook his head. "Not at all. She'll be fine."

I let out a long sigh and gulped the lukewarm tea.

"I can't believe it was Sofia. I thought you might be right about her being the killer's target," Valentina said as we gathered around the fireplace. It wasn't cool enough to light a fire, but there was something comforting about being together. "I should have guessed it was her."

"She had to have the sale go through. Miguel told her

it was off, so she forged his signature and the note. Then she took advantage of the fact that Isabel had tampered with the equipment."

"And she thought I saw her push him," Andy scoffed. "I wish I had. It happened so fast that I never noticed."

"She might have gotten away with it if it hadn't been for your meticulous note-taking and documentation," I said to him with a small smile. "She was convinced you had proof."

"Well, I'm glad she was wrong about that because now we can be sure that the right person has been arrested," Andy said.

I was impressed with his maturity and wisdom. This trip only served to solidify my thoughts about him and his future at Torte.

We lingered for another hour until the sky went from dark black to purple.

"Should we try to take a nap?" Carlos suggested.

"I could sleep," I said, suddenly feeling the weight of the last two days catching up with me.

"Let's plan for a leisurely brunch and a swim later," Valentina suggested. "Your rooms have blackout curtains, so sleep as long as you like."

Knowing Sofia had been caught must have been the antidote to my earlier sleep issues. Carlos closed the shades, and I was out the minute my head hit the soft pillow.

I woke hours later to birds and chatter on the terrace. I rolled over to see that Carlos was gone, and it was nearly eleven. I couldn't believe I'd slept for so long. I stretched, feeling luxuriously restful and equally curious, as if last night had been a dream.

Voice messages from Mom and Lance awaited me.

I listened to Mom's first.

"I'm glad you're sleeping in, honey. Carlos filled us in on what happened. It sounds like the police have made an arrest, which hopefully means you can enjoy the remainder of the trip. Here's my Torte update. I'm sharing pictures from the book club last night. It was a huge hit. Bethany and Rosa transformed the dining room, as you'll see. Aren't the roses and her brownies just the sweetest? They served Uva rosé, and Sequoia made special strawberry lattes. Next month they want to read a mystery novel!

"This won't surprise you, but Doug and I had the time of our lives at *Perfect Crime* last night. Lance has outdone himself with this production. I was on the edge of my seat and the tension left me breathless. At one point, I truly believed there had been a murder. You and Carlos must see it as soon as you get home. Doug and I agree it's one of Lance's best, and we'd love to see it again with you.

"The dining room is already buzzing. Rosa's lemon chiffon cake with lemon curd and Italian buttercream has customers salivating. Marty's doing another flatbread special—an arugula, pesto, goat cheese, and sundried tomato. I need to run a tray of apple cider donuts and butter croissants upstairs. Can't wait to see you in a couple of days. Now, go enjoy the sun and the pool. Love you."

I was happy to hear everything was running like a well-oiled machine at Torte.

Next I listened to Lance's message.

"Congratulations on closing the case, darling. I hear you went tête-à-tête with a crazed killer. Impressive.

Although not the least bit shocking. My bet is always on a Capshaw. I want all the juicy details when you're home, but for the moment, how do you feel about a destination wedding? Fly guests to an exclusive private island? Charter a fleet of luxury yachts? Winter wonderland at a ski lodge?

"No, you're right. It must be Ashland. The question is, where? When?"

"Soak up that tropical sun and that devilishly handsome husband of yours. Kisses."

I sent them both quick responses. Then I took a long shower and made my way downstairs.

Everyone was outside at the pool, enjoying the sun, coffee, and pastries.

"Good morning, Julieta." Carlos ducked from underneath the blue and yellow striped umbrella and greeted me with a kiss. "Come sit. Javier has brought pastries and coffee from his shop."

I smiled at Javier and took the latte.

"We've been replaying last night," Valentina said, motioning to Isabel, Carmen, Alex, and Javier. "None of us can believe it was Sofia, and yet we can all believe it at the same time if that makes sense."

"She works for one of the worst companies," Javier said, offering me a pastry from a pretty pastel pink box. "What Isabel and I discovered about Terra Café International's business practices and treatments of their workers is shocking. The conditions are unlivable."

Carmen shuddered. "I can't imagine that happening here. It would have been devastating."

"What will you do now?" I opted for a slice of raisin cake.

Javier's gaze drifted to Isabel. "We'll continue the fight, protecting our native lands and our people."

Isabel nodded. "The police have been more lenient than expected, especially because Valentina has agreed not to press any charges."

Valentina patted her wrist. "You've learned a serious lesson, and your heart was in the right place. This new team will all move forward together in Miguel's honor."

I appreciated the sentiment and that she suggested we take a moment in silence to honor his memory.

"What were you doing at the processing area yesterday morning?" I asked Javier. A few questions still lingered in my mind, and I knew I couldn't rest until they were answered.

He and Isabel shared a brief glance. Then he removed a silver money clip from his pocket. "I was looking for this. I paid Isabel in cash. She passed the money on to her friends, who helped tamper with the equipment. I must have lost it when we met, and I was concerned that if the police found it, they would associate me with the crime."

So he had helped front the cost. My theory about the two of them working together had been right all along.

Isabel chewed on her fingers. "I felt so terrible. I thought it was my fault. I tried to stop him. I did. Carmen knew, and she and I screamed for him to stop and get away from the machine, but he wouldn't listen. Then he fell . . . and I still can't believe it." She gulped, swallowing hard like she was going to be ill. "I've been sick to my stomach ever since. That's why I erased the board. I tried to do whatever I could to help because I felt so guilty about Miguel and Alex." She reached for Carmen's hand.

"You were so wonderful and supportive. I'm sorry. I'm sorry to everyone."

Carmen squeezed her shoulder. "It's time for us to come together and build a future that all of us and Miguel can be proud of."

Valentina gave her a solemn smile. "I agree. Now we must focus on moving forward in positive ways and put this awful experience behind us."

Her vision for the future of Finca las Nubes matched mine for Torte. After everyone drifted off, Carlos, Andy, and I lingered.

"I think now is as good a time as any to tell him about our ideas," I said to Carlos with a playful smile.

"Please, you've been stringing me along all weekend." Andy waved his hands toward his face. "Time to spill the beans."

I groaned.

Carlos laughed. "We'd like to invest in you. We've priced out roasting equipment and would like to find a commercial space to build out a true roastery. If you're interested, we'd like you to be the head roaster and barista. It will mean reducing some of your hours at Torte because we envision greatly expanding our roasting and moving into distributing."

Andy clapped his hand over his mouth. "Am I interested?" he gushed. "One thousand percent yes. That's a yes if you were wondering. Yes, yes, and yes!"

I grinned. "Good. We'll have a lot of work to do and things to discuss once we get home. We'd like to get this rolling before the twins arrive."

He thumped his chest. "I'm your guy. I'll pour blood, sweat, and tears into this."

"I think we've had enough blood for one weekend," I said, but I was thrilled Andy was as enthusiastic about Torte's future as we were.

Our future was changing, but we were changing and growing together. What a gift. This trip reinforced how lucky we were. What else could I ask for?

Chapter Thirty-two

A week later, we were back at Torte and gathered in the dining room to celebrate Andy's promotion. Late evening light streamed through the front windows in luscious shades of eggplant and primrose. Bethany and Rosa had pushed the tables together to create one long shared dining space. A creamy tablecloth served as a blank canvas for dozens of mason jars filled with vibrant bouquets of dahlias, zinnias, cosmos, and forget-me-nots. The only light was from the beeswax candles between the pretty bunches of flowers, giving everything a soft, ethereal glow.

Bethany and Rosa had leaned into the coffee theme with chocolate- and latte-colored place settings and a generous sprinkling of roasted beans scattered amongst the candles and flowers. Pitchers of cold brew, punch, and bottles of chilled Uva white wine along with gorgeous platters of appetizers filled the table. The espresso bar was lined with coffee-tasting essentials—a variety of house-made simple syrups, chilled creams, and warming spices.

"This is amazing," I told Bethany, setting a plate of

espresso-glazed-bacon-wrapped dates on the table. "I love the coffee menu, by the way." I pointed to personalized menus at each place setting.

"That was a team effort," Bethany said as she made space between the coffee-rubbed crostini with goat cheese and honey, and mocha-spiced nuts. "Marty has gone all in with the coffee food. He's doing a coffee-braised short rib, a coffee-rubbed chicken with hot chili oil, and a chilled pasta with coffee and walnut pesto."

"Andy's going to love it." My eyes drifted to the chalkboard menu. They'd changed the rotating quote to one perfect for tonight's festivities. It was by the author Justina Chen and read "Adventure in life is good; consistency in coffee even better."

"You like the quote?" Bethany filled water glasses. "Rosa found it, and we couldn't resist. It's basically Andy's philosophy for coffee and life, right?"

"It's got Andy written all over it." I nodded in agreement and scanned the dining room, making sure everything else was ready for our staff party. We'd already announced Andy's new role. He and Carlos were making headway on their first task—finding a commercial property near the bakeshop where we could build out a much larger roasting operation. They'd been touring potential spaces and drawing up plans for Andy's dream vision for the roastery.

"Have you had a chance to try my desserts yet?" Bethany tucked her curls behind her ears and brushed off her flowy halter dress. Instead of a punny T-shirt, she'd changed into a pale pink dress with dainty blue flowers and a matching belt. "I made my classic espresso brownies, because—duh—brownies, right?"

"Obviously." I nodded seriously. "What is a dinner party without brownies?"

"Just dinner. Boring dinner." She winked. "But if I do say so myself, I'm super excited for everyone to try the mocha panna cotta and coffee cheesecake. We might need to add them to next week's specials."

"You don't have to twist my arm. I did sneak a taste, and everything was mouthwateringly delicious. Well done." I licked my lips, half wishing we could skip right to the dessert course.

Her dimples became more pronounced as she beamed at my praise. "You're sure?"

"Positive. No notes." I blew a chef's kiss her way. "I considered hoarding portions just for myself and hiding them in the walk-in, but that seemed in poor taste. Not exactly in the spirit of celebrating our team."

"I'll never tell." Bethany pretended to zip her lips. "I hope Andy likes everything. I feel so bad that your trip didn't go exactly as you all intended, so maybe this can be a little reset for everyone. The team is gelling nicely. I can't believe how well the new staff are fitting in, and I just have to say again how excited I am that you're giving me and Andy more responsibility. We won't let you down."

"Absolutely. I have the utmost confidence in both of you. You're crushing it. In fact, Carlos and I were chatting last night about how you're not going to need either of us around. We'll show up for a shift after the twins are born and everyone will be like, 'Who are you?'"

"Oh, my God, never!" Bethany's jaw dropped. "You're like pastry royalty. I'm still worried about you being gone—but we'll find a way to manage, somehow."

I was genuinely touched by how much thought and care she and the rest of the team had put into the celebration and their investment in Torte, but there was no time to dwell in the moment of appreciation because everyone was already filtering into the dining room.

Soon the bakeshop was humming with lively conversation, the sound of clinking glasses, and happy chatter. We gathered at the shared table as light music played overhead, and the sun sank outside. I nibbled on handfuls of sweet and salty nuts and sipped punch, savoring the contrast of flavors and being surrounded by the people I loved. Mom, the Professor, Carlos, Sequoia, Andy, Rosa, Marty, Bethany, and our newest team members chatted animatedly, their voices in a warm, familiar melody. Laughter and conversation wove through the air, mingled with the rustle of passing plates.

The food was stunning, not that I expected anything less. Marty's spicy coffee-crusted herb chicken practically melted in my mouth and paired beautifully with the sweet notes of the honey and goat cheese crostini. Carlos draped his arm around the back of my chair, slowly sipping his wine as he took in the festive scene. "This is good, mi querida. A happy staff makes for happy food and happy customers."

Across the table, Mom caught my eye, placing her hand over her chest in a silent gesture of agreement, her expression filled with warmth.

Marty kicked off a round of toasts, standing up and raising his wineglass. His ruddy cheeks beamed with delight as he addressed Andy with a wide smile. "Let me be the first to say how proud I am to be in the presence of coffee greatness. We'll all be able to reflect on tonight

in the not-so-far-off future and say we knew you when—
you coffee wunderkind."

"To the coffee wunderkind," everyone cheered, holding our glasses high.

Andy's cheeks reddened as he smiled sheepishly and
waved off the barrage of compliments.

"Speech, speech," Bethany chanted, encouraging her
peers to join in.

Carlos clinked his glass with the side of his fork and
cleared his throat. "Sí, Andy, this is the way in Spain. If
your public demands it, you must speak. It would be considered quite rude if you didn't." He winked and gestured
grandly as if rolling out the red carpet for Andy.

Andy sighed and shook his head but pushed back his
chair and stood. "Okay, okay."

This made everyone cheer louder.

I wondered if anyone passing by on the plaza would
think we were hosting a rock concert with that response.

Andy reached into his pocket and pulled out a piece of
paper. He unfolded it carefully like he had won an Academy Award and had prepared his remarks in advance. "I
can't believe I won. I'd like to thank the Coffee Academy
and Jules and Carlos," he kidded, playing it up like he
was holding back tears as he read his note and patted his
chest. "No, in all seriousness, it's great to be home. Costa
Rica was amazing—murder aside, of course—but there's
no place like Ashland. I'm excited about our new venture
and have so many notes and recipes in mind that I don't
even know where to start. I will say that my grandma is
pretty psyched to get her gardening shed back, and Carlos
and I have seen some spaces that will triple or quadruple
our roasting abilities. We're talking about future roastery

tours and special tastings, so if anyone has other ideas or you've heard customer requests, hit me up."

"Can we do a fully immersive coffee dinner like this?" Marty asked, stabbing a tender piece of the coffee-rubbed chicken with his fork. "Maybe a future Sunday Supper at the roastery?"

"I think that would sell out instantly," Bethany replied with a thumbs-up.

"Yeah, we are open to everything. We want the roastery to be an extension of Torte." Andy nodded in agreement, catching my eye briefly. "On that note, I do want to say how grateful I am, to you, Jules and Carlos, for giving me this opportunity and putting your trust in me. It's so cool, and I won't let you down."

His sincerity made my eyes begin to water. I blinked back happy tears, glancing around the full table, thinking of how full my life in Ashland had become. I was the lucky one. To have this staff, family, and friends. There was so much good that lay ahead—coffee adventures, expansions, new staff, weddings, babies—I couldn't contain my joy. Torte was my happy place, and I was oh so very happy to be home.

Recipes

Peach Cobbler

Ingredients:
For the filling:
5 cups sliced peaches (fresh or canned, drained)
½ cup brown sugar
1 teaspoon cinnamon
1 teaspoon salt
1 tablespoon lemon juice
1 tablespoon cornstarch
2 tablespoons water

For the topping:
1 cup all-purpose flour
½ cup old-fashioned rolled oats
½ cup brown sugar
1 teaspoon cinnamon
½ teaspoon nutmeg
½ cup (1 stick) unsalted butter, chilled and cubed

Directions:
Preheat oven to 375°F. and grease a 9-inch square baking dish. Combine peaches, brown sugar, cinnamon, salt, and lemon juice in a mixing bowl. Whisk the cornstarch and water in a small bowl until dissolved, then stir into the peaches.

In a separate bowl, combine the flour, oats, brown sugar, cinnamon, and nutmeg. Add the cold butter cubes and use a fork or your fingers to mix until the texture resembles coarse crumbs. Press about half of the oat mixture into the bottom of the prepared baking dish. Bake for 10 minutes. Pour the peach mixture over the crust. Sprinkle the remaining topping over the peaches. Bake for an additional 30 minutes or until the topping is golden brown and the peaches are bubbling. Serve warm (with vanilla ice cream or homemade whipped cream, if desired).

Torta Chilena with Dulce de Leche

Ingredients:
For the pastry layers:
2½ cups all-purpose flour
1 teaspoon salt
1 teaspoon baking powder
1 cup unsalted butter, chilled and cubed
½ cup cold water
2 egg yolks
1 teaspoon vanilla extract

For the dulce de leche filling:
1 can (14 ounces) sweetened condensed milk
½ teaspoon salt
½ teaspoon vanilla
Powdered sugar, for dusting
Cinnamon, for dusting

Directions:
Preheat oven to 375°F. Line 2 baking sheets with parchment paper. To make the pastry, in a large bowl, whisk together the flour, salt, and baking powder. Add the cubed butter and use a pastry cutter or your hands to combine until the mixture resembles coarse crumbs. In a small bowl, whisk together the cold water, egg yolks, and vanilla. Gradually add this to the flour mixture, stirring until a dough forms. Divide the dough into 8 equal balls. Roll each ball into a thin circle and place on the prepared baking sheets. Prick each dough round with a fork to prevent puffing. Bake 10 minutes or until golden brown and crisp. Set aside and cool completely.

To make the dulce de leche, fill a saucepan with 1 to 2 inches of water and bring it to a simmer. Pour the sweetened condensed milk into a heatproof bowl and place it over the saucepan (make sure the bottom of the bowl doesn't touch the water). Stir occasionally with a heatproof spatula for 1 to 2 hours until it thickens and turns a deep golden brown. Remove from heat and stir in the salt and vanilla. Let it cool slightly before assembling the torta.

To assemble the torta, place one pastry layer on a serving plate and spread it with a thin layer of the dulce de leche.

Stack another pastry layer on top, and spread on more filling. Repeat until the last pastry layer is placed on top. Lightly press down to distribute the filling evenly. Dust the top with powdered sugar and cinnamon. Let the torta chill for an hour before slicing, for best texture.

Pepito Sandwich

Ingredients:
For the steak:
1 tablespoon olive oil
1 teaspoon salt
1 teaspoon black pepper
1 teaspoon cumin
1 teaspoon smoked paprika
1 clove garlic, minced
Juice of 1 lime
½ pound skirt steak

For the black bean spread:
½ cup drained canned black beans
2 tablespoons salsa
1 teaspoon cumin
1 teaspoon lime juice
Salt to taste

To assemble:
1 small baguette or crusty French bread, sliced in half lengthwise
¼ cup caramelized onions

2 slices Muenster cheese
½ avocado, sliced
1 fire-roasted jalapeño, sliced

Directions:
To prepare the steak, in a bowl, mix the olive oil, salt, pepper, cumin, smoked paprika, garlic, and lime juice. Coat the steak with the marinade and let it sit for 30 minutes. Heat a skillet over high heat and cook the steak for 3 minutes on each side. Remove from heat and let rest.

While the steak rests, make the black bean spread by mashing the beans with the salsa, cumin, lime juice, and salt.

To assemble the sandwich, spread the black bean mixture on both halves of the bread. Layer with caramelized onions, sliced steak, and cheese. Top with sliced avocado and jalapeño. Place the sandwich in a panini press and cook for 5 minutes or until the cheese is melted and the bread is crisped.

Arroz con Leche

Ingredients:
1 cup white rice
2 cups water
1 cinnamon stick
Pinch of salt
2 cups whole milk
1 can (12 ounces) evaporated milk

1 can (14 ounces) sweetened condensed milk
⅓ cup raisins
1 teaspoon vanilla extract
1 teaspoon ground cinnamon, plus extra for garnish

Directions:

In a medium saucepan, combine the rice, water, cinnamon stick, and salt over medium heat. Bring to a boil, then reduce heat to low and simmer until the rice absorbs the water (10 to 12 minutes). Stir occasionally. Remove the cinnamon stick. Stir in the whole milk, evaporated milk, and sweetened condensed milk. Cook over low heat, stirring frequently, for 20 to 25 minutes, until the mixture thickens. Stir in the raisins, vanilla, and cinnamon. Cook for another 5 minutes until creamy and thick. Finish with a sprinkling of cinnamon and serve warm.

Suspiros Cookies

Ingredients:

3 large egg whites, at room temperature
¼ teaspoon cream of tartar
Pinch of salt
¾ cup granulated sugar
½ teaspoon vanilla extract (or almond extract for variation)

Directions:

Preheat oven to 225°F. Line a baking sheet with parchment. Beat the egg whites with an electric mixer at medium speed until frothy. Add the cream of tartar and salt and whip until soft peaks form. Gradually add the sugar, 1 tablespoon at a time. Continue beating until glossy peaks form (about 5 minutes). The meringue should hold its shape. Fold in the vanilla or almond extract.

Transfer the meringue to a piping bag. If you don't have a piping bag, you can use a spoon to drop the meringues. Pipe or simply drop small mounds onto the prepared baking sheet. Bake for 1½ to 2 hours or until the cookies are dry and crisp. Turn off the oven and let the meringues cool inside for another hour to prevent cracking.

Empanadas

Ingredients:
3 cups all-purpose flour
½ teaspoon baking powder
1 teaspoon salt
½ cup (1 stick) unsalted butter, chilled and cubed
2 large eggs
½ cup, plus 1 tablespoon cold water
1 tablespoon vinegar
Sweet or savory fillings (Jules used beef, chicken, and cheese, and chorizo and potato for savory fillings, and guava and cream cheese, Nutella and banana, and apple cinnamon for sweet fillings)

Directions:
Preheat oven to 350°F. To make the pastry, whisk together the flour, baking powder, and salt in a large bowl.

Add the cold cubed butter. Using a pastry cutter or your fingers, work the butter into the flour until it resembles coarse crumbs. In a separate bowl, whisk together one of the eggs, ½ cup cold water, and the vinegar. Slowly pour into the flour mixture, stirring with a fork until a dough forms. Knead the dough on a lightly floured surface until smooth. Wrap in plastic wrap and chill for 30 minutes.

To make the empanadas, roll out the dough to about ⅛ inch thick and cut it into 5-inch circles. Place 2 tablespoons of filling in the center of each circle. Fold the dough over and press the edges together, sealing them with a fork. Transfer to a parchment-lined baking sheet. Whisk together the remaining egg and 1 tablespoon water and brush the tops of the empanadas with the egg wash. Bake for 20 minutes or until golden brown.

Andy's Pura Vida Latte

Andy's Pura Vida Latte is inspired by Costa Rica and his love of coffee culture. It will make you feel like you're on a coffee farm, enjoying the warm, gentle breezes and birdsong while you sip this delicious creation.

Ingredients:
2 shots strong espresso
1 cup canned coconut milk
1 tablespoon sugarcane syrup
½ teaspoon cinnamon
½ teaspoon nutmeg
Cinnamon stick for garnish

Directions:
Add warm espresso to a mug. Warm the coconut milk with sugarcane syrup in a small saucepan over medium heat. Stir until fully dissolved but do not boil, then slowly add the frothy coconut milk to the espresso. Sprinkle cinnamon and nutmeg on top and garnish with a cinnamon stick.

Read on for a look ahead to
THE WHISKING HOUR—
the next intriguing Bakeshop Mystery from
Ellie Alexander and St. Martin's Paperbacks!

They say leap and the net will follow. I could trace every good thing in my life to a time when I have done just that. The day I decided to venture away from the safety of my beloved hometown of Ashland, Oregon, and travel across the country to New York for culinary school. Or when I set sail for adventure on the *Amour of the Seas*, visiting far-off ports of call and learning to navigate a floating commercial kitchen. There were even harder times, like packing my bags and leaving Carlos, my husband, behind on the ship to return home to cocoon myself in and figure out what was next. And joyful, happy times like now when my ankles were swollen and my belly so big I could barely bend far enough to fill the pastry cases at our family bakeshop, Torte. I'd entered each experience with a giant leap, flinging myself off a cliffside without a plan and hoping a magical net would somehow appear. Somehow it did, metaphorically speaking.

My hamlet of Ashland, Oregon, had become my safety net. I was equally excited and terrified at the prospect of soon becoming a mom to twins, but I was confident that I'd figure it out just like I had done with everything else.

I wasn't facing this major life change alone. I was surrounded by friends, family, and neighbors who were already clamoring to be first in line to babysit and planning meal deliveries and baby showers.

I smiled at the thought as I watched my footing. I cherished my morning walks to the bakeshop. It was a time to center myself and breathe in the fresh mountain air, but my pregnancy belly made me extra cautious as I descended the steep street that took me past the sprawling grounds of Southern Oregon University and spilled out onto Siskiyou Avenue. The first touches of fall appeared in buttery jewel tones kissing the tips of the leaves with touches of gold. Peachy light illuminated the top of Grizzly Peak in the distance.

Sure, I was probably biased, but no place on the planet was more stunning than Ashland in autumn. The grand Victorians lining the street were bathed in the soft morning light and flush with vibrant fall foliage—sunflowers, asters, and cosmos—that attracted herds of local deer for a bountiful breakfast. They nibbled on the dewy grasses, their ears perking up at my footsteps on the sidewalk.

Once I was farther into town, the architecture shifted to old-world Elizabethan style buildings. Royal eggplant banners with satin trim announcing the current season at OSF fluttered in the slight breeze. Storefronts and restaurants were decked out for the changing weather with lush displays of garlands, pumpkins, and gourds. I paused at London Station to admire a collection of hand-knit scarves and shawls. Soon the temperature would start to dip, flirting with freezing and casting an icy frost over everything.

I continued to the far end of the plaza, past the Lithia

bubblers, omitting a strong sulfur aroma. The historic fountain was a popular spot for tourists and famed for its natural healing properties, but my pregnancy hormones put my nose on high alert. Even from a distance, I couldn't erase the smell.

I crossed the street where Torte sat on the far corner like a pastry beacon with its cheery red-and-blue-striped awning and huge front windows. Bethany, our pastry manager, and Rosa, our front-of-house manager, had outdone themselves with the current window display. Stalks of hearty grasses shot toward the ceiling like a New Year's Eve sparkler. Bunches of fall wildflowers were tucked amongst a bounty of harvest sweets—apple tarts, honey pear galettes, and chai latte cupcakes artfully decorated with buttercream, a sprinkling of cinnamon, and a star anise. They had adorned the window frame with tiny twinkle lights and strings of cinnamon sticks.

I unlocked the front door and stepped inside. An immediate calm rushed through my body as I flipped on the lights and locked the door behind me. We didn't open for another two hours, but I wanted to make sure the dining room and espresso bar were in good shape. Last night, we'd hosted a private party, and my staff had put the tables and chairs back in place and given the dining area a good scrubbing, but I told them to leave the flower arrangements and other little details for the morning.

I fired up the espresso machine and gathered small vases of flowers, setting them on the two- and four-person dining tables and window booths throughout the cozy space. Our large chalkboard menu had a rotating quote, usually from Shakespeare. My parents started this tradition when they first opened Torte. Today's quote was more modern, from Angie Weiland Crosby, but captured the essence of the Bard's spirit: "Autumn dresses up in gold; the richest season of the soul."

Carlos and I had discussed the possibility of giving Torte a refresh, but I was still in love with the corrugated metal siding, touches of red and teal, the long espresso counter, and the shiny pastry cases. It was nearly impossible to be in a bad mood once you stepped inside, especially when there was coffee.

Coffee.

Ah, the sweet nectar of the gods.

I squeezed behind the counter and pulled two strong shots of decaf. Andy, our resident barista and now bona fide coffee roaster, had crafted a special baby blend for me that held the same rich notes of a traditional roast, but without the stimulating effects of caffeine.

Surprisingly I hadn't missed the buzz. Coffee for me had always been a form of morning reverence, an opportunity to embrace the slow, sensory experience of brewing aromatic beans, warming a cup, and adding a splash of luxurious cream.

My mouth started to water as a thick stream of espresso poured into a shot glass like a cascading waterfall. I steamed milk and added Andy's signature cardamom spice syrup to a mug. There was no doubt that when he arrived, he would chastise me for making my own latte, but I couldn't wait. I'd been craving the spicy latte since I woke up. So much for the myth that pregnancy cravings loosened their grip. Mine continued to take hold, even into my third trimester. Carlos had a bevy of midnight snacks on hand to stave off any sudden craving. Last night it was popcorn—salty homemade caramel corn, to be specific. Typically I'm not much of a popcorn fan, but last night I devoured the entire batch and seriously considered asking Carlos to make another.

I sipped the latte and headed downstairs. The bakeshop was divided into two unique areas. The basement housed our commercial kitchen as well as a small seating area with an atomic fireplace, couches, chairs, and a bookcase with board games, puzzles, and coloring supplies for customers to enjoy while they lingered over a chilled orange mocha and slices of hot-from-the-oven zucchini bread.

I went through the opening procedures, warming the bread ovens, lighting a batch of kindling in our wood-fired pizza oven, and reviewing the custom and special orders for the day. As usual, several birthday, anniversary, and celebration cakes were on the docket, along with boxes of pastries for office parties and our wholesale bread orders. The team would be arriving soon, but until they did, I intended to enjoy the quiet of the kitchen and start on a special for the day.

I had just the bake in mind—a pumpkin butter bread with swirls of cinnamon cream cheese. I tied on a fire-engine-red Torte apron with our fleur-de-lis logo and washed my hands with our lemon rosemary soap. Then I gathered the ingredients and blasted Spanish tunes while I creamed butter and sugar together in our industrial mixer.

I already had house-made pumpkin butter on hand. It was similar to a pumpkin puree, but reduced down, so there was less moisture, which gave it a deeper, richer flavor profile.

I slowly incorporated eggs, pumpkin butter, pumpkin

puree, a trio of warming spices, and vanilla, and mixed them until a smooth batter began to form. Then I sifted in the dry ingredients—baking soda, salt, baking powder, and flour. I liberally greased bread pans and spread a layer of the batter on the bottom of each pan.

Next, I turned my attention to the cream cheese swirls, whisking room-temperature cream cheese with a generous dose of pure maple syrup and cinnamon. To create a swirl pattern in the bread, I spooned teaspoons of the cream cheese over the first layer of batter and used a paring knife to thread ribbons through the pumpkin mixture. I repeated the steps again and finished the loaves with a dusting of cinnamon and sugar.

The back door opened as I was sliding the tins into the oven.

"Morning, boss," Andy called with a wave. His freckled cheeks were rosy from the brisk air outside. He tugged off his jacket and hung it on the rack. Then he joined me in the kitchen, inhaling deeply and placing a finger on the side of his nose. "Wait, don't tell me, I smell, uh, pumpkin, yeah?"

"You got it." I grinned, nodding to the oven. "I made pumpkin butter bread with a cream cheese swirl. I was just about to start on a honey butter to serve with it."

"And I see you made a latte? On your own? Jules, are you feeling okay?"

I felt a flush creep up my neck. "Sorry, I couldn't wait." I rubbed my belly. "The twins demanded a hit of your cardamom spice syrup."

"It's so unfair. It's not like I can argue with a pregnant lady, but you know I would have made you something special." He brushed a strand of his auburn hair from his boyish face. "I've still been playing around with ideas from Costa Rica. It's a problem—too many options."

I chuckled. We'd recently returned from a coffee tour in Costa Rica. A dear friend from my days on the cruise ship invited us to her family farm. She'd given Andy a complete education on Costa Rica's coffee culture and walked him through every stage of the growing and roasting process. It had been an incredible trip and served a dual purpose, because Carlos and I offered him a new position. Andy was now Torte's coffee manager. He was responsible for roasting our in-house blends, coffee vendor relations, and overseeing and training our team of baristas. It was a big role, but he was ready for it and so were we. With the twins' imminent arrival, I'd been scaling back and giving my highly competent team more responsibility.

Marty, our favorite bread- and merrymaker, was stepping in to help manage our wholesale accounts and the savory side of the kitchen. During the summer, two of my longtime most beloved staff members, Sterling and Steph, had left to run their own restaurant at a charming family resort on the southern Oregon coast. It was the way of the culinary world—people flowed in and out of the bakeshop. I always wanted my team to pursue their dreams, whether it was here or in a far-off corner somewhere.

"The current lineup seems to be a hit," I said to Andy, polishing off my coffee.

"Yeah, but it's time for a change. Fall is creeping in. I can feel it. Before you know it, Mount A is going to be covered in snow and we'll be traipsing around town in ski boots. Bethany and I were talking at the private event last night about doing a menu refresh for fall."

"Great. How was it, by the way?" That was another sign I was shifting into a new role. I had ensured everything was in good shape last night, but I didn't stay for the event. Truth be told, it was rare that I made it up much past nine p.m. these days.

"Good. Smooth." Andy gestured to the fireplace cranking out heat and the sweet smell of burning applewood. "Marty's twice-baked potatoes were a hit. I think he's planning to do them again for lunch today. People raved about them last night. Oh, by the way, have you seen Lance?"

"You mean this morning?" I glanced at the narrow window on the door. A blush of light seeped inside, but it was way too early for Lance, my best friend and the artistic director at the Oregon Shakespeare Festival. Lance enjoyed his beauty sleep and cast parties that lasted well into the wee hours of the morning.

"No, he dropped by the party. He didn't stay long because he had to introduce a show, but he told me to pass on that he'll be stopping by today to discuss a private event." Andy's eyebrows shot up his hairline.

"Is this about the wedding, because Arlo will kill me if I get mixed up in Lance's schemes."

"I don't think so. He mentioned a cast party, but I'll leave Lance to you." Andy winked and headed for the stairs. "Time to brew the beans."

I didn't blame him. Lance was one of the most tenderhearted people I'd ever known, but he had a larger-than-life persona and a penchant for theatrics. He and his partner, Arlo, had recently gotten engaged. Let's just say they had varying visions about their upcoming nuptials. Arlo preferred a small, understated gathering with family and friends, whereas Lance insisted on an elaborate bash on the scale of a Hollywood production. He'd floated dozens of ideas from a parade of finely costumed llamas who would usher the happy grooms into their reception to transforming one of the OSF venues into a replica of the Palace of Versailles.

When I last checked in, they had agreed upon a custom label of our Uva wine for gifts for their guests, a floral tablescape, and a champagne fountain. They had yet to land on a venue or a date. Those of us who knew and loved Lance—Andy and me included—had given him a wide berth. He thrived on romantic fantasies, but I knew he would meet Arlo wherever Arlo was to create a memorable day for both of them.

My bread timer dinged. I took out the loaves, which had crisped nicely with the cinnamon topping. Hopefully I could keep Lance in check. I had yet to play the pregnancy card, but if push came to shove, I wasn't above it.